I0693142

The Red god

Author

Jenna Recktenwald

Contents

Chapter 1: Invitations

Why is an empty room so boring yet comforting at the same time? The young girl, Mara, thought as she lay on her bed. She idly kicked her feet in the air, pretending to pedal a bike.

Normally she might be reading a book, scribbling on her drawing papers, or playing her Switch. But she wasn't tonight. She wanted to stay quiet and focused so she could try and make out her parents' latest argument, although it was boring waiting between loud remarks. She couldn't hear the softer speaking from her room.

"What's more important?! You know how..." Mara strained her ear and stopped kicking her feet for a moment, but the voice of her mother dissolved into the walls again. She thought she picked up a few more words but wasn't confident enough to make up her mind what the latest outburst was about.

Did she just mention Dad's new car? She resumed her imaginary bicycle, this time a little harder and more frustrated. It was a nice car. It smelled much less than his old red one. The girl didn't understand why her mother would complain about it again. Sure, they had argued about the money it cost at first. They always argued about money. But that argument didn't last a terribly long time.

The Red god

How long had this argument been going again? Mara rolled over to grab her bedside clock and pulled the face towards her. 7:34 p.m. Only about forty minutes, but it didn't seem to be wrapping up. If anything, the snippets she could hear were getting louder and more frequent now.

"Whatever! Just make all the decisions! You'll be happy then!" The latest voice rung out. Her dad usually ended the arguments, so she wasn't surprised to hear his voice this time.

The girl slowly stood up off the bed. She liked to pretend she was a spy, a ninja, or a ballerina at times like these. Tonight she decided she was a detective. Not a big-shot cop one, but one like Sherlock Holmes. She slinked one foot in front of the other, quietly making her way to her bedroom door.

As she put her ear to the crack of the door nearest the knob, she thought more about the latest detective book she read. Listening to doors was completely normal for detectives. She reassured herself and brushed her long brunette hair out of the way of her ear. She needed to maximize her listening powers to be a good detective, after all.

"...and then we'll need a sitter for Marigold too, but the neighbor can probably do that." Mara scrunched up her face in thought after hearing her mother's planning. It sounded to her like they were going somewhere. She wasn't sure how she felt about that yet. She didn't hate trips, but she often didn't love them either.

Planning, packing, and long car trips with both of her parents were usually draining. If they weren't prodding each other with comments, they were uncomfortably silent when it was just the three of them.

The girl looked back to her bed where 'Marigold' lay curled up. She was Mara's cat, a short-haired tortoiseshell. She brought her home after finding the kitten dirty and alone in the woods behind their family house. Hershey was the name Mara started calling her due to her mostly brown coat, but her mother had crinkled her nose and said she could only keep her if she got 'a better name'. After shooting a dozen names down, her mother insisted on Marigold. It wasn't a terrible name, but it didn't suit her.

Mara frowned while remembering that day, but it turned into an impish grin as she walked over and started petting her furry friend. "Hershey," she whispered, so as to avoid any chance of her mother hearing, "it's okay as long as you don't mind me calling you it."

The Red god

Hershey rolled over and let out a soft trill in response, begging for belly pets too. The girl obliged and gently ruffled the cat's stomach fur. After a few moments, Mara turned her head and noted that her parents had been quiet for the past minutes. Her dad's loud remark had been the last of the argument as she had thought. He always seemed to end arguments, but did it count if he did so by giving in to her mother? Mara wasn't sure.

Suddenly, she heard footsteps coming up the stairs. The girl panicked for a split second and grabbed her headphones and a nearby drawing paper. She hurriedly positioned herself on her bed, headphones on and paper in lap.

In one movement, her mother knocked and opened her bedroom door. "Mara, your dad and I want to tell you about your cousin's wedding." Her mother started. She was a slender-built woman, not exactly short, but a head below her husband who stepped into the room behind her.

"Samantha is getting married in January. She and her fiance have invited the whole family to the wedding, but it's a bit far away." Her mother sat on the end of Mara's bed and continued. "Because it's so far away, at a ski resort in Austria, we have to plan to be there for the week."

Chapter 1: Invitations

Mara looked thoughtful, trying to recall where that would be on the globe she and her classmates would take turns spinning around in geography class.

"Is that near Switzerland?" Mara guessed, thinking back to one of her classmates that bragged their dad had gone skiing there.

"It is! You're such a smart kid!" her mother exclaimed, but this compliment only made Mara wary. Her mother always acted nicer when she wanted her to do something, and she thought her own answer wasn't that special to warrant her mother's sudden smile.

She didn't notice or take concern at Mara's lack of response to her praise and continued. "It'll be a great time seeing the whole family! Some of your distant uncles, aunts, and second cousins haven't seen you since you were a baby! I'll get you a few new dresses for the trip, and we'll do both our hair up nice! It'll be a treat for all of us to go."

The girl sunk into her bed slightly. Not enough to visibly sulk, lest she get reprimanded, but enough to put a few extra inches between her and her mother sitting on the bed's edge. She thought for a moment while her mother rattled off more family facts, who on Samantha's fiancé's side would be there, who her mother was most interested in meeting or catching up with, and who she couldn't *believe* would get an invite.

"...and Samantha still talked to them after that. I don't know *why.*"

Mara wanted to break out of the current tangent, so she looked over at her dad, still standing stoically a few feet inside the doorway. "Are kids really allowed there, Dad? It sounds far..." Mara trailed off with a worried expression. She hoped neither parent caught on that it wasn't entirely genuine. Yes, the long trip did worry her a bit, but she wasn't a scaredy baby. It was more the fact that she was sure the trip was entirely the kind of event her mother would enjoy, not her.

Her dad spoke for the first time since entering, "Your cousin specifically included you on the invite, Mara. You don't have to worry about that. We will have to get you a passport before the flight though."

"Oh! The passport photo!" her mother exclaimed, "I'll pick you out something to wear for it, and let's get it done tomorrow!"

Mara didn't have much hope of escaping the trip, but she was stubborn and thought it worth one more attempt. "Do passports cost money? I could stay with Beth instead!"

Chapter 1: Invitations

Her mother stood up from the edge of the bed and crossed her arms. The change in demeanor was one Mara was used to but hated. "Beth is a schoolmate, not your family. You're going on a *family* trip with your *family*." Her mother punctuated the last phrase with an air of finality.

Mara snuck a side glance at her father. He was starting to check his phone, apparently done with the conversation as well. She knew he wouldn't help her out of this, so she faced further away from her mother, reaching to pet Hershey to relieve some of the tension. She replied, "Okay."

"Good. Me and your dad will take care of the appointment for the passport and take you tomorrow." Her mother loosened her crossed arms but kept a serious look on her face. "David, you and your new car can take us tomorrow, right?"

Mara felt bad for her dad after that comment, but she had to hide a little smile knowing her detective skills were top notch. She has been right about her mother bringing up the car in the earlier argument. She liked to imagine Sherlock would have ruffled her hair and told her good job. While lost in that imagined scenario, her dad and mother walked out of her room with some quiet remarks between them.

11

The Red god

Mara was relieved to hear the door shut behind them. She let out a breath she didn't realize she was holding in and relaxed into her bed's headboard. "When am I going to get to decide things?" she whispered to Hershey. The cat trilled a purr in response. Mara liked to talk to her. She let her talk and never got mad at her. Although her half of the conversations left a lot up to translation.

"Yeah, you're probably right," Mara replied to the cat. "Oh! School starts back in three weeks!" Mara loved school. She didn't have too many friends in elementary school, but she had at least two. One was another somewhat quiet girl called Beth. Mara had actually gotten up the courage to talk to her first. Beth reminded her of herself in a lot of ways, quiet in crowds, but very friendly and fun to play with when it was just the two of them.

Mara thought about her other friend too, a boy named Jace. He was the polar opposite of Beth. One day she and Beth were playing imaginary Sailor Moon, complete with tall sticks for magic staff weapons, in a corner of their school's recess area when the taller boy noticed and made a beeline for them. Mara had been nervous he was going to bully them for playing such a silly game away from everyone else.

Chapter 1: Invitations

She raised her 'staff' slightly in anticipation as he jogged up to them. But he was instantly excited and asking rapid fire questions towards the two girls. "Are you sword fighting? Do you play Final Fantasy too? What was the name of that move you just did? Is there another stick I can have? I like yours the best! It has a gnarly knot near the top like a wizard's staff!..."

Mara couldn't help but smile at the memory. She couldn't wait to see them again as she started sixth grade this year. Being able to be herself around them was like a vacation. She turned to pet Hershey more. "But you're my favorite cat ever and forever though, so don't be jealous or sad while I'm at school or this stupid family trip." The fluffy brown mass snuggled deeper into her bed covers in response. Mara translated that as a "Don't worry, I won't!" reply.

The next morning, Mara had her usual non-school routine of getting up, brushing her teeth, and having breakfast with her mother while her dad grabbed his work stuff and ran out the door.

She wished her dad stayed home instead of her mother. Days alone with him were extremely rare but more fun. But he worked a

13

lot. Mara was vaguely aware he led a team of people at a software company but didn't really understand how that could take nine hours a day and even some weekends.

Shortly after her dad left for work, her mother would start up the next routine of the day, complaining about the house's state, what Mara should be helping with, what she shouldn't be doing, and everything in-between. Sometimes Mara caught herself wondering if her dad wanted to work so much or if he just didn't want to be stuck here like she was with her mother.

After completing her chores, Mara approached her mother in their living room. It was an average size room, like much of their house. It was enough to fit a couch on one side, a TV and reclining chair in the corners, and a coffee table near the middle. Every room was decorated by her mother, with the exception of the basement where her dad had older furniture and a big wooden desk for when he worked weekends at home.

Her mother sat on the couch with a basket of laundry near her, folding towels and stacking them neatly on the coffee table. Before her mother noticed her approaching, Mara was struck with a feeling she occasionally had for both of them, but more often for her dad. She felt sad for her.

Chapter 1: Invitations

Her mother's face was sad. Not crying or dramatic, but just... fallen. Why couldn't they all be happy? Why did they have to fight for control and money and cars and Mara and everything? The young girl didn't have much time in that thought before her mother noticed her and changed demeanor.

Sitting straighter and clearing her face of any particular emotion, her mother spoke in a level voice, "Oh, Mara. Have you finished sweeping and cleaning up Marigold's box?"

Mara replied in a more cheerful voice and carefully chosen words, "Yep! Should I do anything else this afternoon?" She knew certain phrases to say or not say to avoid putting her mother in a bad mood. Directly asking if she could go play now would have likely resulted in her mother picking out more chores for her, just for the sake of being contrary.

Her mother sat in thought for a moment. She stared out the window as she did so, leaving Mara shifting uncomfortably. The girl briefly wondered if her mother spaced out and didn't hear her. She turned her head to her daughter suddenly and replied in her previous level voice, "No, you can go play. But remember your dad and I are taking you for your passport picture as soon as he gets home."

The Red god

Relieved, Mara replied before taking off towards her room, "Okay, I'll be ready by then!"

Finally alone in her room, Mara quietly shut the door behind her. She often tried to be quiet. If she was loud, it meant her parents would take notice of her again and have something to say or something for her to do. Quiet meant she was left alone and could get lost in her own company.

She walked across her pink carpeted room (again, a room decorated by her mother) and knelt down by her bedside table. It had a cubby she used for books at the bottom. She flipped through the stack, all of them being stories of fantasy, adventure, puzzles, and heroes and heroines.

Today she felt like another detective book. Most of these she had actually read several times already. But until it was school time again or her grandma dropped by, she didn't have much hope of getting a new book.

Mara didn't see her paternal grandma terribly often, maybe once every few months. But the elderly woman always brought her some book or drawing paper, so she thought very fondly of her and looked forward to her visits. She had another grandma and grandpa on her mother's side, but she saw them even less frequently as they

16

Chapter 1: Invitations

lived across the country in Florida. Her dad's mom lived closer to them in Colorado, although she didn't live in the same city.

The girl laid and stretched out on her bed, grinning widely in anticipation of her story. When she got older, maybe she really could be like Sherlock, smart, confident, bold, making her own way through life and helping people with their problems.

Her book was opened and laid on her chest, but rather than read she imagined a new version with her as the main role. Her clients and city officials alike would thank and praise her as she solved cases impossible for anyone else. She'd have enough pay from her cases to easily take care of her needs without having to worry or argue about money.

No one would yell at her or tell her what to do either. They would need her wit and skill, and they would be polite and friendly to get it. She wouldn't have to do any jobs she didn't want to, and no one would punish or push her to do them either.

This daydream went on for the better part of the afternoon, she realized, as she heard her dad's car pull up in the driveway. She hadn't gotten dressed in what her mother wanted her to wear for the picture yet! In a panic, she jumped off her bed and grabbed the dress laid on her dresser. She didn't want to be the cause of a new fight today, so despite her dislike of the outfit, she hurriedly changed and grabbed her shoes before going downstairs to greet her dad.

"Hey kiddo! You look sharp!" he bellowed as she finished running down the stairs towards her parents standing in the kitchen. Her dad seemed to be in a good mood. This made Mara smile. Maybe they would have a good trip today.

Her mother walked a few steps towards her and started fussing with her dress collar and hair. "It fits you well, but I wish it didn't have these wrinkles..." Her mother was frowning as she fussed with the dress, but Mara didn't pick up an exceptionally bad mood. She still seemed pleased by Mara's wearing of the dress and getting ready to take off for today's appointment.

"What do we have to do for a passport again?" Mara questioned. She mostly remembered about the process, taking a photo and filling out some paperwork before mailing it at the post office, but she wanted her dad to explain it while they drove over. It was a safe question and hopefully one that would keep everyone in a good mood and avoid the usual cold silence.

It worked rather well. They had a pleasant conversation between the three of them. She also learned more about the resort

Chapter 1: Invitations

her cousin was having her wedding at. Apparently it was at an old ski resort in-between two mountains in Austria.

The name was Resort Ruhe. There was a spa, indoor pool, buffet, children's activities, and a large ballroom. Her mother read amenities off the resort's website, and Mara began getting a little excited, not so much at a ballroom and children's activities, but at the thought of seeing bigger mountains and exploring the whole place.

Soon, they pulled up at the post office and entered. Her parents spoke to the man at the desk and were directed to a side office. While they swapped papers back and forth and began filling out whatever was on the clipboard, Mara took a seat and let her mind wander again. A whole week at that resort, that's a long time to spend away from home and with a lot of unfamiliar relatives. She was excited about exploring but not so much about all the showing off her mother would make her do.

She tended to be passed around like a doll by her mother, whether it was at dinner with church members or her dad's company parties. It felt strange. Her mother would brag how pretty she was, how well she was doing in school, and the strangers would nod and agree, saying how nice of a young lady her daughter was.

She should have been happy she supposed, but it all felt so fake, like she was suddenly thrust into the role of a character she didn't want to play.

She did like praise, she admitted, but not the kind her mother sought. Maybe the difference was where the spotlight really shined. It was on her mother in those situations, with her as the role of a prop waiting until her mother was done so she could leave.

While waiting, Mara leaned over and looked at the paperwork her parents were filling out. "Parents: David and Shannon Rockner. Date of birth: 01/06/1984 and 04/26/1985. Permanent address..." Her eyes glazed over as she skimmed the paper. Just for today, she would be glad she was still a kid and not an adult. They had some torturous ideas invented, like paperwork.

The woman in the office who had been helping her parents with the forms stood up and walked around her desk. She had a kindly appearance and bent over slightly to talk to Mara. "Are you ready for your picture, dear? You must be excited! You have a very pretty dress, too."

Mara got a bit shy. The woman seemed genuine in her compliment, and she reminded the girl of one of her teachers. "Yes, whenever it's time," she said in a quieter than usual tone, looking down with an embarrassed smile.

She had Mara line up in front of the wall before pulling a camera out of her desk drawer. "You can smile if you'd like," the woman stated, still with a warm smile.

Mara looked over to her mother and saw her miming a gesture. She stood up straighter and put on a small smile to obey her mother's gestures. The camera's flash went off, and the woman went back to speaking to her parents about specifics on the form.

When the photo was printed out and attached to the paper, Mara unamusedly noticed the dress didn't even show, not one inch. It was so close up only her face and hair were seen. Why do adults bother with these things?

The months leading up to the trip sped by quickly. Mara started school back up and had a shock. Jace and his family had moved away over the break, so he would never again be at their school. She and Beth commiserated in their corner of the cafeteria at lunch. She was still very glad to see Beth, but it was a sad start to the new school year.

Her parents' arguments worsened as the trip drew near, mostly about money. Mara didn't know what plane tickets and other travel expenses cost, but they must have been more than her dad made. Still, the trip was non-negotiable to her mother, and arrangements proceeded.

The morning of their departure was marked by a lot of anxious flitting about by her mother. Everyone's suitcase had to be checked and double checked that they brought the appropriate clothes, shoes, and other accessories.

Mara was relieved she only had to pack her personal backpack. She spent half the morning daydreaming about what the adventurers in her books would bring. Flashlight, check. Notepad and pencil, check. After a few dozen more items, she was left wondering why she didn't own any rope, and if her grandma might be willing to buy her some for her twelfth birthday coming up.

She shook her head. Despite her plans for adventure and exploration of the resort, she probably wouldn't need any rope, or they would have some already there. She nodded in approval at the full backpack and used both arms to stuff it closed and zip it up.

Chapter 1: Invitations

With an exaggerated heave, she lifted the backpack onto her shoulders. Her mother had already instructed her dad to take everyone's suitcases to the car, so she only had one last thing to do in her room before she left.

She gingerly walked over to her windowsill where Hershey lay sleeping in the sun. She kissed her gently on the head, not wanting to wake her up. "I love you, Hershey. Mrs Baker will take good care of you while we're gone. She'll walk over from next door and give you food, water, and I'm sure a few pats every day. Be good, and I'll be back home soon."

The girl had a pang of sadness and anxiety. She wished she could take Hershey with her. She hadn't gone that long without her since the day she brought her home two years ago.

"Honey, we need to get in the car!" her mother shouted from downstairs. Startled, the cat woke up. She looked up, realizing Mara was right beside her, and chirped a high-pitched meow.

The Red god

Mara couldn't stop herself and dropped lower to envelope Hershey in a hug. With a reluctant sniffle she released her and repeated her goodbyes before heeding her mother's prompting to head outside to the car.

The ride to the airport and flight check-in were uneventful, but that didn't stop a knot of anxiety from forming in Mara's chest. She imagined herself quite the adventurer, but going so far away for so long in real life was different.

For once she didn't mind when her mother grabbed her hand among the crowd queuing for their flight. Normally she resisted. Holding hands with your mother was a bit juvenile at her age she thought, but this time... It *was* very crowded. She squeezed her mother's hand and stepped forward as they boarded.

Once near the back of the plane, her parents stopped to bicker over the seats. "Here, I'll sit with you on the first flight, Mara," her dad spoke and gestured to one of the window seats on the right side. Mara shuffled past and sat down.

Chapter 1: Invitations

She had been on planes before, mostly for visits to see her grandparents on her mother's side, but this was going to be different. Her mother told her there were three flights until their destination. The first would be to Frankfurt. The next was taking them to Austria but not close enough to where the resort was. That's why they had to have a third flight to take them to a smaller Austrian airport.

Her dad sat down next to her in the middle seat and sighed. The travel had only begun, but he seemed tired already. Mara was vaguely aware of her mother arguing with a flight attendant about the seats before taking the one nearest but on the left side of the aisle.

As passengers filled in the other seats, her dad leaned closer to Mara and whispered, "Looks like we get a break. The man in the aisle seat next to me didn't want to give his place up for your mother." He grinned, and Mara felt a little less anxious and smiled back.

"What should we do?" she asked.

The grin stayed on his face as he looked around the plane before turning back to Mara. "I spy with my little eye a *very* happy passenger."

The girl put on her best detective face, which apparently involved scrunching her face up and narrowing her eyes, as she scanned what aisles she could see from her seat. "Well, that's definitely not Mom then," she said in a deadpan tone, eliciting a belly laugh from her dad.

"No, definitely not." He chuckled.

After another moment of scanning, Mara sat up in her seat and exclaimed "Oh! There's a puppy on that woman's lap! Awwww, he is very happy."

Her dad nodded. "Correct! Now how about you pick the next game?"

Some time around game three and midway through the flight, the game changed to one where Mara drew on her papers and her dad tried to sleep, but she didn't mind. The few hours alone with her dad had lifted her spirits, and she felt excited about the trip again.

She was going on a mountain adventure after all! She needed to keep herself pumped up for it. What was she going to find there? A rare flower no one has seen for thousands of years? A wild leopard? Ancient artifacts? Maybe all of them. Mara nodded to herself and drew more shading on her sketch.

Chapter 2: Resort Ruhe

After three flights and barely a nap, the family of three trudged out of the last airport towards a waiting bus. The mountains had looked cool from the air, but Mara needed to see them at the resort to tell how big they are. It was a long ride, but after an hour or so the bus began rattling and jostling as they climbed the mountain road. The resort was supposed to be nearer the base of the mountain, but even then they had a bit of a climb during their ride.

Finally, the road evened out, and they turned a corner where the land opened up. Ignoring her mother's calls to sit back down, Mara shot up and stood on tiptoes, grabbing the head of the seat in front of her to look out.

There was fresh snow, but the cobblestone road was well cleared. It continued up a long driveway and widened where the resort entrance was. The resort itself was made of stone and dark wood, giving a very rustic appearance if not for the grand scale of it. It stood three stories tall, a football field long, and had black metal twisted into decorative lights at various heights near the entrance and along the sides.

Her mother stopped her protests for Mara to sit down as she caught sight of the massive building herself. She gasped a little and took a moment to take in the scene. "Well, Samantha has good tastes."

Once the bus was parked, Mara grabbed her backpack and suitcase and took off towards the side where she could see the mountains better behind the resort. They were much bigger than she imagined, taking up ninety percent of the horizon. Mara wondered if they were bigger than most mountains or if they were just closer than she had ever been to one.

She didn't have to wonder long, as her mother called her back. "Mara Jane Rockner! You don't even have your other coat on! Get inside with us now!" The girl stared in awe a few moments more and then reluctantly obliged and headed toward the resort entrance where her mother stood.

They passed her dad as he stood chatting with an older man in the foyer entrance. "Uncle Larry." Her mother scoffed. "He'll talk your dad's ear off for an hour. Let's go ahead and check in." Mara didn't pay much attention to the dozen or so relatives clustered in various groups further in the resort's foyer. Some of them she recognized, some not, but what held her attention was the room itself and a few resort employees.

Chapter 2: Resort Ruhe

The foyer entrance was well lit with crystal chandeliers in a tall, arched ceiling. Between segments of the room there were large dark wood beams. The outer walls and a few inner back segments were made of stone. Two fireplaces lined different walls and brought warmth. The floor was wood, and bright red ornamental carpets covered the most used areas.

Mara took it all in and noticed the wood and stone looked very old and a stark contrast to the fancy lighting and carpet. Altogether it had a very appealing appearance.

The resort employees also caught her eye, although she tried not to stare. Staring was rude, her mother always said. They had a more olive complexion compared to her family, but freckles were also dotted on quite a few of their faces. She thought it might be the amount of sun they get reflected off the snow.

Their hair was mostly dark, and they appeared to have two main uniforms. Both were red and gold in color, but one set was more embellished and had skirts instead of pants for the women. Those employees were greeting guests or standing at the front desk.

The front desk was also made of stone, although it appeared newer than the walls. Behind the desk was 'RESORT RUHE' in gold-colored metal spanning the wall.

The Red god

"Hi, we'd like to check in." Her mother started speaking to the front desk employee. "Shannon and David Rockner. We should have two rooms next to each other."

The woman at the desk smiled and nodded, beginning to check their computer system. Beside her there was another, older woman who spoke. "Welcome. We are glad to have you at Resort Ruhe! Is this your first time?" She was easily understood but with an accent that was hard to place.

Mara noticed she had bright green eyes, and a kind smile that caused wrinkles in the corners of her mouth and eyes. The girl kept quiet as her mother answered. "Yes, we've never been here before, but already I can tell you have a very beautiful resort!"

The woman looked at Mara but spoke in reply to her mother. "Then you must have your daughter join our storytellers in the children's room after you make yourselves comfortable. We insist any children should see it at least once during their stay."

Mara frowned at this. She wanted to explore important things during her week here, not be babysat! But she kept silent still, fiddling with the straps on her backpack, not wanting to upset her mother for talking back in front of a stranger.

Chapter 2: Resort Ruhe

"That sounds lovely. I'm sure she'll love it," her mother replied, taking the keys from the woman as she held them out.

"Our porter will help you with your bags. The rooms are on the second floor, 265 and 266. We hope you enjoy your stay." The woman turned to the porter walking up and spoke something in what Mara assumed was the local language to him.

He nodded and turned to take the bags. "This way, please. We have a shorter route taking the stairs if that is fine."

Her mother agreed. "Shorter is good with us. We've had a very long trip already." The three of them began walking off to the right of the foyer where there was a wide hall, decorated much the same as the foyer's style.

Mara looked over her shoulder to where her dad stood, still nodding at something Uncle Larry was telling him. She only had one parent to sneak away from currently. This should make it easier. She glanced around at various open doors in the hallway as they walked. Some led to brightly lit, large rooms. She saw a few long tables and chairs in some. Others had tables draped in white cloth and appeared to be laid out for dining.

But those weren't very interesting to Mara. They looked like boring adult rooms where adults would have long boring chats.

What excited her were a few dimly lit doorways. An employee walked through one, and the girl noted it was a much smaller hallway branching off.

It was poorly illuminated and had a very old feeling with worn stone walls and old wood floor without the fancy carpet that covered the guest areas. She found her nose almost in the slammed door as it shut behind the worker, oblivious to the young girl sneaking a peek.

The porter seemed to sense her curiosity and spoke again. "There is a children's room where we have a few storytellers gather. You should join the other children there shortly. It is very close to the foyer, only two doors on the left."

Before Mara could respond, her mother cut in and replied for her. "Yes, we heard about it from the front desk. I'm sure Mara will enjoy it."

The man then turned and pointed them up a short staircase. "We will be going up here, please." He then continued but spoke to Mara's mother directly. "If you would like, after your bags are settled in your rooms I can show you to the children's room."

Chapter 2: Resort Ruhe

Shannon gave a little wave. "Thank you, but I have to head back to the entrance to find my husband anyway. I'm sure we'll find the children's room later."

The man nodded and continued a few more paces before stopping in front of a door. "Here is 265, and 266 is the next one. Please ask any employee if you need further assistance." He then turned and left the way they had come.

Mara's mother let out an audible sigh as she pulled out one of the keys and opened the first door. "Let's get changed and go find your dad."

Mara stepped into the room behind her. Here the carpet was entirely dark red with no wood floor seen. There was a small entryway with a closet on one side and a bathroom on the other. Several steps in there were a large bed against the right wall, a desk and TV against the left wall, and a curtain spanning the far wall.

While her mother started opening suitcases on the bed, she ran to the curtain side and pulled it open. She was rewarded with a breathtaking view of the mountain on the right of the resort. It was beginning to darken outside, but there were lit trails dotting the landscape and a few skiers making their way down. The sky was gold blending into dark blue and black above.

The Red god

This is a good vantage point, Mara thought. She could do some initial planning on what areas outside the resort would be worth exploring first.

"Mara, I told you to get changed. We're finding your dad first. Don't even look outside tonight. Ski lessons are scheduled for tomorrow."

Her mother sounded half exasperated already, and she hadn't even tried to sneak off yet.

The woman pointed to a door on the right wall between the bed and the entrance area. "Your room should connect there. Take this key and open it up. Take your suitcase too."

Mara turned away from the window and grabbed the key and suitcase. "Sure! I can be fast."

She ran around to unlock the door. Her room was identical to the other, and Mara grinned from excitement that she got such a big, jumpable bed the same as her parents. She quickly shoved that excitement down though. No jumping in front of her mother. She didn't want to get grounded before she even got one chance to explore.

Chapter 2: Resort Ruhe

The girl quickly changed into the first dress her mother had packed for her, a purple corduroy with brass buttons, and grabbed her black sweater to put over it.

Once dressed, she stopped to listen to the other room. Her mother was still shuffling hangers, so Mara took the opportunity to dig into her backpack. She made it rather heavy, and she realized not all the items were important for adventuring.

Drawing papers and markers were taken out, alongside her Switch and a few other items. She kept her flashlight, small notebook, compass, string, binoculars, and Swiss Army tool in the bag. Most of these items were 'borrowed' from her dad's camping equipment, but he never seemed to miss them.

Satisfied with the reduced weight, she slung the bag back on her shoulder and walked into her parents' side of the door. "I'm ready."

Her mother appeared to be ready too. She was now wearing a long blue dress with a darker blue knit shrug. She walked over to Mara and began looking her over, instructing her to turn around as she looked. "Alright, your hair isn't too bad of a mess, and the dress isn't wrinkled. Let's go find your dad and greet the family."

Back downstairs, the pair entered the foyer and approached David.

"We're checked in, Dear. Here's your key copy." Mara's dad turned to them, briefly pausing his conversation with Larry and an older woman Mara didn't immediately recognize.

"Oh, thanks. Larry and his wife were just telling me about their new vacation home in the Florida Keys."

Shannon put on a wide smile, but Mara could tell it wasn't real. "Congratulations! How long ago was this?"

The older man turned to his wife. "We've been using it about three years, Barbara?" The woman smiled and nodded. "Three years since last summer, yes."

Chapter 2: Resort Ruhe

"Oh!" Shannon interrupted. "Has it been that long since we last saw you? Mara, you must have been only seven? Do you remember meeting Uncle Larry and Aunt Barbara at the last get together?"

Her mother practically pushed her into the circle of adults. She opened her mouth to respond, but Aunt Barbara spoke first. "I remember you! You were such a tiny little thing! You're looking like a young woman now!"

The chatter among adults continued as Mara shut her mouth again. No use speaking if no one actually cares to hear you. There were several compliments made, but Mara began tuning the conversation out, only smiling and nodding as appropriate.

After some time, Mara made an attempt to side step out of view, but her mother silently grabbed her hand and held firm. She was extra cranky today despite the fake smiles, Mara noted. She thought about her next move for a while as the boring chatter continued.

Suddenly, a light bulb went off. Mara saw a few employees holding hands with younger children and walking to the left side of the foyer. "Mom, can I go to the children's room with them? It looks like they're going to start the stories!" A little fake excitement was sprinkled on for luck.

Shannon took a moment to notice her daughter's request. Rather than answer right away, she looked around the room first. "I wanted you to say hi to your grandparents. They should be here soon."

Mara looked to her dad for help, but he only gave her a shrug and looked towards Shannon. Aunt Barbara then cut in. "Our grandson is going to the storytelling. You cousins should hang out!"

Salvation at last! Mara literally jumped and tugged on her mother's hand. "Oh, was he the baby at the last gathering? I'd love to play with him!" Lies, all lies. Mara felt a little guilty, but these were extraordinary situations. She needed a break from her mother's parade of her. It wasn't fair she never got to do what she wanted in times like this!

Barbara looked equally excited and clasped her hands together. "Baby Danny, yes! Although I guess I shouldn't call him a baby anymore. He recently had his fifth birthday!"

Putting on her best begging face, Mara looked up at her mother and continued to swing her arm. "Please can I go hang out with Cousin Danny at the storytelling?"

Chapter 2: Resort Ruhe

Shannon looked to meet her daughter's eyes, and Mara could immediately tell she wasn't buying her fake excitement. It didn't suit Mara's normal distaste for young children. She usually begged in the past to *not* have to hang around the younger relatives.

Shannon outright turned her gaze into a glare. Mara could see her jaw tighten and loosen for a moment before she replied, "Sure! You can go with your Cousin Danny. But be back here after the stories end."

Success! But at what cost? Mara figured her mother only agreed in order to not lose face in front of her aunt and uncle and that she had a talking to waiting when they got back to their room this evening. That all sounded like a problem for future Mara though. She would enjoy the opportunity here and now to leave for her own plans. She nodded and skipped off towards the group of children walking with the employees.

The group looked to be all six and under, Mara thought with a frown. She wouldn't have minded a few kids her own age to talk to. A thought struck her, she didn't even know which one was Danny! This shouldn't have been funny, but the whole ridiculousness caught up with her, and she had to stifle laughter as she walked behind the group.

Well, Danny wouldn't know her either. It could only make it easier for her to sneak off. But Mara had to be careful. She saw what appeared to be the children's room a few doors down a hallway off the left of the foyer. This was almost visible from the group of adults and her parents that she just left.

She looked back and forth between them and carefully paced her steps behind the group. Had either of the two employees walking the kids noticed her? If so, they could come looking for her if she didn't enter the room with the group. Should she enter the room but try to sneak off mid story? Should she tuck and roll now? What would Indiana Jones do?!

She didn't know why her brain picked that particular fictional character to summon for wisdom, but at the last moment before entering the doorway to the room she ducked off to the side and lay flat against the wall. Her heart pounded, and she waited silently to see if the employees or any of the children would notice and look for her. She heard a few of the children babbling excitedly and the sound of chairs being pulled across the wood floor. No questions, no exclamations, no search party looping back into the hallway. She had done it, praise Jones!

Chapter 2: Resort Ruhe

Mara felt her legs wobble ever so slightly as she peeled herself off the wall by the door and began walking further down the left corridor. She mentally scolded herself for it. Now was not the time to be getting nervous. She was... just excited, that was it. She smacked her hands against her legs and put on a determined face. Onward to adventure!

Going down the left corridor to start was an obvious choice. She couldn't go to the right corridor without going past her parents in the foyer. Mara hoped there would be service hallways branching off the left corridor like she had seen on the right. As she walked, she looked carefully at the doors and knobs, trying to determine which would lead to what type of room. If she opened the wrong door and was greeted by a room full of dining adults, someone might try and escort her back to her parents since she's 'lost'. This would have been easier if most of the doors were open.

One doorway stood out and made her abruptly stop. It was on the right side and had a tarnished bronze doorknob. The wood matched the rest of the doors, but it was worn in several places and stained near the bottom. Mara was sure this wouldn't lead to a fancy adult room.

41

The Red god

She looked both ways. No one was around. With a deep breath, she turned the knob and swung the door open. Inside would have disappointed a normal person. It contained a dim hallway devoid of bright carpet, chandeliers, or bustling workers. But for Mara this was perfect! Careful to not make a sound, she stepped inside and slowly closed the door behind her. She learned a lot of things from living with her parents. Quiet kids don't get in trouble was chief among her lessons.

Mara continued slowly down the hallway, stopping to glance in a few open doors. Most were very small closets, consisting of only a water heater, venting, or pipes. Nothing interested her about those, so she quickly dismissed them and carried on. It struck her that she didn't quite know what she was looking for. Adventures and puzzles yes, but what and where? Would she find anything inside the resort itself? Maybe she should go outside and find her adventure there?

She wandered another thirty feet and noticed the hall bent to one side. The walls were more uneven here, and every surface had a fine layer of dust. She touched the walls and felt they themselves were dusty, or rather made of crumbling stone turning to dust. Before she could stop herself, she wiped her hand on her brand new corduroy dress and cringed at the dirt it left. She didn't herself care for the outfit, but she was sure to hear about that stain later...

While wiping at the stain to mitigate the damage, she walked a few feet toward better lighting. Ah! Most of the dirt came free of the fabric. She was pleased with her work and looked up to notice where the brighter light was coming from. There was another open door, but this time it led to a room. It was about the size of her bedroom, but it seemed smaller because it contained tall shelves against three walls and boxes stacked throughout the floor. In the back there was a small, high window where the extra light was coming from.

The sun was mostly set now, but lights along the outside of the resort must have been illuminating the area immediately outside the window. Mara was drawn to it like a moth to a flame. She looked at the floor carefully and made her way around the piles of boxes. She was a few inches shy of being able to see out the window, but she looked around and found a sturdy-enough box to climb on. Once on her tiptoes, she could reach the tall sill.

Outside was hard to see beyond the glow of the resort lights, but she made out some people far back walking back and forth. She squinted and raised her hands to cup her eyes to the window. They were kicking a ball! This was the first time since arriving at the resort that Mara had seen kids close to her own age. She was struck by a yearning to run out and try to join them but was tempered by other thoughts.

How could she get out that side of the resort? She hadn't explored enough to find a door to the outside on this branching hallway. If she did make her way out, would they want to play with her? She thought they looked her age upon first squinting, but the more she looked the more she convinced herself they were older teenagers. Or even if they weren't teenagers, were they kids of the workers? Did they speak English? Would it be rude or stupid of her to ask to play in English if they didn't speak it?

While her head swarmed with conflicting thoughts, she carefully stepped down off the box and turned to walk back to the hallway. If she could find a door leading outside, that would solve half the problem. She gingerly stepped around the stacked boxes and was almost to the hallway entrance when she heard a loud crash. Mara whipped her head around and saw one of the boxes from a tall stack had fallen over.

Anxious about getting in trouble, she quickly closed the door and moved towards the fallen boxes to start putting them back in place. On top were old table-side lamps and cords in dusty tangled piles. While scooping them back into their respective box, she heard a curious click followed by a static sound. Mara was startled by the noise and leaned back away from the pile. What if she had broken something important?

Before she could worry more, a voice sounded out of the static. "Hello? Is this thing on?"

What was that?! It was a male voice and sounded very muffled by the pile. The young girl dove back into the pile and shoved more items into their boxes before getting to something interesting on the top of the bottom box. It was the thing making the static sound, and it must have been where the voice came from too.

She carefully picked it up and began turning it every which way to investigate, being careful not to touch any of the buttons. It was a rectangular device with a clear (but yellowing and dusty) window on the top and several buttons in a row near the side. The static continued, and Mara dusted off the top of the object more.

Oh! It had a tape inside! This was really old! She remembered her grandmother showing her one of these before. What were they? Cassette tapes? That ruled out a stranded skier radioing for help, but it was still a neat find.

The Red god

Her grandmother used her tape player for recording notes, so maybe Mara could use this for narrating the rest of her adventure. She pressed a few buttons, and the static stopped. Now how could she get it to record her? She pressed a few more buttons and tested a dictation. "Hi, this is Mara's adventure story!" After speaking into it, she continued fumbling with buttons to see if it would play it back.

The static started back, but the voice out of it wasn't hers. "Oh, it is recording. Good. Okay!" The same male voice from the first clip continued. "This is Rudy Goodwin speaking. If you've found this cassette player, congratulations! You're in for a treat! I'm making this a story game for any adventurous kids of the resort. You can play by listening and following along!"

A story game? That sounded like it was for little kids, but this thing looked ancient! Mara stared in wonder as she thought. Had this been here for years? Had any of the kids of the resort ever played it? She didn't have to wonder long as the voice continued. "If you complete the story and all parts of the game, you'll receive a special prize at the end! Only one prize exists, so don't share this with the other kids just yet."

46

Chapter 2: Resort Ruhe

A prize? Had anyone else been smart enough to find it? Now this had Mara's full attention. She grinned in excitement and held it up closer to her face as she listened. "I'm going to start with a step of the game first, and the first story segment will come after that. Ready?!"

Mara found herself nodding, although she realized she was silly with no one but a tape recorder to see her movement. It continued. "For the first game step, find the first wooden staircase when entering to the right of the resort entrance. You might want to pause this and unpause it for the clue once you're at the location." She immediately pressed the pause button, not wanting to mess up the game instructions, and jumped up off the floor with the device in hand. This could be a good adventure!

Mara stuffed the tape player in her backpack but paused before zipping it up. Was it really alright to take this? It wasn't stealing if a kid was meant to find it and play the game, right? She assumed the tape must have started out in the children's room when Rudy first made it. It wouldn't make much sense to put it in a storage closet. Her brow furrowed for a minute as she stared at the device in her backpack. It was fine! She was only borrowing it. And she would put it back in the children room after she was done and after she got the prize!

With a nod to herself, she zipped the bag and slung it over her shoulder. She turned and opened the door to leave, but her hand stayed lingering on the doorknob. She thought about the kids outside again. Should she still try to find a door to outside? Or what about finding the first game clue for her adventure?

Mara shook her head. Where were her priorities? Obviously the adventure is better. They always were. How many times did her books let her down? None? Now how many times had people been mean or ignored her? More often at home than at school, but still more times than she'd liked. The kids outside wouldn't miss her, even if they would have been nice and let her play.

She removed her hand from the doorknob and continued down the hall with a new air of direction and confidence. This time she went back the way she came instead of further down the service hallway. If the first step of the game started near the right of the foyer, then she needed to get back to the foyer first.

The trip back was relatively quick with only a few incidents of her pausing to duck in a closet since she thought she heard footsteps. This place could get a tad spooky if you were in it for long, and cold. It seemed colder by the minute but mostly at her back as she walked. But soon she was back in the main left hall off the foyer, with the fancy red carpet and bright lighting.

There were a few adults walking by now, but they didn't pay her too much attention thankfully. She thought of a good plan as she walked. If she timed it just right, she could stop by the children's room and follow her cousin (whichever kid he was!) back to where her parents were chatting with Uncle Larry and Aunt Barbara. Maybe they wouldn't catch on that she wasn't at the storytelling the whole time. That would save her from some trouble, although she still had to face her mother's wrath for forcing her to let her go to the storytelling in the first place.

Mara bounced as she walked. She felt surprisingly daring for someone on borrowed time. She grinned and thought she might get away with more things this vacation. She was pretty smart, after all. She knew how to trick her mother into letting her go, and she found the best adventure game none of the other kids found. She would find the prize too!

A dozen bounces later, she came to the doorway of the children's room. They were clapping with some excited kid babble going on, so she assumed the story was still in progress. Mara didn't care to catch the tail end of it, so she leaned against the nearby wall and waited. Instead, she let her mind wander to another daydream.

She had a cool leather hat and jacket, a brown skin bag across her chest, and a utility belt with all kinds of gadgets and tools. With a smirk she solved the last clue of the game and jumped off a platform just in time. It moved with billowing smoke, revealing a pedestal. On the pedestal was a golden cat statue, encrusted with diamonds, sapphires, and rubies. It just happened to look like Hershey, and Mara stepped forward to claim it as her game prize!

The daydream went on for several minutes and was abruptly ruptured by the sound of chairs scraping the floor and running children. Time to act! Mara turned and positioned herself facing the direction back into the foyer. As the children exited the room, she began walking a few steps behind and tried to remove the post-daydream smile from her face. She had to look a little bored when she met back up with her parents. It would help soften the punishment if her mother already thought she had a bad time.

Mara glanced at the children ahead of her. Cousin Danny? Maybe, no, no, possibly... She had no clue. Oh well! In a minute one of the kids should walk towards Barbara and Larry, and she could put on her planned performance.

Chapter 2: Resort Ruhe

On cue, she saw the group of adults and Aunt Barbara particularly turning towards the kids with a happy face. "Oh, Danny boy! Did you enjoy your story?"

Mara watched as a little blonde boy broke away from the cluster of kids and ran faster towards the crooning grandmother. Oh, that one was Danny. Noted for future reference, blonde with red shirt. Mara walked slower and put on her best dejected face, shoulders slumped as she approached.

Her mother looked over her shoulder towards Mara with a tired frown. "And how'd *you* enjoy the storytelling?"

Mara could feel the annoyance emanating from her mother now, but she had to stick to the plan!

The girl shrugged her shoulders and looked towards her mother's shoes, not up to meet her face, and mumbled a reply. "It was long and full of loud kids."

Her mother's face turned to a subtle smirk. "Oh, you didn't have fun with Cousin Danny after all?"

Mara pushed part of the carpet back and forth with her shoe, still not looking up. "No... It was boring. I don't want to go back there tomorrow. I want to go outside. We're doing skiing tomorrow?"

She stopped fidgeting and finally looked up to meet her mother's face. "The little kids aren't allowed on the hill, right?" Mara laid her act on thick and audibly groaned with the last words. "It should be so much quieter without them."

Her mother held her expression but turned away. "Well, the adult lessons are tomorrow. But now that you've had time to hang out with your cousin, I think it would be good for you to bond more. I was just telling Aunt Barbara that you'd love to help watch him in the resort pool with his parents instead of skiing with us adults tomorrow."

Perfect! Mara had to hide a smile. Being punished by being excluded from ski lessons tomorrow was exactly what she wanted. It would be much easier to do her own thing if her parents and a ski instructor weren't there. Sneaking away from Danny's parents was a small problem, but Mara was feeling puffed up at her recent successes and thought she could manage it easily.

Before she could reply, the conversation between adults moved on. Mara was happy to stand still as they droned on this time. It gave her a chance to glance around the foyer, especially the right main hall, and get an idea of where that staircase was. What did the tape say again? The first wooden staircase off the right of the foyer?

Chapter 2: Resort Ruhe

Her eyes scanned the resort entrance and on to the right hallway. There were a few very short staircases, only two steps really, leading from the outside doors into the foyer. They had metal spindles and handrails and steps covered in carpet. Mara doubted they were the ones, but she also started thinking about the age of the tape. Maybe parts of the resort had changed since then? She might have to check each staircase just in case. Thoroughness leads to greatness! Or so one of her favorite book protagonists said.

Mara was broken out of her thoughts as she heard her name mentioned. "...Mara can sit next to them! Let's find them and get seated." Was her mother talking about the dining area? Now that it was mentioned, Mara did realize she was hungry. She didn't protest as the group continued chatting but started making their way toward the right hall.

Along the way, Mara's dad changed pace and walked alongside her. "Don't worry about the skiing tomorrow." He started leaning towards her and spoke in a lower voice, "It would have been boring for you anyway. And you know how your mother is..." He gave her a wink.

She expected this was to cheer her up, but it also felt... crappy. Yes, Mara did know how her mother was. She was lucky being banned from skiing was her desired outcome so she could sneak off for exploring, but what if it wasn't?

She could only frown and nod in response to her dad. He wasn't here to protect her from her mother's moods. She understood it in part. A husband can't go against his wife because of how marriage works? Or when you love someone you can't disagree with them? No, Mara shook her head. She didn't really understand it at all. Adult logic seemed like the worst thing in the world at this point. She was glad she was still a kid, but even when she grew up she told herself she wouldn't be like they are.

They turned into one of the fancy rooms with lots of tables and chairs that Mara had seen earlier on the way to their rooms. The carpet only extended to the main walk areas here. The rest was dark wood floor where the tables and chairs were grouped. Each table had crystal vases containing purple and white bouquets of flowers. Mara also noticed a banner in the back that she hadn't seen when she first walked past. It read 'Celebrating Ryan and Samantha Jansen!' in cursive letters.

Along one wall there were now large platters and tiered plates of food. Mara smelled it more than she could see it from across the room. Ham? Something smoky? Cheeses? Whatever it was, it made

Chapter 2: Resort Ruhe

her mouth water. Some workers also milled about the already seated guests, pouring drinks.

"Oh, there they are!" Mara's mother exclaimed. The girl looked in the same direction and recognized her grandparents seated at one of the tables. Mara's grandmother wore a silver dress that Mara thought sparkled slightly in the bright dining lights. It had decorative pleats and a matching sash draped across her arms. Her hair was gray blending into white and done up in a braided bun. A green, jeweled pin helped hold her hair and was accompanied by matching earrings and necklace.

She looked very dressed up compared to the last visit Mara remembered with them, but she didn't linger on the thought. Her grandmother always looked well put together no matter where they were visiting, at their estate in Florida, a restaurant, or other family gathering. Her makeup was bolder than Mara remembered, but it suited her look. It wasn't clownish like Mara briefly thought of Aunt Barbara's.

Next to her was her husband, Mara's grandfather, who was dressed in a dark suit and silver tie. He also had the same color green cuff-links, leading Mara to wonder if her grandmother dressed him to match. She giggled at the thought of an old man being made to wear something he didn't want. Maybe Mara wasn't alone in that, she thought as she played with the sides of her dress.

Their group walked up to the table, and Shannon made the first greeting. "Hi Mom! It's good to see you and Dad made it alright."

David stopped beside her and reached out to shake the older man's hand. "Hey Gareth, Mildred, good to see you again."

Mara's grandfather stood to meet the handshake and gave a reply, "You too. We were just wondering where you three were. Milly was anxious to see everyone." He made a motion for them to sit, but Aunt Barbara waved and stated they were seated with their daughter and son-in-law a few tables away. Aunt Barbara, Uncle Larry, and Danny left for the other table as Mara and her parents sat with her grandparents.

Mildred patted the seat next to her. "Mara, Dear, come sit with me. Let me see your outfit." She spoke with a smile, but Mara always had a hard time determining the emotion behind it. It was easy for her to pick up her parents' emotions, but her grandmother was... different.

But not wanting to upset her, Mara obliged and took the seat. "Hi Grandma. I like your dress too."

Chapter 2: Resort Ruhe

Mildred looked her up and down while her smile dropped. "Yes, it's a Francoise dress. I had it shipped in as soon as I heard the engagement news from Samantha. Your dress is... very purple."

The last words were spoken with an air of hesitation, but Mara didn't expect complaints about it or further fussing. Her grandmother was very polite to Mara and never said anything mean to her that she could recall. The young girl wasn't sure if she could categorize her as liking her though. It was almost like there was an invisible barrier that prevented Mara from really knowing or feeling her grandmother's true feelings on their interactions. She supposed that barrier was called politeness, another adult invention that she didn't fully understand. What was the point of visiting someone for years but never being open with them?

Shannon took the pause as an opportunity to jump in. "Oh, Mom, it's from the winter line of that new department store we have near us. I got it new for Mara for the trip as well."

Mara observed her mother as she spoke. The Adult Politeness Barrier didn't seem to be between her mother and grandmother. Shannon looked nervous at every word and movement, and Mildred responded in kind with a deeper frown and sharper tone of voice. "A small town department store? You know if you couldn't

57

afford a decent dress for my granddaughter I would have ordered her something myself."

David had been pulling out a chair next to Shannon to seat himself but thought better of it at that remark. "Oh, I almost forgot food! You ladies stay seated and I'll grab us all plates." He walked off to the tables of food, leaving the now-tense atmosphere.

"It wasn't the cost, Mom," Shannon defended, "David got that promotion last year, you know."

Mildred scoffed but said nothing as she unrolled a new napkin and silverware. She began tucking the napkin on Mara's lap and spoke with a nicer tone, "Well, no matter what your mother dressed you in, you look nice, Dear. You grew a few inches, didn't you?"

Mara smiled and nodded, beginning to tell details about what she had done since their last visit, about school, something cute Marigold did, and a new book she read. Her grandmother kept a polite smile and nodded or occasionally asked a question.

Gareth took the opportunity to catch up with his daughter and asked Shannon a few questions about David's promotion. He wasn't hard to read like Mara's grandmother was. His personality was friendly but quiet or stoic at times. The quiet seemed to coincide with Mildred speaking up, a pattern Mara observed in her own parents as well.

David soon returned with plates of food, much to Mara's delight. She looked hers over and saw an assortment of toasted breads with what smelled like smoked turkey and ham with a generous portion of sliced cheeses on the side. She didn't waste time digging in, and the conversation went back to mostly Shannon and Mildred.

Watching them talk was like a tennis match, Mara thought. Her mother would try to subtly brag on something, but her grandmother would respond with a redirect or put down. Back and forth the conversation went. Mara felt lucky that her grandmother never directed that energy at her, but she started feeling sorry for her mother too. Maybe this was another well-known adult thing? You couldn't be nice to your own kid, but you could be nice to a grand-kid? The pattern would follow. Mara thought much the same comments were given to her but through her mother, not grandmother.

Well, no matter the cause, that wasn't a mystery Mara was interested in solving. She had better mysteries, ones that had prizes at the end. She finished eating first and then spent her time looking for an opportunity to leave for the staircases she had to check.

She thought about lying and saying she didn't feel well so her Dad would walk her back to their room, but that probably wouldn't work. He'd no doubt love the excuse to leave and stay in the room with her. She leaned forward and rested her chin in her hands, deep in imagined scenarios as the adult conversations continued.

What if she told them about the game and asked to go finish it but left out the part that she got it from a storage room instead of the children's room?

No, she couldn't risk it. Her mother would no doubt confiscate the tape as her next punishment.

Mara's gaze drifted to her mother as she thought. She was no longer talking to Mildred and had instead taken to staring towards her lap and fidgeting with her rings. She was unusually sullen and seemed to be out of responses for Mildred, but the older woman continued a steady stream of comments towards her. Mara would see her mother occasionally nod after a comment but nothing more.

Chapter 2: Resort Ruhe

The scene made Mara uncomfortable. She shifted in her seat, unknowingly mirroring her mother's nervous fidgeting. Shannon noticed the movement and turned her attention to Mara. Mildred was cut off mid comment when Shannon spoke. "You must be tired, Mara. I should have noticed sooner and asked if you wanted to go to bed. It was a long trip, and it's past your regular bedtime too."

She used a soft tone, and it caught Mara off guard. She looked between her grandmother frowning at her mother, and her mother giving Mara a concerned look. Before she could think better, the girl blurted out a response, "Mom, can you and Dad come to bed with me too? I don't want to go alone." She was a little too old for needing her parents to tuck her in or check under the bed for monsters, but Mara realized she said that to get her mother away from her grandmother. She felt protective of her for a moment, and she hoped her mother would reciprocate and keep her soft tone... maybe just for tonight.

Shannon pushed her chair out and stood up, motioning for her husband to do the same. "Yes, Sweetie, I think that's a good idea. We're all really tired tonight." Shannon stressed the word 'tired' while glancing back at her mother.

The Red god

"Fine, we'll see you for skiing tomorrow," Mildred replied in a curt tone and took no more notice of the family as they pushed their empty chairs back into the table and turned to leave.

Back in their rooms, Mara put on her pajamas and got ready for bed. She gave her backpack one last glance for the night, but she didn't regret her choice of giving up on sneaking away in favor of having her parents come to the room with her. She could hear her dad in the other room comforting her mother. Mara felt lighter tonight than most nights she spent with her parents. The room seemed at peace, although her mother was still quieter than usual.

After brushing her teeth, Mara hopped into her big bed and started rearranging the large amounts of covers and pillows to her liking. She sculpted a mountain and placed herself in the center. Perfect! She knew she'd sleep well in it.

The girl's eyes began drifting, but her parents knocked and came into the room before she was fully asleep. "Goodnight, Mara. We love you," her dad spoke, and her mother stood beside him with an arm wrapped around. Mara gave a sleepy smile and mumbled,

Chapter 2: Resort Ruhe

"Love you too..." It was a phrase she wasn't much used to, except special occasions like birthdays. It was a good night now.

Chapter 3: Day One

Mara was awakened by loud talking. "No, the other shoes! We're going to be late, and they'll be waiting on us." Her mother's bad mood seemed to be back. Mara rolled out of bed with a groan but straightened up when she saw her backpack and remembered yesterday's events.

She could play the game today! She couldn't help but take the tape recorder out of her backpack and turn it over in her hands again. How long would it take her to finish? Could she get the prize in one day? Her head swirled with daydreams once more before her mother knocked once and opened the door. In a panic, Mara shoved the device behind her back. Shannon took no notice and spoke, "It's time for breakfast and then to meet up with Cousin Danny's parents, Mara. Don't dawdle, get dressed."

Back in the dining room, Mara shoveled waffles and eggs into her face and occasionally chewed and breathed. Her mother had been rushing the family all morning. Apparently they slept late, and their ski lessons were about to start. Mara didn't care about that, but she

Chapter 3: Day One

was glad the rushing meant her parents would be gone soon, leaving her with her next adventure opportunity.

Mara was the first to clear her plate as her mother kept stopping to remind her dad about the day's schedule, and her dad tiredly shoved his food around his plate and sipped coffee. The girl almost threw her fork down in excitement after the last bite and asked, "Can I go find Danny and play now?" Mara thought it would be very easy to leave the dining area now and conveniently forget to find Danny and his parents by the pool.

"No, your dad can walk you over to them when he's done. I don't want you getting lost," her mother replied. Mara's attention shifted to her dad and he sighed before picking up his mug again. She watched in a mix of amazement and horror as he chugged the remaining contents without a break. Another adult mystery, why do they enjoy such a bitter, gross drink?!

Her dad stood up and motioned for Mara to do the same. "It's fine. I'm done anyway. Let's go find them."

Maybe it was the coffee kicking in, but Mara noticed her dad looked happier the further they walked. He broke the silence first. "I know you don't really want to spend your vacation babysitting your cousin, but the pool here is supposedly huge and has a waterslide at

65

one end." He paused to give her a smile. "I'm sure you'll still have fun without the ski lessons today."

Mara shifted her backpack to her other shoulder, noting the heavier weight due to the tape recorder it hid. "Yeah, I'll try. When are you and Mom getting done with the lessons though?" The question was innocent enough, but Mara was wanting to synchronize her watch to know the time limit she had on exploring.

"Hopefully around five o'clock. We have to get changed afterward and have dinner with the family at seven." He began searching his pockets before continuing. "Do you have a keycard for the room? Whenever you and your cousin are done with the pool, your mom wanted you to go straight back and wait for dinner with us."

Mara pulled her card copy out of the side of her backpack and nodded, but she consciously didn't verbally agree that she was going straight back to the room. It wasn't a lie if she didn't really say she was going to do it, right?

The pair took the left hallway and turned a corner. Soon after they found big glass windows and double doors into the pool room. A woman waved towards her dad and her from a lounge chair.

Chapter 3: Day One

David waved back and they walked over. "Hey, Gina, nice seeing you again," David greeted, "Danny got big, didn't he?"

The woman looked a little younger than Mara's parents. She had brunette hair up in a ponytail and wore a red two-piece swimsuit. She took off a pair of sunglasses while looking at Mara. "Oh you got big too! I think you grew a foot since I last saw you."

David replied before Mara could. "A foot? She already had two of them!" He chuckled at his own joke as Gina shook her head.

Mara took the opportunity to return her greeting. "Hi Mrs Gina, I came to hang out with Danny today."

Gina smiled warmly and waved her closer. "I know, Honey, I was waiting for you after I talked to your mom about the playdate last night. I'm glad you two are getting to hang out! Do you want to leave your backpack here with me while you change into your swimsuit and join Danny? He's already in the splash playground over there."

Mara shifted the backpack, suddenly uncomfortable. Gina seemed genuinely nice, so Mara didn't understand why she felt nervous leaving the backpack with her. She would have no reason to take the tape recorder from her. Still, she fought the urge to keep it on.

67

The Red god

Ignorant of her struggle, Mara's dad took it off her shoulder and handed it to Gina. "Thanks for watching Mara today. Me and Shannon appreciate it. We might be back late afternoon from skiing, but Mara has our room key and can stay there whenever you all are done with the pool."

Gina took the backpack and sat it beside the lounge chair with a pile of towels, water bottles, and her own bag. "No problem! I hope you enjoy the slopes!"

David turned and spoke to Mara before leaving. "Alright, you stay out of trouble, and we'll see you in the room when we're done." Mara nodded but again said nothing incriminating. After a last glance at her backpack on the floor, Mara walked to the back wall and entered the women's locker room. As she changed into her swimsuit, she wondered why the pool area would be so cold. Goosebumps formed on her skin. She rubbed her arms and tried to will it away as she walked back to Gina.

Gina smiled as Mara walked up, but her expression became confused as Mara got closer and sat on the next lounge chair. "Are you shivering, Honey? It's so hot and humid in here!"

Chapter 3: Day One

Mara realized she was actually physically shivering and rubbed her arms faster. "Hot? It feels freezing. I don't think I can get in the pool."

Gina shook her head and put her hands on Mara's arm. Her hands felt burning hot in contrast, and Mara flinched. "You are freezing!" Gina exclaimed, "Here, take this towel and warm up next to me for a while. Maybe you just have to get used to the temperature in here since you were in the colder hall before." Mara nodded and looked down as she wrapped the towel closer, feeling a little embarrassed to be babied like this.

Gina went on to make small talk, mostly about Danny or asking Mara questions about herself and school. After fifteen minutes and only a handful of quiet replies or nods from Mara, Gina leaned closer and held her hand against the girl's forehead.

"You don't have a fever, but you don't seem well. You're still shivering, you poor thing!"

Mara didn't exactly feel sick, but she felt frozen, as if ice was on the back of her neck. "I think I should go back to my room early," Mara started, "My parents won't mind." This would have been a good excuse for getting away early to go explore, but she honestly wasn't faking this. She furrowed her brow as she couldn't explain it either.

Gina gently brushed hair out of Mara's face before removing her hand from her forehead. "I should get Danny and we'll walk you up to your room."

At this suggestion, Mara vehemently shook her head. "No! I'll be okay! Our room is only down part of the hall and up one flight of stairs. It'll take me one minute to walk there."

Gina was about to call for Danny anyway, but as soon as she opened her mouth Mara jumped up and grabbed her backpack. "I'll see you and Danny around later! I'll wait in my room for my parents, bye!"

She took off as Gina shouted a reply. "Oh! Well I'll tell your parents if I see them first so they can check on you!"

Once outside the pool area, Mara decided it would be good to go back to the room first. She could get her heavy coat before exploring. That should solve the shivering.

She made her way down the hall and up to the room. Before changing, she noticed she already felt warmer. Maybe just the pool area was cold and Gina was one of those crazy people that wears shorts in winter outside. The girl shrugged and put on her previous outfit, another dress packed by her mother, but at least it wasn't too frilly. She opted to grab a thinner jacket instead and headed back out.

Feeling better, she was now a girl on a mission: Find the first clue at the staircase!

Not wanting to miss anything, Mara went back to the resort foyer to start. There were a few stairs leading from the outer doors down into the foyer. Mara looked around and tried to casually check them out without drawing the attention of the employees. Those stairs were made of stone and had a short metal bar for a handhold. Nothing of them was wood, so she continued down the right hall looking for the next one.

There was the staircase leading to their room on the next floor, using the shortcut the porter had shown them. Mara bent and inspected this one closer since no one was around. It was wood! But it had carpet on the steps covering most of it. She took out the tape recorder and pressed rewind briefly before playing. The voice of Rudy sounded louder this time, but Mara thought it was because she was trying to be sneaky, and everything was louder when you're trying to sneak. It was a law or something.

The Red god

"...find the first wooden staircase to the right of the resort entrance. You might want to pause this and unpause it for the clue once you're at the location." This time, Mara didn't pause it and let it continue. "...Are you there? Alright! Check carefully around the third wooden spindle, near the base, for the clue."

Mara pressed the button on the device and then moved to the third spindle from the bottom. She looked carefully, tried wiggling it, and then dug around in her backpack for the multi tool she had packed. Mara flipped through the tools before pulling out one with a tweezers end. She was so glad she packed tools! This was a very smart idea to think so far ahead. None of the other kids would have had this advantage.

She poked the tool around the spindle base for a few moments before jumping with a startle. "Remember! The third spindle from the top!" The tape recorder spoke. Mara thought she paused it, so the sudden voice scared her.

She was glad it wasn't paused though, because she was definitely checking the wrong one. This time Mara pressed the pause button with more force and then moved to the third spindle from the top. She started over with her process of looking into the base and wiggling it. This one was loose! The girl excitedly pulled the tweezers out and tried them in the tiny space around the bottom. She felt a little resistance on the side facing her, so she grabbed a few times with the tool and pulled. A small yellow stained wad came out.

It seemed old and brittle, so Mara slowly unrolled it. It was a piece of paper with writing on both sides. One side she couldn't read the language, but the other was English. She could read the words, but they didn't make much sense to her. She picked up the recorder and played it again.

"...Did you find it? Amazing! You're on the start of an incredible journey! Now that you found the first clue, I'll give you the first portion of the story." Mara beamed at the praise and pulled it closer to hear every word.

"There once was a young girl, orphaned in a village. The villagers took care of her basic needs since she didn't have anyone close, but besides that they ignored or sneered at her from afar. The villagers were stupid, slow, and fought often. But instead of fixing their own problems, they pointed at the girl and insulted her." Mara frowned, already feeling sorry for the girl.

"The girl was wise though. During her isolated time, she listened to the wind, the rain, the trees. They were older than the villagers. They were from the foundation of this world and took a liking to the girl. For they saw her. They really saw her and knew how special she was. It was like a star was among the villagers, and they were so dull and stupid as to not see it, but nature itself saw her and recognized it. So the wind spoke, and the girl listened. What's written on the piece of paper is but a small part of what the wind said. To progress, you must read it, dozens of times if necessary, and then find the location it speaks of for the next clue."

This was a strange story, Mara thought. Wouldn't the girl still be incredibly lonely with only wind keeping her company? It wasn't like wind could touch your arm or hug you.

Not wanting to ignore the game instructions, Mara looked around and read the paper as instructed, first to herself: "The Wind cares for you. The Wind follows you. Follow the Wind and find. Among the rock boundary you learn."

She felt a little silly, but she supposed repeating and memorizing the clue was supposed to help her later in the game. After three repeats to herself, she did three out loud: "The Wind cares for you. The Wind follows you. Follow the Wind and find. Among the rock boundary you learn."

Chapter 3: Day One

Prickles formed at her neck and arms once she finished. She nervously laughed to herself. It almost seemed like wind blowing on her, but there was an air vent she could see in the ceiling that must have been responsible for the sensation. Mara shook the feeling and checked her watch. It was only 11:38 a.m. She had plenty of time to try finding the next clue. Follow the wind... and a rock boundary.

Naturally, Mara thought it must be somewhere outside. With a confident nod the girl hopped up and grabbed her bag. First stop: Her room again to get her heavy jacket. Second stop: Outside!

With her coat in hand, Mara flew back down the stairs and ran excitedly towards the foyer where she knew she could get to an open door. Rounding a corner, she almost ran headfirst into a woman, but she stopped herself just short of impact.

"I'm sorry!" Mara shouted in surprise, stumbling back. She lifted her head up to see the woman. She was tall, thin, and had red hair that fell into her face as she leaned towards Mara.

"Are you okay?" the woman asked.

Mara nodded, embarrassed. "Yeah, sorry again."

The woman smiled and cocked her head slightly. "You know, if I knew you'd be so excited to come to my wedding I'd have sat you and your parents closer to the head table, Mara. That's why you were running full speed at me, right?" The woman laughed at her own joke and waved her hand in the air. "Oh, it's okay. I see you got your coat and must be excited to play in the snow. I wouldn't expect you to hang out with the adults all day."

Mara hadn't seen her cousin Samantha for a few years. She was very pretty, with green eyes and a sprinkle of freckles across her nose. The girl didn't want to be rude, but she also didn't want to get distracted from her mission. So she chose her words carefully.

"I was going to play outside, Samantha, but I am happy to be invited to your wedding. The resort you picked is very pretty! I just haven't seen the outside much yet."

Samantha smiled so wide her nose crinkled. "I'm really glad almost the whole family could make it. Some of you haven't met Ryan yet, but he is just the sweetest, funniest, kindest man."

The woman closed her eyes and audibly sighed. "Oh, and smart. And charming. And charitable. And..."

Mara began to tune her out at this point. She daydreamed often enough to recognize Samantha was off in her own Ryan-centered dreams. She looked really happy to be getting married, but didn't she know what came after? You have a kid that annoys you, you fight with your husband, you don't have enough money, and no one is happy. Marriages looked miserable. The fairytales Mara watched and the actual married adults she knew were a stark contrast.

After some time, Samantha caught herself. "...Annnd I've been rambling about Ryan for five minutes." She nervously giggled. "You'll have to meet him. How about you and Aunt Shannon sit at our table at dinner tonight?"

Mara was glad she finally finished, but she kept her forced polite composure. "That sounds fun! I'll see you later, Samantha!"

At that, Mara darted off beside her and towards the foyer doors once more. Samantha shouted a final reply, "Have fun outside! I'll see you all at dinner!"

Mara waved to indicate she heard and turned to shove the door open and headed outside.

Once outside, it was very quiet. She could no longer hear the vague hustle and bustle of employees in other rooms, guest chatter, or the hum from the lights and appliances. It was so quiet she could... hear the wind? Or what was she going to do outside to find the next clue?

She pulled her coat on and buttoned it up as she started to walk along the resort's left side. Standing around wouldn't help her find it, so she figured a slow walk around the building was a good start.

The building had stone walkways around it with what looked like solar lights along each side. But it was very sunny out this day, so they weren't on. Snow was piled on the sides, indicating the workers kept it well shoveled and maintained. Mara decided skipping would keep her warmer as she walked, so she did just that as she thought about the next clue and the game prize.

Eventually she turned the corner, following the left side heading towards the back of the resort. Here it was a bit more unkempt, with a few larger bushes that weren't well pruned like in the front. Mara wondered if the stone boundary might be the end of the sidewalk, but it all looked the same. There was nothing to indicate 'wind' or a clue. She didn't get discouraged though. She wasn't lazy or a quitter. Remembering the first story part, she imagined herself like the girl, who the wind thought was a star among the village. Stars shine and continue on!

Chapter 3: Day One

Turning the next corner, she was behind the resort now and had an amazing view of both mountains. She wasn't sure she'd ever get used to that view. It was breathtaking to see up close. After a moment of gawking, she turned her eyes down and started scanning further down the horizon. She saw skiers in the distance and assumed her parents were somewhere in the group. But they were very far away and could only see her as much as she saw them, a dot on the landscape.

Further down there was what looked like a gravel road near the middle between the two mountains. That might have been where she saw the teenagers playing with a ball last night. Where did that road lead to?

Mara scrunched up her face and cupped her chin with her hand, channeling her inner Sherlock for help. The teenagers didn't seem to live at the resort. She hadn't seen any kids that age in the main resort areas or on her behind-the-scenes tour of the service halls.

So there were two roads that Mara knew of that they could have come from: The one that their bus had originally taken them up to the resort entrance and the gravel one leading between the mountains and away from the back of the resort. Considering that she saw them in this spot before, the greatest possibility was that they lived somewhere beyond this road. Did knowing this help her with the clue? Could a rocky road be considered a boundary? Probably not.

What about following the wind? Was there a weathervane nearby? Maybe the wind generally goes one way through the mountains, and that would show her the direction to walk. She turned around and looked over the back of the resort roof.

There were a few satellite dishes and lots of chimneys and vents, but no weathervanes. Further to her right there were a few small buildings or sheds. They must have been for maintenance or utilities judging by their drab, unappealing colors. They had nothing on their roofs.

The girl's game of detective wasn't going well yet. Putting her hands on her hips in a new level of determination, she slowly turned and took in the whole surroundings again. What would Sherlock do next? He, and all her book and movie heroes, always instantly had the right solution. Mara wanted to be like that.

It wasn't fair her reality never matched her dreams. She wanted to blame someone or some circumstance for her not getting this clue easily, but she couldn't think of anyone but herself for her being stuck. This frustrated her more than being stuck!

Oh! What did the last message say? To repeat the first clue dozens of times if necessary? She supposed she should repeat it more. She started out loud this time: "The Wind cares for you. The Wind follows you. Follow the Wind and find. Among the rock boundary you learn."

There was no one nearby, so she was bold and repeated it louder: "The Wind cares for you. The Wind follows you. Follow the Wind and find. Among the rock boundary you learn."

Closing her eyes, she tried to visualize the story and the girl writing down the Wind's whispers.

"*Follow me.*"

Startled, Mara jolted and opened her eyes. She whipped her head around. No one was there. Had she imagined it? She had an amazing ability to get lost in her daydreams, but this hadn't happened before. The prickly sensation returned to the nape of her neck, and a breeze picked up. Her hair flowed in the wind and was swept to her left and in front. On instinct, she stood up and started walking in the direction.

The Red god

She didn't follow a cultivated path and instead crossed it and continued through shrubs and pathway lights before walking into a small patch of trees. The tree branches brushed her face and forearms as she held them up to move through. Red filtered through the trees and onto the snow below for a brief flash. Mara blinked to clear her vision. Inside the grouping of trees it was darker, but she could still see.

Near the middle, there were a few piles of stones that looked tooled and as if they were once stacked. The wind blew past once more and continued out through the other side of the trees. Mara followed and reached an incline with sparse trees and more rocks. As she walked, she saw she was right about the stones being stacked at one time. The clusters of stones were still stacked the further she walked, and they formed a waist-high wall that continued up and around. It looked like an old fence or... boundary.

This was it. The second clue was here.

Mara set her left hand to the stone wall, touching each in the top row as she went. The texture went from smooth to jagged chiseled and finally clear, defined etching. She stopped walking but kept her hand running over the etching and turned to inspect it. The first one looked like the same shapes and scrawls as was on one

Chapter 3: Day One

side of the first paper clue. The next was English, which she read: "The Wind can help you, more than you see, more than your own boundary."

Mara didn't understand merely by reading the words. She hurriedly pulled the tape recorder out of her bag and set it atop the stone wall before playing it. Static sounded for several long seconds before Rudy's now-familiar voice rang out. "...Have you found the clue at the rock wall? You're smart! I know you have! Good, now you can hear the next story portion."

"The girl listened to the Wind and was happy. She didn't grasp how it could help her, but she knew it was wise and powerful, a force that moved across the whole Earth wherever it pleased. 'I promise I'll listen further' the girl whispered back to the wind. It was happy and breezed through her hair in response, speaking more: 'I can help you. But as you see, I don't have a physical body. I will do this through you, if you will continue following.' The girl nodded before the wind resumed. 'You can do extraordinary things with me! First, speak to all the villagers. They are slow and easy to anger, as you know and have felt the brunt of. But I can help them, and they will see how special you are. Speak to them and ask what they desire. With your own knowledge, also inspect and see what prevents them from gaining their own desire and happiness. Tell it all to me.'"

Rudy dropped the 'story telling voice' and resumed in his usual brisk tone. "Now! To get the third clue, follow along with the story and with what the Wind asked of the girl. Talk to your family and friends and get their answers. You can either write these down in a journal or speak them when you're alone before you play this recording again! You can pause it until you're ready to move on! Happy playing!"

Mara pressed pause and lingered her hand on the button. What a strange game this is turning into! She wasn't stupid; she knew Rudy must have taken into account the wind patterns in this region when he made the clues. They were so accurate it was eerie, almost as if the wind itself did lead her here. He must have been a very smart man and put a lot of work into creating this.

She turned and looked back at the etched words in the stone boundary. It could have taken weeks or months to put the message in the stone. If Rudy put this much work into the game, what could the prize be?

The girl briefly thought of Willy Wonka and the Chocolate Factory. That was an amazing game as well, with a lot of work and build-up to what Willy really wanted the goal to be: To give his factory to a deserving child as his legacy. Could the prize be equally amazing here?

She got giddy thinking about the possibilities. Maybe her daydreams were sweeping her away too much, but it was fun to let them go occasionally. Whatever the prize was, she still wanted to race towards it. Onto the next clue!

The girl kneeled to fix one of her boot laces before putting her backpack on and sprinting towards the resort entrance back the way she came. On the way, she thought about how to get the answers from her family. Asking those questions seemed a bit silly. But with how much care Rudy put into the game, she knew it must serve a purpose to do this part.

She was winded and had to stop and catch her breath before she made it into the resort. Spotting a large decorative rock on the side of the resort pathway, she sat and took her notebook out of her bag. The game said she could speak the answers or write them down, but writing things down seemed much more detective-like.

The Red god

Mara decided to start by writing "Clue #3" at the top of a page along with columns and a list of names below it:

"Name, Desire, Problem

Mother

Dad

Grandmother

Grandfather

Aunt Barbara

Uncle Larry

Cousin Samantha

Aunt Gina"

That seemed like a good start. There were a lot of other family members at the resort not on this list yet, but she didn't really know how many she needed to talk to, and at least she had already talked to the people in the list once while here. It would be easier to find and talk to them again.

She checked her watch and noted the time as 2:26 p.m. She still had some time to kill before her parents were done with skiing. They were top on her list, but that didn't mean she needed to talk to them first. She tried to think of who she would have opportunity to ask during dinner and who she wouldn't.

Chapter 3: Day One

Samantha mentioned them eating at her table tonight, but she didn't know who else would be at the table. Well, there's no point wasting time trying to predict it. Mara swung her legs off the rock and stood back up, walking towards the resort entrance at a more normal pace now.

Would Gina still be at the pool? Would it be too awkward if she tried to re-join her and talk? Despite Mara's adventurous spirit, she could be very shy to talk to. Real-life people were very different than her adventure stories. But this was part of her adventure! So she had to try her best!

Making up her mind, Mara began walking that direction after re-entering the resort. She walked several minutes and reached the big windows and double doors into the pool area.

She paused, only peeking inside but not entering yet. Gina was there on the same lounge chair. How should she do this? Just walk inside and say, "Hi Ms Gina, what's your life's desire?"

She grimaced from the awkwardness of even thinking that. She had to be more subtle, more... normal. Plus, Rudy warned her to keep the game secret for now. She couldn't risk Gina or her other family members questioning her behavior.

Mara was a pretty good actor though. She learned throughout the years how to act to stay out of trouble, how to act to avoid most bullies, and how to act to stop some of her parents' fights. If she approached this right, she could do it. With more confidence now that she practiced scenarios in her head, she opened one of the double doors and walked towards Gina.

Gina was a mothering type. She already fussed over Mara earlier this morning, so the girl knew she could play to that. Mara stopped a few feet away and noticed Gina was reading a book and hadn't noticed her presence yet. It was always easier when other people started conversations, but this was no time to be shy and lock up, Mara thought.

The girl gathered her courage and spoke first. "Hey Ms Gina... I went up to my room for a while, but I feel better and got bored. Can I still hang out with you and Danny till my parents are done?"

Gina was visibly startled and slammed her book shut, turning to Mara. "Oh! Haha, hi Honey. Of course, sit down!"

Mara glanced at the cover of the book before Gina set it aside. It was a man with a torn shirt, wolf-like features growing on his face, and blood dripping onto his... defined ab muscles. Her face blushed and she turned away to face the pool. Adults read weird books.

Gina patted the chair next to her. "Sit, sit! I see you got an extra coat. Wow! That cold, huh?"

Mara noticed she was still wearing her outside coat and hurried to take it off, setting it on the chair before she sat herself. "Uhm, yeah, it is pretty cold here. Much colder than home."

Gina smiled and nodded. "I guess it is. There's a ton of snow from the mountains too, but it's a beautiful scene to look at."

The two made small talk for several minutes, as Mara thought how to steer the conversation. At one point Gina switched to talking about Danny, how he was enjoying the stay and the pool. Mara thought this was as good of an opening as any, so she began her prying questions.

"You dote on Danny a lot. Did you always want to be a mom? Even when you were younger?" the girl asked, trying to keep an air of innocence and curiosity.

Gina's smile changed, and she looked out at the group of kids playing in the splash area. "I don't know about always, but certainly after I knew about Danny being on the way I did. I loved him before he was born. I think most mothers do."

The Red god

That was a nice answer, Mara supposed, but it didn't give her any insight into Gina's life desire.

She decided to try again. "Did you want to be something else when you were a kid?"

This elicited a chuckle from Gina. "A million things! I think at one point I wanted to be a race car driving baker. I could never focus on just one thing. But they changed as I got older, and being a mom was definitely one I'm glad I fell into."

The woman turned to face Mara more. "You must be thinking about growing up a lot, huh? I guess being at your cousin's wedding will do that. You two met when you were both still kids, although she was a lot older than you, and here she is getting married."

Gina sighed wistfully at the last words. Mara had to be careful here. She needed to make sure the conversation didn't redirect to herself too much or she'd lose her line of questioning.

The young girl looked towards her lap and fiddled with a loose thread on her dress. "Yeah, I am, but it's confusing. I don't know much about it. Like, how do you make sure you're happy? Is there a specific job or goal you have that you focus on?"

She didn't get an answer right away and had to turn to look at Gina. The woman was staring out towards the pool again, lost in thought. Mara hoped she hadn't asked too weird of a question. She didn't want to gain suspicion and get questioned herself.

Finally, Gina started again. "I think... happiness isn't a thing you attain all at once like a prize. It's a journey. I'm happy now with my husband and son, my little family. And our few pets and my job keep me busy too. But I also think I'll be happy in the future, maybe with more climbing in my career, more free time to hang out with my girlfriends, more time to read when Danny gets older and needs me less. I think things will change, and I'll keep finding happiness in different places."

She turned and grabbed Mara's hands in her own. "And, Honey, I'm sure you'll find your own happiness in whatever you want to pursue."

This answer made Mara... angry, confused. She had to stop herself from snatching her hands away from Gina. She must be lying, like adults do.

People weren't happy that easily. Her parents weren't. Her grandparents weren't. And Samantha wouldn't be either. Mara thought Gina must have been talking in polite terms to her since she was still a kid. Her real answer had to be somewhere hidden.

But she didn't want to offend Gina and cause trouble, so she nodded and put on a fake smile. "I guess I'll have to see. I still won't be an adult for a long time."

Gina didn't notice the girl's change in demeanor and went back to talking. The woman shared a few stories from her own childhood, but Mara mostly tuned her out at this point, only keeping a polite appearance of listening and nodding.

At one point Gina's husband returned and joined them in the next chair over. The two adults took over talking as Mara got out her notebook and started taking notes under the pretense of doodling.

She noticed Gina's husband giving her a mental list of things to do at one point: Get Danny lunch, go back to the room and make sure the clothes were pressed and ready for dinner, reply back to the pet sitter about something, remember his parents were coming the week after they got back, and on.

Gina continued smiling as they talked, but Mara thought she saw something beneath it. Tiredness. What was hidden in Gina's 'happiness' speech? She mentioned having more time in the future. Maybe that was her main desire, beneath the lies of happiness.

Chapter 3: Day One

Mara wrote "more time" besides Gina's name in her journal's list. She still had the 'problem' column to fill out for her though. What was Gina's problem? Gina's blocker to getting her desire?

Mara tapped her pencil against her chin while thinking. Well, for one she wasn't honest about wanting it now. Mara thought she definitely lied to her with her answer. She wrote down "honesty" in the problem column and shut her notebook. That should be enough for her.

At this point, Gina was getting up and grabbing her things. "I'm going to take Danny back to our room to get dressed and start getting ready for dinner later. Would you like us to walk you back to your room first, Mara?"

The girl shook her head and stood up to gather her coat and backpack. "Thanks, but I'm okay. I can walk back by myself."

Gina gave a thoughtful look. "You know, you're a lot more mature than I was at your age, more independent and thinking too. But remember, you're never too adult to spend time with us."

Mara nodded and smiled. "I know, I just want to beat my parents back to our room faster. But I'll see you and Danny later, bye!"

The Red god

Mara thought about Gina's last words as she ran back to her room. She seemed more mature? More independent? Maybe this talk did have Gina seeing Mara differently. Did the villagers see the girl differently after she asked the questions the Wind wanted her to? Maybe that was the point of this game step? She shook her head. She'd have to finish the task first and get the next story segment from Rudy, then she'd know what happened.

Back in her room, Mara doodled in her notebook while waiting for her parents. She thought she may be able to write out part of their answers even before asking them. The problem columns for them already had some apparent answers.

She wrote down "controlling, anger, and selfish" for her mother's entry and "avoidant, cowardly" for her dad's. Now that she thought about it, she didn't really know what her dad wanted out of life. It obviously wasn't what he had now. He wasn't happy with his wife or most of their home life. He worked a lot, but that didn't make him happy either. His constant working seemed to fit more into the avoidant term Mara put as his problem.

Chapter 3: Day One

Thinking about them for too long made Mara frustrated, so eventually she flipped to another page in her notebook and began drawing Hershey. Mara missed her, even though it was only a few days ago that she saw her. Whenever her parents made her upset, she was always there to pet, always purring in response. She was a good cat.

Mara was halfway through doodling a background for Hershey's page when the door to her parents' room was unlocked and they entered. "...you better. Those are clean clothes I packed for each evening. They need to stay clean. Goodness knows my mother will comment on anything."

Mara noted her mother's mood as she heard her talking first. Her task might be hard to complete tonight, but she had to try. She put her notebook back in her bag and walked over to the doorway separating the rooms. "Hi Mom, how was skiing?" Mara thought some diplomacy first would help her reach her answers easier. David gave Mara a pitying look before walking into the bathroom of their room and shutting the door.

Unfortunately Mara was used to that look. It meant "She's in a bad mood, good luck." She heard the shower start and figured her dad was trying to get some peace before tonight's dinner.

The Red god

Shannon scoffed. "That ski instructor didn't know what he was doing, and neither did your dad. He fell twice and got a tear in his new jacket." Her mother shuffled through dresses on hangers as she ranted. It wasn't directed towards Mara yet, but she knew that was coming next, so she stayed quiet and checked her own dress for any traces of lint or hairs to get ahead of her mother's complaints.

After throwing a dress hanger on their bed, Shannon turned her attention to Mara as predicted. "And? Are you ready for dinner? I told you what time it was at and what dress you should wear."

Mara nodded. "I know... I got back to the room early and I've been ready."

Her mother motioned for her to spin, and she begrudgingly did so. The woman couldn't find anything to nitpick, so she waved Mara off. "Well, the dress looks good. Alright, just wait while your dad and I finish getting ready."

Mara was nervous but wanted to be brave and get her mother's answer out of the way, so she didn't leave and instead sat on the side of her parents' bed as her mother dressed. She tried to think about her mother outside of their typical interactions. Did anything make her happy? Did she have daydreams of her own? Her only goal

96

Chapter 3: Day One

seemed to be keeping up good appearances for family, but did that count as her life's desire?

Mara didn't know, but she formulated a few careful questions to get there. "Cousin Samantha said we'd sit with her tonight. Will Grandma be at our table too?"

Her mother struggled with her dress zipper and sighed. "Samantha didn't tell me she changed the seating. I don't know. Maybe."

Mara was encouraged it wasn't an angry reply at least. She continued with her next question. "Would it make you happy if Grandma can join us?" This question made her mother visibly flinch. She jerked open a jewelry box and started putting on a set of gold earrings. Mara thought the movements used more force than required, which was a bad sign for their talk.

"Your grandma doesn't make anyone happy" Shannon finally replied. The woman suddenly turned and faced her daughter. "And why would you ask that!? Did Samantha ask about your grandma and me?"

Mara vigorously shook her head. "No! No one talked about you. I just wanted to find out what would make you happy." This

97

explanation didn't deter her mother from her start of an interrogation.

She leaned in closer but spoke in a lower tone. "Did your dad ask you to bring this up?"

Mara knew how the rest of this conversation was going to go. Her mother was spiraling and would only stop when it was time to put on a fake face for the family at dinner.

The girl did her best to assuage her mother anyway. "No... I was alone after the pool, and I came up here. I was drawing and thinking about things."

Shannon remained postured in front of her. "Thinking about what? How to make tonight worse?" Mara shook her head but didn't reply this time. The woman continued. "You know what would make me happy? If you didn't lie. Someone put you up to this. Someone needs to mind their FUCKING BUSINESS!"

Mara flinched and turned away, partially because the last words were loud and partially because her mother was so close her breath was offensive in her face.

The bathroom door lock clicked, and Mara's father came out, dressed for dinner except a missing tie. He seemed oblivious to the mood of the room as he asked Shannon where his matching tie was hung. Mara didn't dare make eye contact with either of them, hoping to be forgotten and escape the rest of the episode.

Shannon grabbed a tie off a nearby hanger and grabbed David's arm as she drug him back into the bathroom and began her next interrogation of the night. Harsh whispering was heard, ninety percent from Mara's mother, but she couldn't make out the words. Mara waited a few moments, trying to stay very quiet and still, until she was sure her movement wouldn't bring her mother's attention back to her.

She seemed entirely engrossed in her argument with her husband now, so Mara carefully got off the bed's edge and crept back to her room through the shared doorway.

The girl slowly shut the door, making sure to pre-turn the doorknob so it didn't click when it met the door jam. She sighed in relief when she had it closed and removed her hand from the knob.

Well that didn't work! Mara strode angrily across the room and climbed into her bed, pulling the covers over her head. She was stupid for thinking that would work! That all she needed was to be brave and ask the questions anyway! Stupid!

Despite knowing she needed to remain quiet, she began sobbing in frustration. She hoped the covers muffled the sounds enough. The last thing she needed was her mother hearing and turning her anger on her again tonight.

She began mocking her mother's responses in her head: "Mara, you shouldn't cry! You'll make the family look bad! Mara, you shouldn't ask stupid questions! You'll make me mad! Mara, you shouldn't try to make things better! You'll fuck THEM UP!"

A loud gasping sob escaped her, and she covered her mouth to quiet the next one. She had to get a hold of herself. This wasn't the first episode her mother ever had, and it wouldn't be the last. Mara had to do better. She needed to read the mood ahead of time and keep her mouth shut. She knew this. She already learned this lesson a dozen times. She needed to stop thinking things could change or that she would be the one to make them better. What could a stupid girl like her do!

After several minutes of trying to control her breathing, the sobs stopped and she was calm enough to think. She removed the covers from her head and grabbed her backpack from the floor. After Mara cleaned her face up with a wad of tissues, she turned her attention to her notebook. Her hands traced the sketch of Hershey. Looking at it made her more calm, but she couldn't bring herself to smile.

Chapter 3: Day One

She flipped back to her notes for the third clue. There was no way she was going to try asking her mother further questions. But what should she write for her 'Desire' answer? She didn't have any new information to go off of. Mara sighed and wrote "A better family?". This wasn't a perfect answer, but maybe it was good enough for the game.

She looked at her watch and noted it was still twenty minutes until dinner, but Mara was already exhausted. She idly thought about claiming she was sick to get out of going downstairs with her parents, but there was no way her mother would allow that or not punish her for it.

She wanted Mara dressed correctly and with a happy face to present to family tonight. There was no getting out of it, so she spent those twenty minutes staring out the window in thought.

She imagined the prize at the end of the game was citizenship to a hidden village. A village where everyone was nice and happy. Her parents weren't at the village, but there was a man and a woman there that looked similar to them, and they warmly welcomed Mara to live with them. Hershey was allowed to join her, and they lived together without fighting or arguing.

101

The Red god

While still mid daydream, her mother opened the door and curtly told her it was time to leave for dinner.

Walking the halls to the dining room, the trio was very quiet. This was typical after an episode, but Mara wondered if her dad was mad at her too. She did cause this, so she supposed she deserved it.

If she was able to hear the argument between her parents before she ran off and hid in her bed, then maybe she'd know what to say to calm her mother and divert most of the anger away from her dad. At least she could have one of them not mad at her.

But if Mara didn't know the exact thing to say, then it was better to say nothing. She decided to only answer direct questions tonight, at least while her mother was present. That was the safest.

They arrived at the dining room, and Mara snuck a peek at the banquet line-up while her mother looked around for Samantha's table. Similar to last night they had a dozen tall platters with meats, cheeses, bread rolls, and what smelled like apple pastries. There were also two serving containers with stews.

Chapter 3: Day One

The layout looked very appealing, but Mara didn't find herself very hungry after the evening she had. She felt a sudden tug on her hand and dutifully turned to follow her parents over to Samantha's table.

It was near the middle of the room, and while walking Mara spotted her grandparents two tables away. She felt relieved knowing her mother and grandmother wouldn't have an opportunity to fight tonight.

Samantha's table itself had a dark purple tablecloth and bigger centerpiece composed of white Baby's Breath and purple flowers Mara didn't recognize. The table was full of adults except for three seats. Mara recognized Samantha and her parents. The older couple was well dressed with the man in a dark gray suit and the woman in a dark purple collared dress. She assumed the young man sitting next to Samantha was Ryan.

It might have been rude, but Mara scrunched up her face while she overtly stared at him. He was okay looking, tall, short dark brown hair, a well groomed beard, wearing a black suit with white shirt and purple handkerchief. But Mara still didn't know what Samantha saw in him to rave that much. She made him sound like a celebrity or supermodel. He looked very human.

The Red god

Ryan caught Mara's stare and gave a grin and a wave. Samantha stood up and greeted Shannon first. "I'm glad you guys could make it! Please sit! We'll move this chair to make more room." She giggled as she began moving an empty chair. "It's crazy how crowded it gets when you're getting married. I've never entertained this many people before."

Ryan stood up too. "Sam, please sit. I'll move them. You've been up and down all day." Samantha visibly blushed and sat back in her seat at his insistence.

Oh boy, it was going to be a long night, Mara thought. They were already doing the lovebird act.

Shannon put on her usual fake smile and replied to Samantha. "Thank you for inviting us to join you tonight! I'm sorry we didn't get to greet you and your parents last night."

Samantha wrapped her arm around Ryan's as he sat back down next to her. "Oh, don't worry about it! Everyone had such long flights! Me and Ryan fell in love with this venue after looking through the ski resorts my parents suggested, but I felt bad asking everyone to travel so far!"

Samantha shifted her hand before continuing. "Speaking of Ryan... I'm excited to introduce him to you! And have you seen the

Chapter 3: Day One

ring he proposed with?" She grinned widely and leaned closer to show Shannon. "It's a sapphire, passed down from his mother. God rest her, she had beautiful tastes." Samantha turned to Ryan for the last comment. "I wish I got to meet her."

Ryan patted her arm. "She would have loved you; trust me." The young man gestured to an older man sitting to the left of him. "Sorry, I'm being rude. Let me introduce my father. I keep forgetting which of Sam's family already met him."

The man extended a hairy hand to Mara's dad and firmly shook his. "Bruce! Nice to meet you and your lovely wife!"

Mara didn't want to be rude, but she wondered if Ryan was going to look like his dad when he got older. Bruce was mostly bald with wisps of gray hair on the sides and an abundance of hair on his hands and coming out of his ears. He dressed well in a black suit, but some of the buttons held on for dear life over a very apparent gut.

Would Samantha be miserable married to Ryan if he did change? Something would make them miserable after marriage. Despite her harsh judgment of his appearance, Mara thought he had a kind face and tried to not stare at his ear hair further.

105

The Red god

The adults settled into further small talk, and Mara picked at the food on her plate. She took a bite every so often to avoid being scolded by her mother for playing with it, but she still wasn't very hungry. She thought about her notebook in her backpack. She wanted to pull it out and look over her list or doodle, but she didn't dare in front of her parents. They were seated on either side of her and could easily look over her shoulder from their vantage.

She settled for pushing carrots around her plate, pretending to write with her fork. Samantha's 'Desire' answer seemed obvious even without asking her. She wanted love and she wanted to love. Her infatuation with Ryan showed that. Mara planned to write that answer in her notes later.

Mara tried to follow some of the adult talk when it concerned Samantha. She was on her mind for her notes currently, so she might as well see if she can finish her row for the 'Problems' column. Mostly the adults were talking about her and Ryan's future plans, honeymoon, the house they were buying, finishing her degree, and if they liked kids or not. Samantha animatedly answered most questions, with Ryan gladly answering a few but in a more reserved manner.

Chapter 3: Day One

Mara tried to think of what she knew of Cousin Samantha from earlier years. She always got a lot of family attention. She was pretty, somewhat athletic, and smart. She graduated valedictorian in a private high school, and Mara's parents had to send her a graduation present. It was a big deal.

From Mara's personal interactions, she remembered Samantha playing with her during several family gatherings. She was always nice and didn't seem to mind playing with a young kid despite being so much older.

Mara liked her more before she knew Ryan though. It was like her head became filled with tweeting birds carrying around heart decorated banners with Ryan's name on them. Maybe being naive of growing up, marriage, and what it all meant for her future reality was the 'Problem' answer.

Samantha certainly didn't seem to see any potential problems in her future. She didn't know anything. Mara was younger, but she already knew a lot about adults and how marriage goes. She didn't have to experience it herself yet to see it in the adults around her. Mara shoved the last chunk of bread roll to the other side of her plate, satisfied with her answer.

The Red god

The rest of dinner droned on. Mara almost forgot how angry her mother was tonight by the way she put on a happy face for Samantha and family. She found herself wishing this was real happy instead of fake happy. As much as she wanted to go back to her room for the night, she was dreading when the mask would drop from her mother after they were alone. It probably wouldn't be as bad as the initial yelling she did, but it still was a tense atmosphere.

Eventually Mara was freed from the adult talking marathon as Samantha's parents stated it was time for them to retire to their room. The rest of the adults politely followed, scooting out their chairs and saying more drawn-out goodnights.

Mara followed behind her parents as they left the dining area and began down the hall. The silence predictably descended upon them as soon as they were out of earshot of the family remaining at the tables. Neither Mara nor her dad wanted to be the first one to test the waters and see what mood Shannon was in. The safe route was to wait and let her say something first.

"Damn it..." Shannon tiredly muttered, "My bag is still at the table. I'll be right back."

As she strode back to the dining room, David spoke next. "Mara?"

Chapter 3: Day One

She stopped looking down at the carpet and turned to her dad hesitantly. "Yeah...?"

He looked unsure and took a moment to continue. "I don't know what you actually asked your mother earlier, because she always skews things when she's in a mood, but please don't do it again. She nearly took my head off."

He sighed and hunched over slightly, forehead in hand. "It's better if we aren't seen talking much either. She thinks we're ganging up on her. Try to not talk to me, at least until she calms down. It's not really your fault, but you know how she is."

He turned to give Mara a sad half smirk, thinking the last line was like an inside joke between them, but Mara didn't return the attempted smile. Her face remained a tired, pained frown. She nodded instead of verbally replying to avoid breaking his new rule.

Shannon returned after a few moments. They walked back in silence, but she began criticizing various things about the dinner conversation and guests after they reached the room. David let her do most of the talking, only nodding and agreeing occasionally.

Her attention wasn't on Mara, so the girl took the opportunity to retreat to her own bedroom and close the door between their rooms.

The Red god

Mara felt like she hadn't slept in a week from the day's events and long dinner. Despite her exhaustion, she wanted to write in her notebook before bed. She took it out and hopped on the bed, pausing to move the pillows and covers around to an acceptable coziness level. Satisfied with her work, she pulled the paper onto her lap and started writing out Samantha's answers she had decided on earlier.

She stared at the page, tapping her pencil. She had three rows filled out, but one answer for her dad and all answers for her grandparents and Aunt Barbara and Uncle Larry were still blank.

She had thought she'd ask her dad after her mother's was done, but that was hard when she was banned from talking to him. Her mother ruins everything!

Mara scowled and was tempted to draw a sketch of her mother. It should have crazy flying hair, an open yelling mouth, and a snake as the tongue. That would suit her tonight. But the more she thought, the more she didn't want to see her face or make the effort to draw it.

One thing was for certain, her mother was not going to prevent her from winning the game's prize! Mara knew she couldn't change her mother, but she could be sneaky and finish this far away from her.

If she couldn't ask her dad for his answer directly, then she'd have to write her best guess down. He always avoided his wife, but he was never brave enough to make her stop or leave entirely.

Mara knew a few kids from school that had divorced parents. Supposedly they were both happier after that. But Mara's dad never brought it up in their arguments, or not the ones Mara eavesdropped on at least. So freedom might be a good answer. But it was more of an immediate wish. What would he want in his life if he was already free? That was hard.

Mara suddenly felt too restricted by her cover pile and shoved and stretched out until she had more room. A nagging feeling grew in her stomach as she thought. What did she know about her dad?

They hardly talked, except if he was complaining about Mara's mother to her. When he talked to Shannon, really talked and not just nodded along to her talking, he usually bragged about something at work: His team got a big project done, his boss gave a good review, or his recent raise. Mara was tempted to say success at work in that case, but he already had a lot, and it never made him happier.

The Red god

Her parents did argue about money regularly. That was one topic that actually made Mara's dad angry. He hated to be insulted about how much money his job made for the family, especially when compared to Shannon's parents who had a lot. The answer of money seemed to check a lot of boxes for a life's desire, at least in Mara's limited view. She wrote down "money" for her dad's answer and shut the notebook. It was time to sleep. She did enough tonight.

Chapter 4: Day Two

The morning came quietly. Mara wasn't woken up by any noise. She wasn't woken up by movement nor light. It was a rare morning where dreams gently fade into warm covers and soft pillows. She stretched and removed covers from her face to look out the large window facing the mountain. The sun was half risen, cresting the side of the mountain and showering golden rays on the otherwise white and blue landscape.

It was still early morning, but Mara had slept straight through the night and felt rested. A lingering feeling from her dreams gave her a rare sense of peace, but she couldn't recall the actual dream. She guessed it was of Hershey or Beth and Jace.

After watching the sun climb higher for ten or twenty minutes, Mara was reminded of her small dinner the night before. She was hungry enough this morning to make up for it. Despite her appetite though, she didn't want to be the one to wake up her parents for breakfast. She wanted the peace to last more than she wanted to eat.

Mara rolled, burying her face in her pillow. Sometimes closing her eyes and blocking out light helped her to think. She wished she could remember her dream if she had time to kill. Trying to remember dreams always reminded her of a book she read.

The Red god

The main character was a man in a coma for years, his entire teenage to adult life. The story followed his consciousness as he dreamed, and his dreams incorporated parts of real life occurring around his hospital bed.

But what was most interesting to Mara was a doctor that came in to study the man's case. The doctor was a sleep specialist who thought he could use his knowledge of the brain and dream functions to help long-term coma patients. He eventually hooked the man up to a machine of his that could manipulate brain waves in such a way to communicate with and alter the dreams of patients. Using this, the doctor guided the man to dream of the events surrounding the accident that led to his comatose state, work through his denial and emotions, and eventually accept what happened and the reality of his past ten years of life.

The man woke up at the end and felt peace and hope, but he did not remember the years of dreams or work of the doctor at all! Yet despite the memories not being accessible, the result of the work, success of acceptance and peace remained. Mara liked the book even though it didn't include her usual hero, detective, or adventurer type. When she felt especially stressed by her parents, she likes to escape to sleep and pretend a sleep doctor would fix her by the time she woke up.

Sometimes it helped. The worst emotions got sorted and put away into boxes in her brain, removing their fresh, prominent presence by the time morning rolled around. Mara didn't know when she drifted back to sleep, but she awoke to knocking this time. "Mara," her dad's voice called out, "it's time to head down for breakfast."

After getting cleaned up and dressed, Mara joined her parents, and they walked to the dining room together.

On the way, Shannon talked to her husband about the day's plans. "Since we're splitting up for the day, I was thinking Mara should stay with the other kids. They have activities planned for them in the children's room."

Mara grimaced, walking behind them. The activities probably included patty-cake and nap time, not that she was planning on sticking around to join them.

"Isn't she a little old for that group?" David replied. Shannon huffed. "She's too young for the women's spa day. The spa here is sixteen and older."

Mara took note of her mother's walk, how she held her arms, and the speed of her movements as they walked in silence for another minute. The girl took it in and estimated it would be safe to speak up with a suggestion. "Mom, what if I hung out with someone not joining the activities today? Like Aunt Gina?"

David turned his head just enough to give Mara a glance. She didn't make eye contact long enough to determine if it meant "don't do that", "are you sure?", or something else.

Shannon luckily didn't catch it and replied, "Gina is going to the spa... but I don't know what your grandparents are doing. If your dad wants to ask around, he can."

Mara wasn't relieved at this answer. Her dad wasn't the type of person to take control, so she figured there was a good chance he would decline and follow Shannon's initial idea of Mara staying in the children's room.

But to her surprise he replied, "Yeah, I'll ask them." Maybe he thought her current mood was good enough to risk it. Whatever the reason, Mara was grateful and got a slight bounce in her step the rest of the way.

Once in the dining room, they sat at the first empty table with their food. Mara's appetite was unrestrained by the buffet of waffles, eggs, sausage, biscuits, and fruit, so she piled her plate high. Mara didn't want to push her luck by questioning when her dad was going to ask her grandparents about watching her. Instead she busied herself working through her food mountain.

The silence between her parents as they ate would have been considered awkward to other people, but it was something Mara was used to. It was a predictable silence after a particularly bad night last night.

Mara took the time to look around the dining room and watch some of the other family members. There were some other distant cousins that Mara was vaguely aware of, but she only knew the names and faces from brief introductions at previous family events. She didn't talk to them or really know them.

One was a husband and wife with two small children, a boy younger than Danny and a baby girl. The mother was fussing over them both, cutting up food for the boy and spoon feeding the baby girl. The woman would smile and babble back at the baby to encourage each bite of food. Her husband also smiled as he chatted with their young boy and sipped his coffee.

Mara felt a slow burning make its way into her chest while watching them. It was a confusing, uncomfortable feeling. She wanted to be angry at them, but she didn't understand why. They weren't doing anything wrong. They looked very happy with each other, but watching it didn't make her happy.

Mara turned away and focused back on her plate. She'd nearly emptied it, but a few vestiges of waffles remained. True to her appetite, she had eaten enough to make up for last night's light dinner, but her eyes had been bigger than her stomach while going through the buffet line. She hoped her mother wasn't paying too much attention and wouldn't scold her for not finishing it.

While thinking of her mother, Mara snuck a glance at her. Shannon was reading through a booklet she had picked up at the resort. It had a big picture on the front with the gold RESORT RUHE sign that had been behind the check-in desk. Further down, it had Samantha and Ryan's name on it.

Mara began wondering how much they spent on this wedding. She didn't have a great concept of actual costs for the resort rooms, food, events, and these fancy custom booklet schedules. But if she had to guess, it was probably at least two cars' worth. Cars were expensive. She learned this from her parents' last big argument when her dad bought his new one.

But Samantha's parents and Ryan's dad didn't seem bothered by anything last night. If the cost were a lot for them, they probably would have been tense. Maybe they had a lot more money than Mara's parents, and cars weren't a big deal to them. The girl mentally shrugged the thought off. She was glad she didn't have to personally worry about adult things like money yet. It never seemed pleasant.

"What's the next thing on the schedule again?" Mara's dad broke the long silence. Her mother seemed annoyed at this question but began answering. "I told you the schedule before. Also you're capable of picking one of the booklets up and reading it yourself."

David thought better of replying and went back to quietly sipping his coffee. Despite his silence, Shannon picked the topic back up with an audible sigh. "Today is Guy-Girl Day. I'll be going to the spa with the other women, as I said. The guys will be meeting outside the resort at ten o'clock to do some mountain hike. Then dinner starts at 6 p.m."

Mara wasn't too interested in the schedule, but she flip through it when her mother set it down. Tomorrow was sledding and tubing, movies and wine bar the next day, a culture and shopping experience, and then finally the wedding day.

The sledding sounded fun, but Mara didn't know if she'd be allowed by her parents to join in or if she needed the day to solve more clues. There was no use planning far ahead though. She knew what she needed to do today to get the next clue, and that was enough.

With an exaggerated stretch, her dad put his empty coffee down and started getting up from the table. "I see Gareth and Mildred walked in. I'll ask them about watching Mara."

Mara wanted to jump up and follow him, but her mother gave her a glare, so she sat back in her seat and waited. She was glad they were splitting up for the day. The sooner her mother leaves for the spa the better. Mara didn't want to be around her any longer today. It was stifling.

Despite having to sit still next to her mother, Mara tried to focus all her energy into listening to her dad's conversation with her grandparents. She made out a word or two but nothing she could string together into an answer.

Chapter 4: Day Two

After a few moments, her dad left her grandparents and walked back over. "Mildred wants to rest in this morning, but they'll join you for lunch and watch you the rest of the afternoon, Mara. I guess you'll have to join the children's activities until then." The girl slid down further in her chair, disappointed at the answer, but she nodded understanding to not be rude.

After another twenty minutes of silence, Shannon got up and began clearing her and Mara's plate. "I have to join up with the women first because the sauna starts at 9:30. David, can you walk Mara to the children's room?"

David got back up, seeming eager to leave. "Sure, I'll take her right now so I have time to change before the hike. C'mon kiddo, let's go."

Shannon left them, and David and Mara began walking down the hall the opposite direction. He made a few comments as they went, trying to talk up the kids' activities and cheer Mara up, knowing she didn't want to go.

But Mara was only half listening and nodding. Her mind was on her notebook clue entries instead. She would have opportunity to write down entries for her grandparents later in the afternoon,

121

but she still had empty fields for Aunt Barbara and Uncle Larry. It would be ideal to talk to them first.

As if her thinking made them appear, Mara saw them standing outside the children's room, waving goodbye to Danny in the cluster of kids entering the room. This could be a good opportunity!

As they started walking away, Mara darted away from her dad and greeted them. "Hi Aunt Barbara, Uncle Larry! Are you watching Danny today?"

"Oh! Hi, Dear!" Barbara started, "We're actually dropping him off. You can hang out with him in the children's room! I hear they have a full schedule of games and stories!"

Mara had to hold back a grimace at this. She had to think fast to get to her goal. "Well, I wanted to spend the day with family instead of the kids' room today, but my grandparents can only watch me later afternoon... I guess most of the adults have more important things going on today." She put on her best sad face and fidgeted with her hands.

"Awwww, aren't you a dear!" Barbara exclaimed, "We'd love to spend time with you if your mom and dad can't this morning. I know most of them are splitting up for the day's activities."

Chapter 4: Day Two

Mara had to physically keep herself from jumping and striking a success pose. Instead she lifted her head and softened her sad expression. "Really? You'd have time to let me hang out with you?"

David finished walking up in time to hear. He seemed to awkwardly debate stopping Mara's plan to ensure Shannon wouldn't be angry, but he sighed and kept quiet for another moment as Barbara jumped back in. "Of course! I'll be joining the ladies later afternoon, but your uncle isn't one for mountain hikes you see." She gently elbowed Uncle Larry's gut to illustrate her point and laughed. "So we wanted to stay together most of today anyway."

Mara's dad finally spoke up. "Well we appreciate the offer, but are you all sure? I was planning on dropping Mara off with the kids' activities anyway."

Barbara quickly waved her hand. "Yes, yes! It's fine! Gareth and Milly are watching her in the afternoon too?"

David nodded. "Yeah, they'll meet up in the dining area at lunchtime."

Larry perked up at the mention of lunch. "We can drop her off when we go to lunch then. It's not a problem." The adults exchanged a few more pleasantries before David left Mara with them and walked off to prepare for his guys' hike.

This was working out well, Mara thought. Now she had to carefully get answers from them on what they desired in life and what problems kept them from it. While Mara thought, Aunt Barbara rattled off their plans for the morning. Uncle Larry hadn't gotten his coffee yet, so that explained his more quiet demeanor. They walked back to the dining area, grabbed a few coffees for both of them, and then walked to one of the resort lounges that had a fireplace and large windows facing the mountain.

Mara settled into a comfortable couch next to them as Larry pulled out a tablet and Barbara opened a book.

"I hope this morning won't be too boring for you." Barbara smiled at Mara. "We're old folks, so we're used to calm days, except when we have Danny."

Mara pulled her notepad and pencil out of her backpack. "That's okay! I can work on my drawings." She was careful not to show her clue notes and instead showed Barbara her latest drawing of Hershey.

"That's so good!" She praised. "You're quite the artist!"

Chapter 4: Day Two

It seemed genuine, so Mara couldn't help but blush and become shy. "Thanks. I don't know if I want to be an artist when I grow up, but I like drawing."

They chatted for a few more minutes before Mara gathered the courage to start steering the conversation. "What about you and Uncle Larry? How did you know what you wanted to do when you grew up? And did you get to do it?"

Larry joined in. "Now that's quite a question. I don't know if I thought about that at your age." He paused to scratch his chin. "I guess it's something that changes."

"What do you mean?" Mara inquired, hoping for a concrete answer and not generalizations.

"Well when I was fourteen I know I wanted to be a Forest Ranger. I loved the outdoors. I loved hunting, fishing, and camping." Larry paused briefly and looked towards the ceiling, smiling and seemingly visiting a good memory. "But when I turned eighteen things in the US were changing. The Vietnam War was going on, and some of us had our futures chosen for us in those times."

Mara looked puzzled, so Larry continued. "I went to the war instead of being a Forest Ranger, but my mind wasn't that of a fourteen-year-old anymore. War is never a pleasant experience, but I did make the best of it with the men. We forged strong bonds and had each other's backs. I don't regret that time with them, even if I hadn't planned it."

"So..." Mara started, still trying to confirm his answers for the clue, "Your goal changed as you grew up, and you actually accomplished it during the war?"

Larry let out a gut laugh, startling Mara at the suddenness of it. He took a moment to catch his breath and replied, "I wouldn't say anything was accomplished during that war! But, I didn't feel the need to be a Forest Ranger after that. I had enough of trees and underbrush for a lifetime."

He paused to scratch his chin. "I think I was about twenty-four before I had my next real goal turning over in my mind. I wanted to go back to school, university, to make something more of myself. I had big dreams of being a politician and making changes."

Mara leaned forward, excited to be getting somewhere. "So is that what you did for a job afterward?"

Larry shook his head. "No, I never got that far. I did graduate with a degree in economics, but right around that time I switched dreams again."

Chapter 4: Day Two

Mara visibly deflated. None of this made much sense for the answer she was looking for. But Larry was very happy to keep talking, so she let him.

"Or I should say, a dream walked into my life." He grinned at Barbara, but she only gave him a side-eyed glance before jumping in. "You tell that story, but every time you leave out the fact that it took you three months to stop dating that blonde before you talked to me."

Mara shrunk in her seat at that, expecting a fight to start between the two older adults, but to her surprise they both burst out laughing.

Larry choked out a reply between laughing and wiping tears. "I don't mention her because I never want to tell the next part! I was scared to break up with that woman! And when I finally did, she set half my belongings on fire in the dorm courtyard."

Barbara's laughter faded, but she remained smiling at her husband. "I know, but I love that part. I actually helped you shop for more clothes after we started talking. I had fun dragging you from shop to shop."

The Red god

The two adults must have noticed Mara's wide-eyed stare, as Barbara turned to her and changed tones quickly. "Oh, it was a small fire. Nothing really. Everyone ended up safe!"

Larry coughed and tried to change the subject. "Anyway, me and Barb met and got married not long after. I needed money for our soon-to-be family, so I started work at a bank. I don't regret it, as I did get use out of my degree studying the stock market and investment funds."

Mara absentmindedly pushed her pencil around her notebook page, trying to formulate a better question to get to her answer. "So... is being with Aunt Barbara your real life goal in the end?"

Larry chuckled. "You are a very literal kid, Mara. You don't read many allegories, do you?"

Mara looked offended, considering herself an advanced reader for her age, but Larry continued. "It's okay! I tell long-winded stories and have trouble getting to the point. What I meant was life isn't always one single goal, one purpose in life. I took what life gave me and embraced it. I enjoyed each part the best I could. I never had a regret, except getting old!"

Barbara nodded. "That's a good way of putting it. I didn't envision everything my life would have, but it has been a good one.

Chapter 4: Day Two

I've had a good husband, two lovely children, an adorable grandson, and many friends. But, I do have to admit I have some regrets, things I didn't do or say that I should have in my younger years."

Barbara sat her book down in her lap and turned towards Mara with a serious expression. "I'll tell you one, Dear. You're a very bright kid, but maybe some wisdom from an old lady can help you. Cherish the loved ones you have, and let them know you care regularly."

Barbara paused with a sad smile. "I had a very good friend in my younger years, and I didn't do that often enough for her before it was too late. I wish I could go back in time and have fixed that. But life moves fast, and you move on."

Mara thought of Jace and how he wouldn't be coming back to their school since he moved away. A heavy feeling settled in her chest, but she breathed against it, not wanting to cry. "I think I understand," Mara replied, "Thanks for the stories."

Mara wanted to be polite with her response, but her mind was conflicted on their answers. Were they actually happy? Can you be happy with some regret, or with getting older and facing your death? That was a long way off for Mara, so she had a hard time thinking about it. She knew how it worked of course; a few hamsters taught her early lessons on death when she was six. But knowing the basics and facing something yourself were very different. Well, regardless of how happy they seemed, Mara thought the two points they brought up were valid desires of theirs.

She flipped her notebook to her clue page, making sure to angle herself where Uncle Larry and Aunt Barbara couldn't read the page, and filled in their answers. For Larry's 'Desire' column she wrote "Not to age", and for Barbara's she wrote "Undo regret with friend". For both of their 'Problem' columns she wrote "Can't control".

Chapter 4: Day Two

Unless either of them could invent a time machine or anti-aging serum, Mara didn't think their desires had any chance of happening. They were very hard ones, but she hoped the written answers were enough to move her forward. She reviewed her page and noted that only her Grandmother's and Grandfather's rows remained blank. She would have to hope that hanging out with them later in the afternoon would be enough time to get their answers. She also hoped her Grandmother's Adult Politeness Barrier didn't prevent Mara from getting a genuine answer.

The rest of the morning went by quickly as Mara doodled, Larry checked stock prices on his tablet, and Barbara read her book. Soon they were walking her to the dining area where she would meet up with her grandparents and spend the rest of the afternoon with them.

Mara spotted her grandfather sitting at a table near the back first. She headed towards him but turned to wave her goodbyes to Aunt Barbara and Uncle Larry. Her grandfather was facing away and was hunched over a small laptop, typing. Mara looked around but didn't see her grandmother yet.

She reached the table and greeted her grandfather as he hadn't noticed her yet. "Hi, Grandpa."

He promptly stood up and pulled out a chair for Mara. "Hello, Dear. Take a seat." He motioned towards a restroom door on the side of the room. "Milly will be back in a minute. Then I'll grab some lunch plates for us."

Mara sat down and slid her backpack off. "Thanks! Lunch smells good already." Gareth sat back down and turned his attention to his laptop, leaving Mara wondering if it was going to be hard to get answers from him. She never talked to her grandfather much. During past visits, it was mostly her grandmother who talked with her.

While her grandmother was still away, she thought this might be her best opportunity to ask him questions. Mara took out her notebook and nervously tested her pen on a page with doodles. This was the hardest clue to get yet! It involved so many forced conversations. Mara wasn't used to things like this. But the game prize, Mara had to get it! She took a deep breath and forced herself to start. "What's the computer for?"

Chapter 4: Day Two

He chuckled but didn't look up. "Boring work programs. No games."

That was at least an opening, Mara thought. She leaned over the table, resting her elbows in front of her and chin in hands. "What kind of work stuff?" she questioned. She knew from overheard conversations that her grandfather did something with insurance, but she didn't really understand what he did.

He again replied without looking at Mara. "Oh, spreadsheets and reports." Mara began getting frustrated. She hated being treated like a little kid that wouldn't understand. She knew some things about insurance!

She thought sharing her knowledge might get her grandfather to take her seriously. "Soo spreadsheets for insurance... do you decide and track who you don't give medical help there?" Mara's insurance knowledge came from news anchors on TV and a few rants and arguments between her parents. She hadn't intended her question to be offensive, but she knew she said something bad based on her grandfather's reaction.

He lowered the lid of the laptop and peered at her from above it. His expression was hard to read. It wasn't exactly angry, but it wasn't pleased. His face gained a deeper crease where his gray beard

133

and mustache ended. "Mara, Dear, did your father tell you about my company?"

Mara sheepishly shook her head. "No one really told me about your job, but sometimes I overheard stuff... So I got curious."

He sighed, closed his laptop the rest of the way, and folded his hands together on top of it. "Insurance isn't about declining medical treatments for people. It actually helps more people get care than normally could. Let me give you an example."

He gathered the salt and pepper shakers and got some coins from his pockets. "See," he started, "Ms Salt and Mr Pepper each have Hausfeld Insurance. They pay us what's called a premium each month." He moved several pennies, nickels, and quarters to the center of the table in a pile. "We take some of this premium to pay out employees." Some of the coins were moved out of the pile towards Gareth. "And the rest is left in the pool to pay out treatment claims."

"Now, Mr Pepper unfortunately has a heart attack and requires a lot of medical care. We review the situation and approve the medical claims to be compensated." He moved most of the coins from the pile towards the pepper shaker, leaving a few pennies behind.

Chapter 4: Day Two

"Later, Ms Salt has a headache and visits a doctor. The doctor is inexperienced and does a lot of expensive and unnecessary tests. Because of this..." He paused to move a single penny from the pile towards the salt shaker. "Ms Salt gets some of the unnecessary tests declined, and only part of the initial visit is covered." He leaned back with a satisfied smile. "So you see, we help people. The things we decline are the things that weren't really necessary."

Mara thought for a moment, hoping to not anger him with her next questions. She leaned over and picked up the salt shaker. "Then Ms Salt still got the tests but didn't have to pay for them?"

Her grandfather's smile faltered. "Well, no. Ms Salt had to pay for the tests herself since the doctor already did them."

Mara tilted her head, trying to follow. "Then she paid for insurance and the doctor bills herself, mostly?"

Gareth moved to take the salt shaker from her. "Yes, but she needed to because her doctor made bad decisions."

Mara stubbornly held the salt despite his movement. "Then Ms Salt should have dealt with her headache herself and not paid for insurance since the doctor and insurance didn't help?"

The Red god

He let out an audible sigh and closed his outstretched hand that had been reaching for the shaker. "No, she has to have medical insurance. So she still needed to pay for it."

Mara furrowed her brow but relinquished the salt shaker. "Then Ms Salt was always going to have a bad result no matter what, and Mr Pepper just got lucky? So insurance is like the lottery. Some people win and some people lose?"

"That's... It's not like the lottery. We have smart people working for my company. We call them Claim Auditors. They use a lot of math to figure out what we pay for and what we don't."

Mara thought that was what she said in the first place: They decide who got help and who shouldn't. But she held her tongue, not wanting to ruin her purpose for this conversation just to figure out something stupid like what insurance was. Instead she nodded and made a vague 'oh' and 'uh huh' sound.

This seemed to please him, as his smile returned. "So, you see, we help a lot of people, including the community because we employ so many." He leaned back in his chair and began reopening his laptop. "When I started the company, it was only five employees, but it's nearing a thousand now."

136

Chapter 4: Day Two

Mara was worried she'd lose his interest if he went back to his work, so she kept the questions coming. "That's a lot! Was starting the company always your dream? Are you really happy that you got to do it?"

"I'm very proud of it, yes. I started out as a bag-boy for my father's grocery store, Hausfeld Market. You don't get a lot of respect as a bag-boy. I knew I wanted something of my own someday." He paused to type for a moment but continued his story. "Something respectable. I didn't know at the time that it would be in insurance, but the vehicle for getting there didn't matter much."

Mara eagerly flipped through her notebook pages and readied her pen to fill in his answers. "Your life goal was respect then, Grandpa?"

The blunt question elicited a chuckle from him. "Your mom is right. You're smart for your age. You get right down to it! Sure, that's a fine way of putting it. Respect is a good goal for anyone in life. Remember that!"

Mara nodded and wrote down "respect" in her grandfather's 'desire' column, excited to be closing in on the game's next clue.

She stopped asking him questions after that, and he seemed relieved to have silence and to be able to turn his attention fully to his work.

Shortly after, her grandmother returned to the dining area. Mara was made aware of this fact by the harsh sound of her heels on the wood floor. She didn't need to turn her head to know her grandmother was in a mood. Sounds often gave emotions away if you were used to listening for them. Mara was surprised when her grandfather bolted up and pulled out a chair. The movement was sudden, but she supposed he had the 'gift' of reading emotions from sounds too. He seemed to shift in demeanor to try and manage his wife's.

"I can't believe the gall that attendant had," Mildred started without a proper greeting. "They closed the restroom for cleaning but then stood there waiting for a separate janitorial worker. I had to get two supervisors before they made the first attendant clean it herself."

Gareth pushed the chair in as she sat before retaking his own seat. He nodded approval as she continued regaling her story. "This is supposed to be a starred resort. You'd think they'd teach their workers better English as well."

Chapter 4: Day Two

Mara was quietly pushing her pen around her doodle page during her rant. She was glad it wasn't directed towards her, but she couldn't help but feel for the resort employee.

"Mara, let this be a lesson for you too, Dear. Don't pay people good money for bad service and let them get away with it. You get your last name from your father, but you're a Hausfeld and can act like it."

Mara didn't know quite how to react to that statement, so she merely nodded. What did a last name have to do with anything in that story?

Gareth excused himself to grab the lunch plates, and Mildred seemed to be simmering down. She took notice of Mara's drawings and moved the conversation on. "Some of those have an edge to them, Dear. Shannon tells me you spend a lot of time reading and drawing. You're getting older, you know. What are your ambitions for your schooling?" Her grandmother spoke in a calm, polite tone, but the question made Mara uneasy.

"Uhmm... There's a writing contest at school that I might enter. But my grades are already good. I get mostly A's..."

Her attempt at answering the question didn't seem to meet her grandmother's expectation. The older woman tapped her fingers on the table in front of Mara. "No, Dear, I mean what higher school are you planning on attending? I hope Shannon wasn't exaggerating when she told me she and your father are looking at private schools next."

Mara nervously shrugged. "I don't know anything about changing schools."

Mildred looked like she wanted to say something more, but she held herself back, her mouth slightly puckered from the unsaid words.

Mara thought the moment's silence might allow her to change the subject and get closer to her grandmother's answers. "Grandpa was telling me about his job earlier. It sounded really neat. I've been thinking about future stuff too, just not changing schools I don't think." Mara looked up to gauge her grandmother's reaction before finishing. "Did you know what you wanted to do with your future when you were my age?"

Mara thought her segue was perfect, but Mildred didn't break her current expression. Instead, the older woman continued her previous thought. "Your school change is important. You won't get anywhere in a public school."

Chapter 4: Day Two

Mara wondered if she heard her, so she tried changing the topic once more. "Did private school help you know what you wanted to do when you grew up?"

She barely got the question out when her grandmother started again. "If Shannon won't see to your schooling properly, I'll enroll you in a good one myself."

Ah, Mara thought, she heard but was ignoring her. She was really stuck on her school... Mara thought she went to a good one already. The teachers always gave her lots of homework, so she was at least never bored.

The thought of being made to switch schools and lose her last remaining friend, Beth, scared her. Luckily Mara thought this unlikely to happen. She remembered past times her grandma and mother argued about something related to her, what dress she should wear for a certain family gathering or what she should do during her school breaks. Usually her mother didn't end up making her do exactly what her grandmother said. Her mother would make her do something, but not the exact thing.

Mara began tuning her grandmother out as she talked at her husband about this. She was throwing out what Mara assumed were specific schools she had in mind, but Mara didn't care to remember them or get back into this part of the conversation. Maybe her mother would yell and lecture her before making her do extra homework or another after school activity once they were back home. That wasn't a pleasant thought, but it wasn't as bad as moving states and going to a private school.

While Mildred talked at Gareth, Mara looked back over her notebook's clue page. She filled out her grandfather's desire, but not his problem column. She had no chance of talking to him further as long as her grandmother was here. Did he have an obvious problem keeping him from getting his desired respect? She didn't know how he felt at work, but around his wife he wasn't someone Mara would call respected.

Compared to when she wasn't around, he appeared to shrivel in his seat, making himself smaller, less talkative, and less independent. His earlier chuckles were replaced with hollow sounds of agreement and nods. He reminded Mara a lot of her dad. If respect was something he wanted at home and not only at work, then his problem was much the same. Mara wrote "avoidant and cowardly" in his 'problem' column.

The page was becoming depressing to look at. She was eager to reach her next clue, but thinking about her family and all their many problems was not pleasant. She wanted action, adventure, puzzles! Not family arguments. She thought hard about speeding it along. All she needed was her grandmother's answers, but she was hard to talk to. It was almost like Mara wasn't a real person to her. She was a blank doll she might have some say in forming.

Mara didn't want to compliment her mother, but she did treat her slightly more like an individual. She would have gotten angry at Mara's questions if she was here. But she wouldn't have completely ignored them like her grandmother did. Why were people so complicated? It would be easy if her mother was always mean, or if her grandmother was always nice. But they both had moments of making her feel good, ignored, stupid, smart, small, and big. It frustrated her. She wanted the good without the bad, but one always followed the other like a cycle.

The more Mara stared at the page and the more her grandmother talked, the more her eyes stung. She hated moments like this. She didn't have any real reason to cry! Why did thinking about her mother and comparing her grandmother make her react? She sometimes had to hold herself back when her mother talked at her for long periods as well. She got used to practicing techniques for it. Where did she first learn them? She didn't remember but knew the steps well.

First she'd pretend she wasn't actually in front of her mother. She'd briefly close her eyes and imagine she was alone at a beach, in a park, or somewhere, anywhere else. She would watch her breathing and slow it down. Next she would focus her eyes on a particular spot, somewhere away from her mother. It was true she wasn't in front of her mother now, but she figured the technique would work if her grandmother was upsetting her too.

She decided to pick the nearby salt shaker as her focus. She stared at it, not looking away to let her grandmother in her vision again. She breathed once, twice, three times in a steady rhythm. She wasn't at the table. She wasn't at the resort. She was in her bedroom instead, with Hershey curled up at the foot of the bed, softly purring. And if Mara wasn't really there, nothing could be upsetting her. She also sometimes pretended she was a rock, like a pet rock sitting on a shelf watching the scene. Rocks don't cry. Rocks don't react. Rocks just sit there, and it doesn't matter what's happening around them.

Mara didn't know how much time had passed since she focused herself, but she was brought back by her grandfather shaking her arm. She was startled and whipped her head up to look at him. He looked perplexed. Mara was about to ask what was wrong, but she first turned to look at her grandmother.

She looked disturbed and was staring straight at Mara. "Mara? Are you listening now? Has that happened before?"

"Uhm, has what happened before?" Mara replied, concerned she offended her. Maybe she was asking Mara questions when she focused herself. She hadn't meant to ignore her grandmother.

Mildred looked to where Mara was looking before and pointed. "That! You stared and wouldn't respond to me. It was like you were asleep with your eyes open! Good grief, Dear. What was that?"

Mara felt very self-conscious at her grandparents' stares. She did this all the time around her mother, but her mother never got concerned about it. She probably just yelled louder, but Mara wouldn't know since she got good at focusing and tuning it out.

"I guess I'm tired after eating lunch," was the lame excuse she could think to say. Her grandmother didn't say anything in response, but she remained watching Mara with furrowed brows. Her grandfather took chance at the rare silence to speak up.

"Should we move away from the dining hall and find more comfortable seats in the lounge?"

Mara followed her grandparents into a different lounge area than she had been in this morning. This one was closer to the back of the resort building, and it had big doors closing it off from the hallway. Inside was a grand stone fireplace, a wall lined with books, and two large sectional couches, one facing the fireplace and one facing the large picture window with view of the mountains. The room smelled of leather, and Mara thought this place probably didn't normally allow children inside.

Her grandmother took a seat near the fire first and patted the leather couch next to her. Mara dutifully followed and took the seat. Gareth sat in a nearby armchair and pulled out his laptop once more.

"Mara," her grandmother started, "I realize all the talk of school must be boring to a child your age, but it is important. I'll speak to Shannon about it later." Mara nodded, hoping her

Chapter 4: Day Two

grandmother's use of the word 'boring' meant she believed her excuse of being tired when she zoned out earlier.

"I'm sure it is, Grandma. But I don't know why a specific school is important." Mara figured if she stayed on the school topic, she might have better luck at getting her grandmother to talk to her instead of at her.

Mildred smiled before replying. "Because, everything early in life is so important! The school, the clothes, the family, the hobbies, the friends. Everything will lead you to making something more of yourself!"

Mara saw an opening with that phrase. "Something more of yourself? I don't really understand what that is. Is that what you want to do for a job? Or what family you want when you grow up and get married...?"

The older woman took her questions seriously this time. "To make something of yourself is to make yourself higher. Higher than the people around you. That's not in any one thing like a job or money, it's in everything. To have the higher job. To have the higher wealth. To have the higher family standing."

She took Mara's hand in her own and made her look at her as she continued. "When you have that, Mara, you have power. Power is whatever you want it to be. It doesn't matter if you want to be a doctor, lawyer, author, or anything else when you grow up. If you have power you can do that and more. Nothing stops you."

Mara still wasn't sure she understood, but she was glad her grandmother was talking more on the topic. She thought for a moment before posing her next question. "And you accomplished it? Through private school and everything else you did in your life?"

Mildred laughed and let go of her hand to wipe her eye. "Nothing is accomplished and done, Dear. There is always more, always higher. You never get to stop, but it is much better than stopping, than settling."

Mara asked a dangerous question next. She didn't want to derail the conversation, but she was honestly curious of this answer. "Did my mom settle? Is that why you always fight?"

Her grandmother took on a serious tone. "Yes, I believe she did. I'm sure you love your father, but she could have done better. She should have done better. Not just in the marriage she chose but in her own school, her own work. Don't be like her and settle, Dear. You can reach higher."

Chapter 4: Day Two

The answer didn't surprise Mara. Her grandmother always seemed disappointed in her mother, but hearing it plainly spoken felt odd. It was a mix of relief at getting a true answer out of an adult and despair at the finality she spoke it with. They would never be happy as mother and daughter. Her mother would never be good enough for her grandmother. They would fight and argue until one of them died. Was that her same fate with her mother? To always tune out her screaming until her mother aged and died? Or until she couldn't take it anymore?

Mara couldn't focus on the conversation anymore. Mildred sensed her unease but misplaced the source. "Don't worry, Dear. Your grandfather and I won't let that happen to you. You're a Hausfeld. You're destined for greater things, beginning with a private school. We'll speak to your mother."

Mara numbly nodded and asked if she could get back to her drawings. Mildred had no argument, so the trio fell into silence. Mara drew, and Mildred checked news and her readings on her phone.

Later in the afternoon, Mara switched from her drawings to her clue page. She filled in the final answers: "Power" for her grandmother's desire and "it's never enough" for her problem column. Despite the roaring fire in the stone fireplace several feet away, the room felt cold.

When three o'clock rolled around, Mara got antsy to leave the company of her grandparents. They were still absorbed in their own reading and work for the most part, save a few more small-talk conversation attempts.

Asking to go back to her room to rest seemed like a good enough excuse they'd buy, but Mara always overthought her plans. Should she feign yawning for several minutes before asking? Should she pretend to nod off on the lounge couch and wait for one of them to suggest she go to the room for a nap? What about if she had a headache or stomachache?

Another ten minutes passed as Mara weighed percentages of success of her imagined escape plans, and the lounge door opened. An older woman walked in. She appeared younger than Mara's grandmother, but she still had wrinkles near her eyes and mouth and walked with a slow gait.

Chapter 4: Day Two

"Milly, there you are!" the woman spoke with a spirited tone, "You missed the facials and seaweed wraps! Don't I look younger?" The woman paused her walk towards the couch Mildred sat on to strike a pose and grin.

"Facials don't make you look younger, Patricia, Botox does." Mildred returned a wry smile.

Mara thought they must be good friends for her grandmother to joke with her. It was a rare sight, as she couldn't recall her joking with her mother or herself.

The two women chatted for a few moments more before Patricia turned to Mara. "And who is this lovely young lady?"

Mildred cut Mara off as she opened her mouth to answer, an action very familiar to Mara who had her mother speak for her often. "This is Mara, my granddaughter. Shannon is her mother."

"Oh," Patricia crooned, "Aren't you a dear? You have such pretty hair and good posture for your age."

Mara mumbled thanks and looked towards her lap, unsure what else to say. She didn't have to think for long, as Mildred took the conversation over immediately with talk of another recent trip and her latest going-ons.

151

Mara sat in silence as the two chatted, wondering if she should still feign her yawning and ask to leave.

Before she could decide, her grandmother abruptly stood up and motioned to her husband. "Gareth, take Mara to the pool or something. Me and Patricia might be catching up for a while."

He obediently closed his laptop and slowly stood up. "Fine, you two have fun. Mara, grab your bag please. Don't leave your things here."

Mara wondered if she was getting kicked out of the lounge now because the older women didn't want to talk around a kid, but whatever the reason she was happy to leave. She grabbed her bag and notebook and followed her grandfather out with a quick wave goodbye to her grandmother.

Once outside the lounge door and alone with her grandfather, Mara felt braver. She didn't hesitate asking her desired question. "Grandpa, can I go to my room to rest instead? I don't really need a babysitter the last few hours before dinner. My parents will be back at the room soon enough, and I was at the pool a lot already..."

Gareth shrugged. "Sure, that's okay. Saving your strength for the sledding day tomorrow, eh?"

Chapter 4: Day Two

Mara nodded but didn't verbally agree, her usual tactic to avoid an outright lie. "I can walk back to the room myself too. It's not that far."

He eyed her suspiciously at this, "Are you going straight to your room? You're not ditching an old man to go to the pool alone, are you? That would be dangerous."

Mara vigorously shook her head. "Straight to my room! Promise!"

He chuckled and playfully shoved her shoulder. "Alright then, off with you. I need to get back to my work anyway."

He barely blinked before Mara darted down the hallway. "Okay, bye! See you later, Grandpa!"

Back in her room, Mara dropped her backpack off her shoulders onto the floor with a resounding thump and made a beeline for her bed. She didn't care to properly place her belongings; she had an important task finally at hand.

She jumped onto the bed and sat cross-legged with her notebook in lap. How should she do this? Review the clue answers she wrote down and then resume playing the tape recorder? Oh! The tape! She hopped off the bed and grabbed the device from her backpack before returning to her seat.

Excitement filled her as she flipped through the notebook pages to land on the clue page. She paused to take a breath and then recited the answers she gathered. "Gina's desire is more time. Her problem is she isn't honest. Samantha's desire is love. Her problem is she's naive. Uncle Larry's desire is not to age. His problem is that's not controllable. Aunt Barbara's desire is to undo regret with a friend. Her problem is also that she can't control that in the past." Mara paused to take another breath. Saying these out loud made her feel odd.

"Grandfather's desire is respect, but his problem is that he's avoidant and cowardly. Grandmother's desire is power, and her problem is that it's never enough. Dad's desire is money, and his problem is also that he's avoidant and cowardly."

Mara stared at the last words on the paper and looked around first, as if making sure there was no way her mother could be close by listening. "Mother's desire is a better family. Her problem is she's controlling, always angry, and selfish. In everything she thinks of herself first! And we have to go along with it... even when!" Mara caught herself mid-rant and stopped. Complaining more wouldn't change anything, and this is all she needed for the clue. Moving on with the game was the important thing.

She closed her notebook with as loud of a thump as she could muster, happy to be done with that part. Her fingers reached to the tape recorder and pressed play.

"Did you get the answers?" Rudy's voice almost tickled her ear as it sounded from the tape. "Good job! I knew you would be good at following! Now! Let me tell you the next story portion!"

She eagerly leaned in. The story was weird at first. Mara wasn't used to hero stories involving elements like wind, but it was starting to get interesting.

"After the girl told the Wind the answers, the Wind promised that through the girl it could solve those problems and make the girl adored by all and live in peace. 'There are more steps to get there though,' it whispered, 'and these require you to trust and obey. You don't listen to the villagers anymore. You listen to me. You must next get a key. I'll guide you to it, but you must not trust, listen to, or obey the villagers, only me.'"

Mara thought the 'story voice' for the Wind sounded very feminine this time. She wondered how Rudy had that vocal range!

The Red god

He was a good storyteller. The voice switched back to Rudy's normal one next.

"Now! Behind where you are greeted lies a doorway. Make your way through it at any cost! From there seek the oldest thing you see, then older still. Go until you see the key and take it!"

Rudy's voice had an intensity to it today... It was normally a happy, excited tone, but by the end of those instructions he had almost begun to yell. Mara supposed all the voice acting was to hype up the player even more. She pressed pause and sat in silence, thinking.

Behind where you are greeted... Mara immediately thought of the check-in desk when they first entered the resort. There were a few employees there that greeted them and the large 'Resort Ruhe' sign on the wall behind them.

Was there a door though? There might have been, but Mara didn't remember. If there was, then this clue seemed pretty easy! It wasn't hard to figure out like the last one was. She had to walk around outside for a while before she found which direction the wind went. This one would be too easy.

She looked at the time and noted she had about an hour and some change before her parents would be done with their activities

Chapter 4: Day Two

and expect to find her with her grandparents or getting ready for dinner. She didn't want to waste time overthinking the clue, so she gathered her things back in her backpack and slung it over her shoulder before heading out.

On the walk to the foyer where the reception desk was, Mara thought about the story portion. There was so much emphasis on trusting and obeying the Wind. Did that mean anything in context of her getting the next clue? It had to have been a hint about something she needed to do. The game was too well put together for something like that to be meaningless to the player.

She passed a few people she didn't recognize that tried to greet her. They might have been from Ryan's side. Mara was worried about getting caught on her adventure, so she discouraged a conversation by only nodding and smiling, keeping a brisk walk. Were the villagers from the story supposed to be her relatives here at the resort? If so, not trusting them would be pretty easy. Mara already had plenty of trust issues.

The Red god

Upon reaching the junction of the hallway into the foyer, Mara slowed her walk and peeked around for who was there. She saw a few relatives she vaguely recognized talking with one employee at the reception desk. She couldn't see if there was a door behind the desk at this angle. She'd have to move further in the foyer, but she didn't want to look suspicious and have either relatives or the employee try walking her to the dreaded children's room.

There were a few small couches at one end of the foyer. Mara figured they would be her safest bet to hang out at and watch the room without looking too odd. She mustered her confidence and walked across the foyer to them. One of the relatives stopped talking to the employee and gave her a glance, but she purposely pretended not to notice them and took out her notebook as she sat on one of the couches. She started a new doodle page, hoping to look busy. Luckily this seemed to work. They went back to talking and paid her no mind.

Mara glanced up and saw there was a door behind the desk! It was off to the right side, but that must be it! It was closed and had the appearance of an employee-only door, but she was confident she could find a way to sneak in. For now, she pretended to be very invested in her doodling and waited for a good opportunity.

Chapter 4: Day Two

While waiting, she listened in on their conversation. It wasn't too interesting. The employee seemed to be explaining to them that one of the ski lifts was closed for maintenance today. The relatives, a couple a little older than her parents, kept asking questions about it, when it would be open, why it needed maintenance, why today, and on and on.

They weren't raising their voices in anger, but they seemed to not understand that their dozens of questions wouldn't cause the lift to magically be available sooner. Mara caught herself rolling her eyes as she listened, hoping they would give up and go somewhere else. The less people in the foyer, the higher chance she had of sneaking in that door.

Several agonizing minutes passed before the couple accepted their lift-less fate and walked off into one of the halls. Mara was now left alone with the single employee behind the desk. She tried to still appear busy with her drawing, but after a moment the older woman left the desk and approached her anyway.

"Do you need help, young miss?" the woman asked. She had a thicker accent than some of the younger employees.

The Red god

Mara tried to sound confident in her reply, but it came out a bit quiet. "Uhmm... no. I'm okay. My dad is out on the guys' hike today, and I'm waiting for him."

"Oh! You don't need to wait here then." The woman smiled. "You know where the children's room is? You must have gone with the group of other children for storytime yesterday? You can play there. The hiking group might not be back for hours!"

Mara had to think fast. She didn't want to get pushed into that. What was with the adults and always shoving her off with the toddlers! "Well, I was there for a while... But the other kids are so much younger than me. I'd rather draw alone. I'm fine here, really!"

The woman didn't seem to buy Mara's excuse. She looked concerned and sat down next to Mara instead of leaving. "You know, the group I saw was much younger. But do you not have another family member to spend time with?"

The familiarity the woman showed by sitting right next to her startled Mara. "I have plenty of family here. I just want to draw." This was a partial lie, of course, and Mara said it in a tone ruder than she expected from herself. Something about the woman's question made her defensive.

160

Chapter 4: Day Two

The woman either didn't notice or didn't care as she continued. "I see. You must be a good artist to have that dedication. I have a few grandchildren your age, but they never sit still enough to practice a hobby like that!"

This piqued Mara's curiosity. "Do your grand-kids live near the resort? I saw older kids playing with a ball the other day..."

The woman smiled and nodded. "Yes, that was probably them. We have a small town further in the mountains behind the resort. A lot of our workers live there. Did you try to join their game then?"

That was one mystery solved, but now Mara felt embarrassed for having asked. "No, I just saw them."

"Ah, that's a shame. They love playing with new kids. You know, some of them might join the sledding tomorrow too. What is your name, Dear? I'll tell them you were looking for kids your age to play with."

Mara didn't answer right away. The pushiness made her wary, even though she had very friendly mannerisms and tone. The woman looked at her expectantly until she answered. "My name is Mara."

"Mara, that is a very beautiful name. I'm Alma." The woman pointed to her name tag. It read 'Alma' and below it 'Front Desk

Manager'. "Let me know if you need anything. We don't like guests at Resort Ruhe to want for anything, but especially company. It is not good to spend time alone here."

Mara was confused at that last statement but nodded. Alma then stood up and walked back behind the desk, busying herself on one of the computers.

Mara went back to her half-hearted doodles as she thought. Would she get to play with those older kids tomorrow? The prospect did sound fun. Maybe she could take a break from the game and join the sledding then, just for a few hours. She began to daydream of how the day might go:

A bright sun shone down on smooth blankets of white snow. Multicolored birds tweeted cheerfully as they raced from tree to tree and around the hill slopes. Mara was wearing her favorite color purple jacket, striped pink and white gloves, and thick fur-lined boots. She wouldn't be cold despite the winter wonderland around her. Her imagination placed people around the slopes, happy families and laughing kids zipping by with brightly colored sleds of various sizes and shapes. Mara's own sled would be a teal blue, long, and slightly pointed in the front for better speed.

Chapter 4: Day Two

The older kids from the village would find her easily and gladly initiate the introductions. After exchanging names they'd compliment her sled and take turns riding in the back of it with her. They'd start on the small hills and run to the larger and steeper ones next. Mara could almost feel the cold breeze whipping past her face as she imagined.

"Don't trust the villagers," a voice whispered in her mind. The daydream stopped, but the cold feeling against her face remained. Was it wrong to want to hang out with the village's kids? Why would not trusting them be a component of the game? Mara looked to Alma, the kind older lady still busy at the front desk.

She said guests shouldn't be alone here, but what if that was what Mara needed to distrust to finish the game? Could the employees and village inhabitants know about the game but not want any guests' children to be able to follow it? Who was the game made for then?

No matter her theories on the last clue's meaning, Mara knew she had to get through that door. She had to make it to the next thing. If anyone didn't want her to succeed, she'd find a way around it. Adults in her life are selfish. Adults in her life don't mean well. Adults in her life lie. Maybe Mara needed to grow up.

Before she knew quite what she was doing, Mara's legs slid off the couch and she was walking towards the desk.

"Uhm, Ms Alma? I get lost in the halls sometimes. Can I get a cup of water?"

The gray-haired woman smiled and nodded. "Sure, it is not that busy at the desk right now. I will walk you to the dining area where we always have drinks available."

Mara beamed at the offer. She thought herself very clever at this moment. The two began walking down the hall together, leaving no one at the desk.

"So, who is the lucky bride or groom to you, Miss Mara?"

Mara's mind was on her scheming, but she guessed small talk was unavoidable. "Oh, my cousin, Samantha. She's really excited about everything and invited my whole family here."

Alma chuckled. "I imagine she is. A person should be excited for their wedding and marriage."

Mara tried to hide her scowl. Now she knew the woman couldn't be counted on for truths. Marriages weren't happy things. Mara knew that.

Chapter 4: Day Two

The two made it to the dining hall, and Alma pointed towards a stack of cups and pitchers filled with ice water and what appeared to be different kinds of fruit juice.

"Please get whatever you like, and I'll walk you back to the front so you don't get lost and miss your father when he returns." The woman then turned and walked further in to fill her own drink from the coffee station.

Mara saw her opportunity. She slowly stepped back out of the room and then bolted once she was out of sight. She wouldn't have long before Alma turned and saw her missing. She had to reach the door! Her foot slipped halfway down the hall and she stumbled, but she picked herself back up and sprinted.

She was lucky there was no one else on her route to the front. She reached the desk and ducked underneath the part of the counter that was open. The door! Mara didn't get a good look at its doorknob from her prior viewpoint, but up close she now saw it required a keycard to unlock. She frantically jiggled the handle anyway to no effect.

Where could she get a card? Maybe one of the room cards would work? Mara tried her own, but the door lock lit up a small red button indicating it didn't work. Mara spun in place thinking of what to do. The back of the desk had a computer, stacks of paper, miscellaneous office supplies, and drawers. The drawers had small keyholes on them, but Mara tugged one and found it unlocked. Success? No! It only had resort letterhead and pens in it!

She yanked several more open before seeing a keycard. It had an employee's name and photo on it. Mara picked it up but hesitated. How much trouble could she get in for this? Wasn't this stealing? Could there be any good excuse for what she just did?

"Don't trust them!" Her thoughts urged her on. She turned and used it to unlock the door. The light turned green, and the handle swung open. Mara flung herself inside and closed the door.

Inside, it was quiet. Mara rested her back against the door and slowed her breathing. The floor here looked older, and the walls had a slightly crumbling appearance to the stone. But it was clean and lit well enough. The employees must use this hallway and the connecting rooms often.

Mara turned and put her ear against the door, carefully listening for Alma's footsteps or anyone else that might catch her. Satisfied that she seemed to be alone, she lifted her back off the door and began walking.

Chapter 4: Day Two

She was supposed to seek the oldest door, then the next oldest thing, then find a key. Mara carefully inspected each of the five doors lining the hallway. They all had signs of wear on them, but one was worse. The wood was almost carved near the doorknob where one's nails would bump the wood when grabbing it to turn. How many people had to have gone through it to do that?

Mara swallowed against her racing heart and turned the knob. It opened with a jarring creak and darkness inside.

Mara wasn't normally afraid of the dark, but it gave her pause. A cold draft passed her neck, and she finally stepped in. She closed this door behind her as well before fumbling for a light switch along the wall. One turned on with a very audible click.

The first thing Mara noticed was an intricate area rug in the middle back of the room. It was mostly red but swirled with scrolling patterns of gold and black. On top of it was a large dark wood desk. It had small cracks in several areas. There were also a few chairs, filing cabinets, and a stack of boxes off to the side.

With her apprehension about the dark gone, Mara noted the air smelled musty here. Not wanting to waste time, she walked to the back of the desk and began looking at the items on top and drawers. Despite the wood's worn appearance, everything here looked new. It had a computer, printed papers, folders, paperclips, nothing interesting.

Mara frowned and tried to channel her inner detective again. What would Sherlock do?

"Not steal and break into a nice lady's private office" was the first thing to come to mind. Her frown turned into a grimace as she tried to shake the thought. This was all for a good reason! The game meant for her to do this! If Sherlock couldn't help her, she had to help herself.

Mara slowly turned and looked over the other items in the room. The chairs looked recently upholstered. The boxes were cardboard, unopened, and labeled with a popular company's logo. The filing cabinets were modern and metal. But... one of the end tables in the corner looked worn. It was made of carved wood with dark metal hammered pulls on each drawer.

She walked over and noticed a coating of dust on the top surface. It looked right. Mara pulled the bottom drawer open on instinct and was rewarded with a metal key. It wasn't quite the length of her palm, but it was heavy. It looked manually shaped, with some imperfections and changes in texture across the handle. The teeth of the key were notched out and didn't look anything like the modern house or car keys Mara was used to seeing. At the end of the handle the metal was bent into spirals forming an oval shape.

She turned it over in her hand, mesmerized. The metal chilled her hand. She did it. She found the next clue and was another step closer. It was worth it. It was going to be worth it!

Mara heard a door suddenly open. It must have been the front desk door! She pocketed the key and leapt up to turn the light switch off. Once enveloped in darkness, she flattened herself beside the door leading back to the hall.

Her heart pounded, and she did her best to hold her breath. Footsteps echoed. Mara was sure the shoes sounded like Alma's, or at least someone in heels.

They seemed to step towards a door and creaking was heard. Were they checking the other doors? Mara stayed still for what seemed like several minutes. The door to her room swung open last. She exhaled slowly to get even one percent flatter against the wall. In her periphery, she could see a woman's hand on the knob, but they didn't enter or turn on the light.

After a moment, they closed the door and walked back out towards the front desk area. Mara resumed breathing but didn't move. Were they sitting at the front desk now? Was she trapped?

They must have suspected something if they were checking the rooms.

Mara didn't want to stay in the dark room, but she didn't feel safe leaving yet. She slid to the floor in frustration and pulled her knees to her chest, closing her eyes tight.

Crying wouldn't help anything. She didn't need to cry. She was a small, gray rock. Rocks don't cry. Rocks don't feel panicked. Rocks are just sitting there okay. She repeated her self-soothing technique and stayed like that for some time.

After a while she unfurled herself and checked her watch, luckily it had a button with a small light. She'd been here over an hour. Her dad was going to be back and looking for her soon. She had to do something. Mara hoped the door's creaking couldn't be heard from the front desk. She slowly opened the door and slipped out into the hallway.

There were five doors here, and she had explored one. Maybe one of the others had some way outside or into another part of the resort.

She crept around and opened the next closest one. It had large metal shelves lining the walls. They contained stacks of cardboard boxes and assorted rags or cleaning supplies. No window, no other

Chapter 4: Day Two

door inside. She closed it and checked the second, then the third, and the fourth. There was no escape any other way than the door behind the front desk where she came in.

Well this wasn't going well! Mara became angry at herself and frustration overtook her. She walked to the front desk door and put her ear to it quietly.

Clacking of computer keys could be heard, along with occasional sipping sounds and a barely audible thud that Mara assumed was a coffee mug being put back down. It was either Alma or another employee.

What were her options? Walk right out and make a run for it? Alma knew her face and name and would surely tell her parents if nothing else. Even another employee would tell Alma as the Front Desk Manager, and then Alma would know from the description that it was her.

What about creeping out quietly? Unless the employee was wearing headphones, she didn't have a chance. Mara never saw the front desk people with headphones. They likely weren't allowed to wear them even.

Her only choice was to wait and see if they left for a few moments. But she was running out of time. Once the guy/girl activity groups finished, the front desk would likely be busy with people walking past, asking the employees questions.

Mara found herself desperate, wishing the wind really did exist like in the story or that Rudy Goodwin was still at the resort and could help her.

She rubbed her knee through her dress and winced in surprise. She must have scraped it during her fall in the hall. Blood didn't show through the thick fabric, but it stung.

Why did she have to get hurt to play the game? Wasn't this too hard for a kid? It all might be over if she was caught now. An employee would want the stolen keycard back, and they'd find the metal key and tape recorder on her.

This wasn't fair! If part of the clue was true about not trusting anyone from the village, then the part about trusting the wind and getting help should have been true too! Rudy Goodwin set the game up with great care. She had to believe he had something planned to help her.

Mara put her hand in her pocket and turned the metal key around in her fingers. "C'mon Rudy, help me" she thought. Her vision suddenly darkened for a moment, and she slumped to her knees. A horrendous crash sounded from beyond the door!

Chapter 4: Day Two

Mara heard someone scream and rapid footsteps carried away. What was that?! She gathered herself and stood up, her vision returning. Was that glass breaking? There was silence when she put her ear to the door, save for the audible pounding of her heart. The employee left!

Mara opened the door and exited. In the center of the foyer was one of the crystal chandeliers smashed on the floor. That explained the crash, but she didn't have time to gawk. She removed the employee's keycard from her other pocket and shakily jammed it in one of the desk drawers before running down the guest hall beyond the foyer. She heard rapid footsteps coming her way, so she ducked into the door that led upstairs and towards her room.

She could hear multiple employees speaking in their native language and sounds of the broken glass being moved. They were probably in a hurry to clean it before any guests saw. Mara didn't stick around to listen more. She now had a free path back to her room, and no evidence besides the metal key to prove she snuck in the private office.

Back in her room, she hid the key under the mattress and slid her backpack off before laying down. She felt dizzy and so tired. What was that timing? Was Rudy actually in the resort, hiding between walls and pulling chandelier cords to help her? She was scared. Her fingers trembled, and she held her hands together to stop it. This didn't seem like a good thing for an adult to do. This didn't seem safe. What game was she playing?

Despite her fatigue she took the tape recorder out of her backpack and stuffed it into the room's closet beneath a stack of extra blankets. She needed a break. She needed to calm down. Her parents would be back soon and they'd have dinner together, right? Then tomorrow she would sled with the other kids? That sounded good. She wanted that. She hoped her mother held her hand as they walked to the dining room together soon. Mara wouldn't shirk it away this time.

Mara laid back down and rested her eyes, repeating to herself that her parents would be back at her room soon.

Mara was aware she fell asleep only because she was startled awake by a slamming door. Her mother's muffled voice immediately followed in the other room. She sounded annoyed, so Mara assumed she met up with her dad and they both returned.

Normally this would have been a tense atmosphere Mara would have avoided, but the lingering fear from her earlier adventure made her glad she wasn't alone anymore. Mara hopped off her bed, smoothed her dress and hair, and walked to the dividing door.

She knocked first. "Mom? Are we going to dinner now? Can I come in?"

Shannon yanked the door open before responding. "Weren't you supposed to still be with your grandmother?!"

Mara looked up to meet her annoyed gaze and noticed her dad quietly gathering his evening clothes and walking into the bathroom. "I was, but Grandma started talking to a friend, and I came back to the room to wait for you."

An awkward silence followed as her mother crossed her arms and looked Mara up and down. "Alright, but comb your hair better. It looks like a mess."

Mara complied and fetched her brush before walking back to sit on her parents' bed as she fixed her hair. Her mother was busy fussing with her own dress collar in-between fixing her makeup.

Mara hoped she could keep on her good side tonight. She tried to make small talk to gauge her mood. "How was the spa day?"

Shannon sighed and replied in an exasperated tone. "The woman doing the seaweed wraps didn't know what she was doing. And cousin Janice wouldn't shut up about her daughter dating a doctor. You'd think she was going to marry him tomorrow from all her bragging." She shifted as she applied more mascara and continued. "Samantha shouldn't have invited her. She does this at every family event."

Chapter 4: Day Two

Mara nodded as if she agreed, but she had very little recollection of cousin Janice and her daughter, certainly not enough to judge her.

"Did Samantha have fun with you guys? She must have complained about missing Ryan a dozen times!" Mara made a mock pouting face, hoping to lighten the mood. Occasionally she could make her mother laugh, but it was rare.

Shannon simply scoffed. "I guess. If I didn't have Janice talking my ear off, maybe I would have chatted with her."

Mara's careful conversation steering seemed to work. Her mother took over with a monologue about cousin Janice, but she wasn't directing any anger towards Mara or her dad. After ten minutes, David exited the restroom, cleaned up and dressed in his evening wear of a white shirt, blue tie, and blue slacks.

Shannon walked over and fussed with his tie, leaving Mara quietly watching them, waiting until they were ready to walk to the dinning room with her.

As she watched she began to wonder something strange. Was her dad a strong guy? He was taller than a few other male relatives. He wasn't especially muscular, but he wasn't stick thin or weak either. Could he take someone on like Rudy if he was putting Mara

177

in danger? Or more importantly, would he? It made Mara nervous that this thought even entered her head. No one would have to fight or get hurt. The chandelier was probably an accident. Everything would be fine. It had to be fine!

"Kiddo! C'mon, we'll be late, let's go." David held the door open as Shannon already began walking out. Mara shook herself of her thoughts and hopped off the bed to follow.

She ran to catch up and walk next to her mother.

"You know," David started, "the event planners really should have planned a kids' hike instead of a guys' hike. I was about dead when we weren't even halfway back. My feet still ache something terrible. But you probably could have sprinted circles around us, Mara."

He gave her a lazy smile but didn't appear to be joking about his body pains. He walked a little stiffly behind them. Shannon didn't waste the opportunity to interject with a fresh barb. "Maybe if you lost some weight you wouldn't be in such pain from a one-day hike."

David straightened up and dropped his smile but continued walking steadily behind them.

Chapter 4: Day Two

Mara didn't want tension to return, so she tried to change the topic. "The sledding day is tomorrow! I can sled with the other kids, right? I'm okay if you both need to watch me too."

She watched her mother's footsteps and hands as they walked, trying to determine her mood and if it would be okay to hold hands as they walked the rest of the way. Shannon had a brisk walk, swinging her arms as she went. She appeared anxious to get there on time, so Mara thought this wouldn't be good timing to push her luck with seeking her mother's attention. She settled for gripping the fabric of her own dress pockets to keep her hands busy.

"We'll definitely have to watch you tomorrow." Shannon answered. "You can sled with the other kids, but I don't want you getting hurt. There are trees and rocks everywhere on the slopes. If you scratch your face right before Samantha's wedding photos, I'll never hear the end of it from your grandmother."

Mara thought that answer was better than it could have been. At least she was going to be allowed to join in on the fun, and her parents would be there too. She recalled her earlier daydream about the perfect sledding day and was feeling more hopeful than she had in the past few days.

The Red god

Once they reached the dining room, the trio bumped into Aunt Barbara first. She chatted with Shannon for a few minutes about the spa day and asked David how the hike went.

Mara's nose wanted to lead her off to the side where the banquet tables had roast ham tonight, but she caught sight of her grandmother at a table first. Mildred noticed Mara as well and shook her husband's arm and pointed towards her.

Mara was too far away to hear what she said, but Gareth stood up and began walking towards them.

"Hi, Dear, how was the spa day?" Gareth greeted his daughter but didn't wait for her answer. "Milly would really like it if you sat at our table tonight."

Shannon turned away from the conversation with Barbara. "Sure, Dad. We'll sit with you."

Mara noted her tone lacked enthusiasm, but she didn't appear ready to argue. What grandmother wanted, grandmother got, Mara supposed.

Before they walked that way, Barbara turned to Mara. "Oh! Danny is so excited to sled with you tomorrow, Mara! I'll be inside with Larry. My knees aren't what they used to be! But Gina will be with Danny on the smaller slopes tomorrow. I hope you kids have fun!"

At that, Barbara waved and returned to her table as Shannon gave her father a look and then walked to their table. Mara followed while her dad promised to return with plates soon. Mildred sat at the table watching them as they walked up.

Tonight she wore a dark purple dress with multiple layers folded at the collar, giving a ruffled effect. Mara thought her dress and jewelry looked very pretty, but her unpleasant scowl ruined the effect. Mildred tapped her glass in annoyance as Shannon took her time setting her sweater on the back of a chair and pulling it out to sit.

There was no small talk tonight as she launched into a topic Mara had hoped would be forgotten. "Evergreen Premier. That's a top school that would give Mara the best advantage. I was talking to Mara about it earlier."

Shannon took a slow sip from her glass before replying. "That's not in Colorado. And I have Mara's schooling covered. Me and David specifically chose our house because of the school district it was in. It's the best in the city. We've had no complaints."

"You've had no complaints because your standards are practically in the gutter already," Mildred shot back, cutting her daughter off. "It's a public school." She emphasized public as if it was a dirty word. "It will never compare to a private school, and certainly not Evergreen. You're right it's not in Colorado, but Mara is not an infant. She doesn't need you every moment. Students board at Evergreen all the time."

Mara began watching their argument like one would watch a tennis match. She wanted her chair to swallow her up, or at least for her dad to return with their food and hopefully change the topic. He wouldn't let her be shipped off to a boarding school, right?

She liked her school! As much as she didn't like her home life with her fighting parents, being alone somewhere strange was an even scarier prospect. She wouldn't even have Beth anymore or... Hershey! No, leaving Hershey wasn't an option. Mara would run away or smuggle her feline best friend with her if it ever came to that.

"-and you are not her parent! I am!" Shannon was practically whisper yelling at this point, but Mildred kept a cool composure.

The older woman took a moment to wipe her fork with a cloth and inspect it before replying. "Why don't you just admit that

Chapter 4: Day Two

you and David don't have the money? That he has a mediocre management position at a mediocre company, and you can't afford anything better for Mara?"

Mara's eyes shot to her mother's for her response, but she only opened and closed her mouth a few times. Anger left Shannon as a look of shock and shame set in.

"Ahem..." David's throat clearing startled Mara. He stood behind her and sat her plate down first before turning and setting Shannon's down too. He took a seat and looked to Mildred and then Shannon. Mara expected him to say something. To be angry. To defend his wife. He must have overheard that last comment when he walked up!

But he turned to look at Gareth and changed the subject instead, pretending he didn't hear it. "Boy, you made a good decision skipping the hike, Gareth. It was rough. Did you hear Michael had a pretty good fall during it too?"

Gareth looked nervously at Mildred before returning the small talk to David. Mara didn't understand until she looked back at her grandmother. She was smirking at Shannon. She said that knowing David was walking up. Both of Mara's parents didn't want to argue, or couldn't argue, that they were well-off and could afford a private school. Mara didn't care at all about the money or the school quality. She didn't want to go anyway. But their loss of the argument made her afraid. Were they both going to go along with her grandmother's plans? Mara wasn't very hungry anymore.

Shannon was quiet the rest of the dinner. Gareth and David both seemed happy to relieve some tension with their stories of Michael's injury and painful knees, and Mildred occasionally asked Mara questions about her favorite school subjects and interjected with more facts about Evergreen. Mara quietly answered what she had to, but she didn't elaborate or look up from her plate much as she pushed her food around.

When David cleared his plate first, he gently nudged Shannon with his arm and glanced at Mara. "Are you both done now? Man, I wouldn't mind turning in early. My back needs a rest."

Shannon had a half-finished plate, but she nodded and stood up to grab her sweater. "Have a good night, Mom, Dad."

Mara jolted up to follow, very eager to be leaving the table. "Bye, Grandma, Grandpa!"

Chapter 4: Day Two

Mildred put on a bored face, not wanting to appear bothered by their sudden early departure. She went back to her own food rather than acknowledge their goodbyes further.

In the hallway, the three of them walked in silence for a few moments. Mara's stomach ached, and she felt her chest tighten as she thought about the possibility of leaving her home and school if her grandmother got her way. A million bad predictions flooded her imagination. Mara's hands painfully gripped her dress fabric, trying to calm herself.

Her mother had been very quiet. Her walk was slow, and she hardly swung her arms as they made their way back towards their rooms. Mara thought now was a good opportunity to reach for her mother's hand. She needed something, some comfort to make this day better.

She planned her timing to match her mother's steps and watched her gait for a moment before removing her hand from its clenched position and reaching for Shannon's hand. She made contact and felt her warmth for a brief second before Shannon

185

recoiled and removed her arm. Before Mara could pull back, an audible smack rung out and Shannon stopped and stood staring down at her.

The woman said no words, but her glare and the sting in Mara's hand said it all. Mara's breathing picked up, but she was too startled to audibly cry. Her eyes watered and she stood, eyes locked with her mother for several seconds.

David stopped and waited. He was visibly uncomfortable but didn't move to stand between the two or defend Mara. Instead he touched Shannon's shoulder after she made no move to break her stare. "We should talk in the room. Let's keep walking." Shannon moved to shrug his hand off her shoulder, or slap him too, Mara wasn't sure which, but David removed it quickly. She then turned and briskly continued walking.

Chapter 4: Day Two

Mara finally blinked at this point and felt the tears roll down her cheeks, although she still did not audibly cry. Her dad gave her a pitying look but said nothing and walked after Shannon.

Back in their respective rooms, Mara let out her cries. She tightly pulled her pillow to her face to muffle the wracking sobs. Why was she like this?! Why was he like this?! Why did no one actually LOVE HER? Her breathing was rapid and shallow. Her face was suddenly burning hot and wet despite the pillow absorbing most of the tears.

Maybe it would be better if they shipped her off to a boarding school! No one cared! No one asked what she wanted! No one felt anything but annoyance, indifference, or outright contempt for her! Even her own mother-! A shuddering breath cut off her thought as she struggled to inhale. Even her own mother didn't love her. That was it. That was always the answer. She was stupid to ever think otherwise. Or to ever think that her dad would care enough to defend her.

The Red god

She removed her face from the pillow to better breathe. In the other room her parents were arguing loudly about how the night went. Surprisingly they weren't mentioning the school issue itself. Instead Shannon was attacking David's job, salary, and how he wasn't man enough to defend her at dinner.

Despite the volume, their argument faded into the background for Mara. She was used to the noise. Instead she focused on the sound of her breathing. She felt a strange calm overtake her, and a cooling sensation on her burning face. Rudy. He did defend her today. He was the only one who did. Mara wasn't sure how he saved her earlier with the chandelier, but she was sure it was him.

At the time the events were terrifying, but Mara thought she saw them more clearly now, more in context with her revelation about her mother. Rudy did show her care. It wasn't supposed to be scary. The crash and breaking glass were loud, but he did it for her. Someone did something FOR her.

Mara's sobs had quieted, and she wiped her face before standing up. She walked to the closet and carefully removed the tape recorder from her earlier hiding place. Rudy was on her side.

Chapter 4: Day Two

He believed in her and cared. Mara had to believe that. It was the only thing she had proof of.

She tightly gripped the recorder to her chest and looked out at the dark mountain landscape from the picture window. Tomorrow she was going to continue the game. She was going to finish it before her time ran out, and Rudy would be proud of her. He was going to help her, and she would trust him.

He had to love her...

Chapter 5: Day Three

Mara was awake before morning officially dawned. The room was cold, dark, and still, but she had things to do, and she wasn't going to wait. She removed her covers in one swift move and stepped off the bed.

Last night her sleep didn't wipe away the emotions of the day. They were instead replayed on a loop. She knew she had to listen to the next clue before her parents woke up and started the day of pretend. Pretending they wanted to play in the snow with her. Pretending they liked the relatives gathered for Samantha's wedding. Pretending they cared about family.

She carefully stepped to the chair where she had laid the recorder down. How could she ensure she listened to it quietly enough? The device didn't seem to have a volume button, or at least not one that looked obvious to Mara. There were some dials and unrecognized buttons on one side, but now was not the time to press everything and risk blasting the volume.

She looked around the room before deciding on a simple strategy. Mara pulled the bed covers off and drug them into the bathroom. She carefully pre-turned the doorknob and shut it successfully without a sound. This was the furthest point from her parents' room.

She flicked the light on and climbed into the bathtub with the covers, pulling them over her head to muffle the tape recorder sound as much as possible. She wondered what Rudy would have her do next.

If he crashed the chandelier for her, then that meant he was watching from somewhere in the resort, right? The hallways and common areas did have security cameras. Maybe he watched from those. There were no cameras in the guest rooms or bathrooms, so she supposed he couldn't see her now.

After she listened to the next clue and started the day with her family, she thought she should nod to a camera in the hall so he knew she was continuing the game. So he would watch her and continue to help. Mara liked that idea.

Not wanting to procrastinate any longer, Mara tugged one last time to secure the covers around her and pressed the play button.

"I'm not going to ask if you got the clue successfully this time," Rudy's voice started, "I know you did. Keep the key safe. You'll need it soon after you complete this next task."

The Red god

Mara sighed, relieved that the volume for this recording was pretty low. She could hear it fine, but she didn't think there was any risk that her parents would be woken up by it. Rudy was very calm in this segment, not his usual animated self, but he sounded pleased.

"You're getting closer to the end. You should be proud of yourself. I'm proud of you. You might wonder at this point what the end of the game will be and what the end of the story will be. I'll tell you one secret now: The end of the game and story are the same. You are writing this story with me, the Wind."

Rudy is the wind? Mara was confused again, but she was happy that Rudy was happy. And if he was the wind in the story, she supposed that made her the girl neglected by the villagers.

"I won't forget my promises to you. Your life will be better with me. But you can't forget your part in this either. I'll tell you this next step plainly. You're smart and no longer have need of rhyming clues. Go to the village. There is a box you MUST retrieve for me! It is important!"

Rudy's rising voice startled Mara, but it must have been necessary to highlight how important this part is. She listened closely.

Chapter 5: Day Three

"In the village there is an old, long-abandoned dwelling. It is near the southeast corner. Inside you will find a stone stove in the middle. There is a loose rock, and there you will find the box. Don't let anyone see it. Don't tell the villagers what you are doing. Retrieve the box and make sure you are alone when you play this next. I look forward to meeting you at the end..."

Meeting her...? She was going to meet Rudy? It was a promise! She pressed the pause button and removed the covers from her face. Leaning back in the tub, she smiled towards the ceiling thinking about his promise. Things were going to be better. Rudy would meet her in person. Something good would happen instead of the constant bad she experienced with her parents. She was excited again. She wouldn't let him down!

Mara stayed awake despite the early hour and passed the time with her notebook. She had sketched out a plan for today to make the task go smoothly. She already knew the road behind the resort led toward the village. But there would be a lot of pretending on her side to get through the prep work of getting there.

The Red god

Around 7 a.m., the sun had risen, and she heard her parents stirring in the next room. Not wanting to waste time on her mother's moods, Mara quickly got cleaned up and dressed for breakfast. When 7:30 arrived and her mother knocked and swung open the dividing door, Mara was sat waiting on the edge of her bed.

"Morning... Are we going to the dining hall for breakfast now?" Her voice was calm and practiced. She felt like a different girl compared to last night. She wasn't afraid. She wasn't desperate for her parents' company. She was a little more grown up, detached, and ready to move on. Rudy was waiting for her, after all.

Shannon noticed the changed mood and eyed her suspiciously. She looked Mara up and down slowly, likely looking for an unkempt strand of hair or incorrect clothes to nitpick. Mara smiled when Shannon gave up and became visibly frustrated.

"You must have gotten up early to be waiting like this." Shannon sneered. "In that much of a rush to see your grandmother and talk about Evergreen again? It didn't slip by me that you two talked about it behind my back before the ambush at dinner."

The older woman stared expectantly at Mara, but she gave no indication of being upset at the accusation. But what an accusation

194

Chapter 5: Day Three

it was! As if Mara plotted to be ripped from her home and forced to attend a boarding school! Like most things in her life, she had no say in it! Not when it was her grandmother making decisions nor her mother.

Mara normally would have felt shame or seething anger at this provocation, but a cold dullness had been covering her since her revelation last night. Nothing her mother said or didn't say would make any difference. It was like watching a tiny bird peck at an enormous boulder. Shannon would tire herself out without even a single chip being possible.

Still, she didn't want to provoke her back, so she replied with safe answers to get the interrogation over with. No point wasting time when she had a plan to enact for today.

"I don't want to go to Evergreen. Grandma doesn't listen to me though. I woke up early because I was hungry." Half lies, but it didn't matter. Her parents lied to her often. She would lie to them back now.

"Maybe you should go to Evergreen. I'm sure she'd pay for it. Then you can grow up quicker, be more successful than me, marry a man with more money than me, and make her prouder than me!"

Mara winced at this, but less because of the content of the words and more because a few droplets of spit escaped Shannon's last hissed words. She didn't know of a safe reply to this, so she put her head down to give a more demure appearance and placed her bets on the bird tiring out after a few more pecks.

"I know you have a goal here, Mara." Shannon paused for a long moment. This got Mara's attention, although she kept her head down and didn't visibly panic yet. Could her mother know about the game?! Is Rudy known to other people? Maybe one of the employees took notice and told her mother? A dozen lies to cover up her game goal began firing off in her mind. Which one would she be the most likely to believe?

Mara held her tongue, but more out of uncertainty of saying the wrong thing. Shannon continued. "You keep sneaking off and spending more time with your grandmother. You probably think she's nicer than me, more successful than me, and that she'll continue to take a special interest in you and you'll get something out of it. But I'm your mother! Not her! It's too bad you're stuck with me!"

So... she didn't know anything. These were just more paranoid accusations. Mara was glad she kept her mouth shut. She wanted to

Chapter 5: Day Three

breathe a sigh of relief and laugh at the absurdity, but she couldn't do it yet. She had to keep her poker face until her mother was done and out of the room.

What an idiot her mother was! Just like the stupid, evil villagers of the story! She would never see Mara's true goal, her problem-solving, her tenacity, and her bravery with finishing the previous game clue. Rudy saw it, but not her.

Before Shannon could rant much more, David knocked on the already-open door. "Uh, I thought you'd like to know it's getting closer to 8. I'm ready when you are." He looked nervous to be interrupting his wife. Normally Mara would have guessed he spoke up to save her from the last dregs of her mother's mood, but she didn't care anymore. Her dad didn't really defend her. He never would, just like he didn't last night.

Regardless of his good or neutral intentions, his interruption had the desired effect. Shannon angrily huffed and moved back through the doorway to their bedroom and snatched up her sweater before exiting the other door into the hallway. "Let's go then! Like you care about being late."

The Red god

David gave Mara a pitying smile before following his wife out. Mara only held a blank look in response and scooted off her bed to join them.

The trio walked down the hall together to the dining room but with a more noticeable space between each this morning. When they arrived, Mildred was nowhere to be seen to Mara's relief. Not many people were seated yet, but some older relatives milled about the coffee station. Mara took the peaceful opportunity to break away from her parents and start filling up a plate with waffles and fruit.

She finished assembling her plate before her parents did. Her mother was waiting for the coffee station, and her dad was slowly picking through the buffet options. Mara wanted to sit down and start eating, but she wasn't sure if her picking a table first would set her mother off. So she stood awkwardly holding her plate off to the side of the buffet.

After a few moments, Mara was startled by a voice. "Hey! Girl! Why don't you take a seat. You look like you might drop your waffle tower." She spun around to see Samantha giggling behind her. "If your parents haven't picked a table yet, come sit with me, Mara!"

Chapter 5: Day Three

Behind Samantha she saw Ryan taking a seat at a nearby table and waving. That... should be fine? Mara didn't think her mother could be mad at her for sitting with her cousin. Samantha was the whole reason the family was here. She nodded and started following her to the table. "Thanks. Sitting with you guys sounds fun. And it's a waffle castle, actually."

Samantha let out another giggle and patted the girl's back as she led her to the table. "Oh, I'm sorry. My mistake. I always mix up mid-century waffle architecture styles. But you did a good job on it!"

Mara wanted to enjoy the good mood at Samantha and Ryan's table, but as they chatted and ate she saw her parents begin making their way over. She knew her mother would behave better in front of Samantha, but it was still a big game of pretend. She was looking forward to a day when she could stop pretending. Maybe she could do that with Rudy...?

"Hi Samantha, good morning." Shannon predictably put on a calm, happy facade. "I see Mara already made herself at home at your table. Did you care if we joined you?"

Samantha noticed nothing out of the usual and beamed back. "Of course! Please take a seat! I'm sorry I missed you at the spa day

199

so much. Oh, how did you enjoy that seaweed wrap?! I'm still feeling my skin today because of how smooth it feels!"

Mara noticed an ever-so-slight twitch in her mother's eye at the mention of the seaweed wraps, but she kept her act up. "Yes, the seaweed was lovely. You picked a great resort for the activities you planned."

The two women continued chatting, leaving David and Ryan to their own conversation. Mara idly listened as she worked through her waffle castle. Apparently Ryan helped Michael back after his fall during the guys' hike. The young man apologized twice during the talk with Mara's dad for choosing such a risky, physically challenging activity for the guys' day.

Mara could only imagine he must have apologized a million more times during the hike back. It made Mara look at him a little differently today. Maybe Ryan was a nice person overall. Samantha certainly thought the world of him. But still, Mara thought, marriage was a doomed thing to begin with. They might be nice people now. They might be happy now. But things didn't stay that way.

Chapter 5: Day Three

Her dark thoughts were starting to depress her, so she tried to think about her game instead. Once she was on the slopes later, she could start her plan.

After everyone cleared their plates, David stood up first. "Well, are we going to see you two outside in a bit? We'll be taking Mara to pick out a sled with the rest of the kids."

Samantha tried to speak but still had a large mouthful of her last bite of food. Halfway through her muffled attempt, she switched to vigorously nodding. Ryan heartily laughed. "I'll translate. That's Sam for 'Yes we're going sledding too!' We'll see you as soon as we grab our winter gear. I hope you get a fast sled, Mara!"

"Not too fast," Shannon cut in, "We don't need any more injuries this trip."

Ryan sheepishly grinned, sensing the reference to poor Michael. "No, of course not. I'm sure the sledding hills are small and safe!"

The two groups parted ways, and Mara and her parents headed back towards their room first to get their boots and coats.

For the first time in a while, Mara left her backpack in the room. She didn't need to bring the tape recorder or notebook today.

The Red god

Her next goal was seared into her mind already. Rudy was very explicit about the next task, where she should go, and what she should look for. Instead she suited up in her winter clothes and firmly tugged on her toboggan cap as if she were a soldier gearing up for war.

They went out a side door of the resort, following a steady stream of family members and excited children. Mara was sure Danny was among them, but she hoped she didn't have to play with him too much. She had a different target in mind.

Once outside, they saw several cordoned off areas with employees in front handing out a variety of sleds and inner tubes. There were rounded rectangular plastic ones in bright orange and blue, longer black ones that looked to fit adults, small circular ones, older looking wood ones, and multi-colored inflatables that looked little-kid sized.

Despite being here for part of her goal, Mara immediately eyed one of the bright blue sleds. It wasn't quite teal; the color was more azure, but she badly wanted it.

Chapter 5: Day Three

Besides the sledding equipment, there were also several tables and temporary tents set up with hot drinks, first aid, and chairs for guests surrounding some carefully placed firepits. The area was swarmed with people already, with lots of screams and laughter from the kids. Objectively, it was a very happy scene.

Mara looked back at her mother to gauge her mood. Was it safe to go for her blue sled and run off to the hills? Shannon was turned away, seemingly distracted by the hot coffee set up on a nearby table.

David nudged Mara. "Let's get your sled, Kiddo!" She followed his lead and walked behind to the line of kids currently waiting for them. Mara watched as the two employees sized up each kid and handed them a suitable sled. They picked from the piles of types and colors at seeming random except for the size. The little kids didn't seem to care, besides the occasional pointing at another sled as the parents drug them away. But Mara cared. She wanted her BLUE sled.

As they waited, she studied the employees. They were young, around Samantha's age, but looked quite tired. The screaming kids all around probably weren't helping. Maybe if Mara was very polite and asked she could get her blue sled. She was a lot older than the other kids.

Surely the employees would appreciate dealing with someone older and less loud for a moment? But... that would be relying on the employees to treat her kindly. She wasn't supposed to trust them anymore, right? Mara was torn between what she should do when the last kid in front got their sled and stepped aside. In a split-second decision she dove for the rope of a blue sled barely behind the sectioned off area. The employee closest stepped forward and went to grab her hand, but she tugged the sled out of the pile toward her.

"Whoa, Mara!" her dad exclaimed. "I'm sure the nice worker would have handed you yours! I know you're excited."

The employee gave her a very annoyed look, and her dad stood behind her to steady the sled. "Is this one okay?" he sheepishly asked. Mara mumbled an apology but kept a tight hold on the sled reins. After a brief up-and-down look from the cross-armed employee, he nodded and waved them off. Mara breathed a sigh of relief. This not trusting people was really working for her. She was sure she would have ended up with an ugly orange sled if she hadn't done that.

Chapter 5: Day Three

With her prize in hand, she skipped out of the line trailing the sled behind. Her dad only shook his head and followed.

The pair saw Shannon in line for coffee still. David waved and pointed towards the small hills, but she gave a blank look and turned away. Sensing she wanted to be left alone, David shrugged and continued walking with Mara.

There were five hills that Mara saw people using today, or maybe six if you counted the one that was barely a bump where a few young parents had toddlers sliding down in the colorful inflatables. The further up they went, the larger and more advanced they looked.

If Mara was really here for sledding she would have been excitedly comparing hills before choosing the fastest looking one, but she was here for something else. Her eyes scanned the horizon for another group of kids, older ones, ones that she saw on her first night here. The front desk employee, Alma, had said they were kids from the village down the road and would be here today.

Mara needed to meet them and make friends. If she did, she had a much better chance at getting to their village and the box that Rudy wanted.

She recognized a lot of relatives and their kids but not the group she was looking for. It was early in the day though. Perhaps they would show up later. If they weren't here yet, then Mara's fallback plan was to pretend sledding was the funnest thing ever and beg her parents to let her stay out as long as possible. That would give her a better chance of seeing the kids later.

Mara headed up to the third hill in the meantime and readied her fated blue sled. Her dad trudged up behind her and waved. "Have fun! I think I'll stay at the top and let you go down and run back up. Otherwise I can't do this all day, whew."

In a flurry of kicked up fresh snow, Mara jumped aboard her ship and accelerated down the hill! She squinted as her sled raced, partly because of the cold wind in her eyes, and partly because it looked like she was going warp speed with blurs of falling snowflakes speeding past her vision. Faster, faster! She was giddy at the physical feeling and found herself laughing as she reached the bottom.

Okay, she knew 'pretending' sledding was the funnest thing was a lie. It actually was the funnest thing. But she would get serious once the group of kids was here. In the meantime, it was fine if she enjoyed herself, right?

Chapter 5: Day Three

Mara ran back up the hill with her sled wildly whipping behind as she zigzagged around smaller children. This time she was going to try going down head first!

She went down, and up, and down, and up until it hurt to breathe. The cold air now stung her sinuses and lungs, but her core was burning hot as she began to sweat.

Mara reached the top again but sat down to catch her breath. David chuckled and crouched beside her. "Only five trips has you tired out? You must be getting old! When we took you sledding on that old church's hill when you were eight, you didn't sit down for the whole two hours. I had to practically grab you by the coat to make you take a break between sprinting up and going down."

Mara remembered that day. It was a rare good one. Her parents didn't argue that day, and her mother wasn't overbearing and didn't make her stop having fun early. She was sure her dad was right that she'd sledded for two hours straight. But she also remembered the next day where her mother screamed because Mara forgot a piece of homework till the day before it was due. Her voice went hoarse from it. Good days were always eclipsed by the ones before or after.

The Red god

Mara mused that it was like someone offering you a slice of your favorite cake, but then seeing flecks of garbage baked into it. It wasn't worth it.

A few moments passed, and Mara was almost caught up with her breathing. But she stayed silent and didn't reply to her dad's reminiscing.

David looked around carefully and then spoke again in a lower voice. "Y'know, about last night. Your mom is really stressed, Mara. You gotta give her some room to deal with herself. You know how she is. Just... leave her alone next time. Or ask her what she wants." He smiled, as though the things he was saying made sense and would fix the situation.

Mara didn't return the sentiment, but he continued. "We can be a team, even. The more we work to keep her happy, the happier the whole house is. Next time, agree with your mom whenever Grandma Milly is asking something. Okay?"

He looked at her expectantly. Mara wanted to disagree. She wanted to say how stupid that was, and that her mother would never be happy with anything she did! She briefly thought of yelling and shoving her dad backwards. He was unbalanced as it was, crouching on snow. She could probably shove him completely down the hill! But... none of that anger was useful. And nothing her dad said mattered anyway. She was going to find Rudy. He mattered. He could help.

Mara settled for a small nod, a lie to get him off her case. David grinned and patted her on the back. "You're a good girl, Mara. Way more mature than I was at your age. Keep what I said in mind, and things will calm down once this week is over and we're back at home, away from Mildred."

She nodded again. "Can I go back to playing now?" She felt suffocated by his speech and really wanted to get away.

He paid no mind to her uncomfortable look. "Of course! Have fun today while you can! Some of the next days' events might be boring for you and the other kids."

Mara picked up her sled and rode back down.

The next few hours were spent on the same routine, sledding down and running up. Although the running was more of a slow jog now to save her breath. Mara was starting to get tired again when her dad suggested taking a break for lunch.

Mara had kept a careful eye out for the group of older kids, but there was still no sign of them.

The Red god

Mara and David walked back towards the various booths and tables close to the side of the resort. One was serving roasted sausages, and David got in line for them.

Mara noticed her mother was seated a few tables away next to one of the fire pits. She was talking to Ryan's dad and a few other adults Mara didn't know. They briefly locked eyes, but Mara looked away and back towards her dad. Shannon made no move to leave her current conversation, which was fine with Mara. She could sit there all day and leave her alone.

David reached the front of the line and got two large sticks of sausages for them both. He handed Mara hers and noticed Shannon seated nearby at the same time. "Oh, there's your mom. Let's find a seat while we're eating."

Mara desperately wanted to *not* do that. "Can I try and find Cousin Danny instead? Gina and him should be nearby..."

David shrugged. "Sure, but after you play with Danny come and find us. I'm going to join your mom." Mara nodded and raced off the opposite direction.

She wasn't really going to look for Danny, but her dad didn't need to know that. She walked behind the booths and off towards the back of the resort. She didn't want to go too far away. She had to keep an eye out for those kids still, but she wanted a break from the busy area.

She found a nice landscaping rock to sit on and began eating her lunch. No one was near this end, so it was quiet except for the occasional loud scream from a sledding kid.

Mara found herself daydreaming that there was a little cottage nearby, hidden in the mountains. It had a dark stone exterior and pink tiled roof. There was a fence around it, and out back it had a large greenhouse with all kind of flowers and butterflies despite the snowy scene around it.

Rudy was there, and he invited Mara to come live in it as her game prize. Hershey was there too, enjoying the sun in the greenhouse and chasing butterflies.

Mara had barely eaten half her lunch, but she leaned back and smiled as she imagined the scene details more. Oh Hershey. Mara missed her so much already. It had been a long week despite it only being Thursday.

Was Mrs Cook feeding her right? Was she petting her enough? Mara wondered if Hershey missed her back.

A new scene came into her mind of Hershey dejectedly walking throughout their empty house, caterwauling as she went. It made Mara sadder to think about. She had to shake the thought away before she got teary-eyed. Hershey was fine back home! Mrs Cook probably overfed her if anything and fussed about how pretty she was. She wouldn't be alone all week.

"Mmmmrrrioooowww!" a loud cry from Mara's right startled her. She nearly fell off her seat!

She quickly straightened herself and looked for the source of the sound. It had to have been close!

"Mrrrow!" it sounded again. This time Mara caught sight of the origin. Ten feet off was a dark gray cat, half hiding behind a bush. He was much larger than Hershey and extremely fluffy!

Mara excitedly grinned. "Oh, you look like you have a winter coat on with all that fur! You're so cute!"

The cat was unaffected by her praise, but he was holding an intense staring contest with her remaining sausage piece.

"Do you want some?" Mara scooted off her rock and inched closer, extending the meaty peace offering. The cat retreated into the bush in response. "No, it's okay!" She kneeled down to appear less frightening. "I won't hurt you! Here, have some."

She ripped off a chunk of meat and gently tossed it in front of the bush, hoping she hadn't run the cat off already.

Chapter 5: Day Three

How had he been surviving in this cold? He looked fairly husky, so Mara wondered if the employees fed and sheltered him occasionally.

Mara waited patiently until he poked his head back out and quickly grabbed the meat. Instead of eating it where it was, he pulled it into the bush and ate it out of sight.

Mara would have been disappointed it if weren't for the obvious chewing sounds coming from the shaking bush. "You are so funny!" Mara laughed. Immediately after the sounds finished, he popped his head back out and stared, waiting.

Mara obliged and tore off another chunk. She threw it slightly further away from the cat this time. The ruse worked, and the cat came closer. "I wonder if you have a name," Mara mused. "You certainly don't have a collar." The cat noisily ate his food, not paying attention to Mara. She took the opportunity to creep closer.

"Boy, you were hungry! I guess you have to eat a lot to handle this cold." Mara was only a few feet away now, and she crouched back down just as the cat finished his mouthful. He was startled to notice Mara closer, but he didn't run this time.

Mara sheepishly grinned and offered the last sausage piece from her hand. "I won't hurt you. I love cats! You... are always nice to me. And cute. And good company." The cat eyed her suspiciously but crept closer to gingerly take the piece from her hand.

For her kindness, Mara was rewarded with another round of noisy chewing from her new friend. She giggled and reached out to gently stroke the side of his face. Mara was good at making friends with cats, more so than people. Cats were simple. They wanted calmness, warmth, food, and a gentle touch. Mara enjoyed their quiet company back.

"Gravy," Mara said with a resolute nod, still stroking the large gray cat. "You look like a Gravy. How about that for your name?" Gravy let out a muffled meow that sounded strangely like a grunt. "Mrffft!" The sound caused Mara to squeal in happiness.

"You like it! I'm glad!" Gravy leaned into the pets now, despite the food being gone. Mara was still careful and slow in her strokes to avoid scaring him. "I'm sorry I didn't have more for you, Gravy. But if you're out here later, I'll bring you food again. You're a good kitty."

The two sat like that for several more minutes before Gravy stretched and sauntered off towards the other side of the resort. Mara gave a cheerful wave as he went.

Chapter 5: Day Three

She supposed it was about time for her to head off too. She wanted to procrastinate more in this quiet area, but she needed to not anger her parents or miss the kids from the village. With a heavy sigh, she began dragging her feet back towards the crowded booths.

On her way back, Mara spotted Gina standing near one of the small hills. "You can do it, Baby! Go, go!" She was cheering Danny on as he pushed off the hill in a small red sled. At least, Mara assumed that was Danny. The small kid was bundled up in such a puffy jacket and hood, she was surprised he could move to sled. But down he went!

"Hi, Gina," Mara greeted. "Oh hey!" Gina turned around. "I saw you and your dad on the big hill earlier! You were super fast!"

Mara grinned, remembering her blue sled's first trip down. "I got a good sled! How about you, Danny?" Some muffled reply came from him as he struggled to disembark at the bottom. Mara noticed he also had a big scarf covering most of his face. Gina wasn't taking any chances with the cold... "Well, you got a good color. I bet the red one goes fast!"

Gina laughed and helped Danny off the sled. "You went very fast, Baby! How are you holding up? Did you want a drink or a break?"

Danny nodded as much as his scarf and jacket would allow. Mara couldn't help but laugh too. "We're going to stop by some of the booths," Gina said, "Would you like to go with us, Mara?"

"I'll walk that way with you, but I have to find my parents. My dad held on to my sled while I sat for lunch."

Gina nodded. "I'm sure I saw them over there a little bit ago. We'll find them."

The three started walking down. Mara noticed Danny holding Gina's hand and stared for a moment before looking away. She shouldn't focus on stupid things like that. Mara wasn't a little kid. She didn't need that. She had things to do, her game to win.

They got water bottles and hot chocolate from a stall before walking towards one of the firepit areas. Mara spotted her parents, so she reluctantly said goodbye to Gina and Danny and headed over.

As Mara got closer, she saw Samantha and Ryan had joined his dad seated next to Mara's parents. They were engrossed in conversation and didn't notice her right away, but she walked and stood next to her dad's chair.

"The only thing I'm telling him is that it's white!" Samantha exclaimed. "Other than that, no dress peeks!"

Chapter 5: Day Three

Ryan was laughing. "I wouldn't look anyway! I only have to wait 39 more hours to see you in it."

"Aw, you two are in it deep. Counting the hours even, Ryan?" Ryan's dad, Bruce interjected.

Samantha was the first to notice Mara. "Hey girl! Did you want to take a seat close to the fire? You must be freezing after all that sledding!" She moved to grab another chair and set it in their circle around the firepit.

"Sure, thanks," Mara replied, keeping her gaze down. She didn't want to catch her mother's face and know her current mood. She hoped she could sit, rest, and let the adults talk. Upon taking her seat, she noticed she had a good vantage point looking out to the hills.

"Did you have fun with Danny?" David asked. Mara nodded, and despite her earlier efforts caught sight of her mother's expression. She wasn't mad looking at least, but she had a fake smile as she chatted with the couple and Bruce. Mara looked away and fixed her eyes back on the hills. She had a job to do today.

The adults went back to their conversation. "Where's the ceremony taking place? The resort has that big ballroom, but I haven't seen the employees prepping anything in there." Shannon remarked.

Samantha gave Ryan a grin before turning back to Shannon. "I hope this isn't a bad idea, but I talked Ryan into having the ceremony outside. I really loved the look of the snowy backdrop! But don't worry! The resort has done that before, and they have heating lamps, a roll-out carpet for the walkway, and canopies to go over the seated areas in case it snows!"

Ryan patted her hand and smiled back. "I'm sure it'll be fine. We told the pastor to keep the ceremony very short! We'll be outside for 10 minutes, plus some photos, and everyone else can head inside the ballroom for pre-dinner drinks. No one is going to freeze, we promise!"

"Oh I don't blame you." David gestured towards the mountain. "It is a beautiful scene they have here. We can put up with the cold for a bit. I'm sure the drinks will warm us up afterward."

Ryan grinned. "I did say open bar! We want everyone to enjoy themselves."

The conversation from there dissolved into who liked what alcohol types and which relative was going to get the most money's

Chapter 5: Day Three

worth out of the open bar. Mara tuned them out at that point. She didn't understand adults and alcohol. It smelled bad; why did they force themselves to drink it? She was fine with her hot chocolate.

She was keeping an eye on her watch and the hills, and at three o'clock a group of older kids walked into view from behind the resort. It must have been them! She wanted to shoot out of her chair and run over, but she had to safely get away from her parents first.

"Dad, can I have my sled and go back out now?" Before David could reply, Shannon spoke. "It's getting later in the day, Mara. You've been sledding a long time. You should probably stay here and let David hand the sled back in before we get ready for dinner."

No! Mara thought, she could ruin everything! She waited all day for this chance!

"But the other kids are still playing. Dinner isn't for hours," she whined. Mara didn't want to sound like a whiny brat, but if she argued with the anger she actually felt, she would definitely get shot down. The whining had a possibility of getting the other adults on her side.

"Sledding officially ends at five." Samantha spoke up. "But until then everyone is welcome to enjoy the hills, refreshments, and

219

food out here! Don't worry about being late for dinner, Shannon. None of us will mind if you guys need extra time to change after hanging out here!"

Samantha was beaming her normal smile, not understanding the power play she was stepping in the middle of. But Mara understood. She saw her mother bite her tongue and give her a look. Mara would be in trouble for this later.

"Use the energy while you have it, kid!" Bruce jumped in, also not noticing Shannon's tensing. "You'll get old one day and have to sit around in chairs all day like us!" He laughed heartily, and the group chuckled along with him, all but Shannon.

Mara took the opportunity to grab the sled that was lying near her dad's chair and run off towards the hills. "I'll be back before five!" She waved.

Mara had to work fast. She had just under two hours to enact phase one of her plan. She needed a way to get to the village, and the box.

Upon walking closer, she noticed the older group of kids had brought their own sleds instead of the colorful ones provided by the resort employees. Most appeared weathered, cracked, or made of old wood.

Chapter 5: Day Three

Mara suddenly felt odd about her bright blue sled. She hoped they wouldn't snub her for it. She wasn't very good at socializing with other kids as it was. But she had to put in her best effort.

The group consisted of five boys and two girls. They looked to range in age from eleven to older teenagers, maybe even sixteen? They had the same olive skin tone as the resort employees, but a few of the boys had blond highlights, and one of the girls had purple streaks in her hair.

Mara was getting more nervous as she watched the group. They looked like cool kids. She wasn't sure if she looked cool or interesting enough for them to hang out with. But Mara remembered Alma's words, that she would tell her grand-kids about Mara looking to play with kids her age. She felt bad about using Alma's kindness a second time to further her own goals, but she wasn't supposed to trust her anyway... Rudy must have a reason for that.

The girl with purple hair turned and briefly made eye contact with her. Mara supposed it was now or never. She jogged closer and put on her best smile despite her nerves. "Hi! I'm Mara. I haven't seen many older kids here. What's your name?"

The Red god

The girl didn't say anything for a moment, but looked her up and down. Mara was struck with a thought she had earlier, when she had first seen the group outside that window: What if they didn't speak English! She must sound like a weirdo to them! Mara was debating what she could do in that scenario. Gesture more? Get her drawing pad and try to talk through that? They'd probably laugh and walk away!

Her spiraling thoughts were broken by the girl. "I'm Anna. Are you with the latest resort tourists?"

Mara smiled wider, relieved that she'd be able to talk to them. The girl had an accent, but like the employees she was still easily understood.

The word tourist sounded odd to her, but she supposed the girl was right. "Yep, I'm here with my family for my cousin's wedding."

Anna's expression changed to a smirk. "Then your family only has babies?" She gestured to the nearby small hill, where Aunt Gina and other relatives had their young kids and toddlers sliding down.

"Uh, I guess. I'm the oldest of my cousins, except for Samantha who's the one getting married. She's in her twenties..." Mara trailed off, unsure if Anna was making fun of her.

Chapter 5: Day Three

One of the boys noticed their conversation and jumped in. "How old?" His accent was a little thicker, but Mara assumed he was asking her age. "I'm gonna be twelve in June. What about you?"

The boy looked puzzled for a moment, and Anna sharply jabbed him with her elbow. The boy groaned and held his rib cage while shouting something Mara didn't catch.

The two argued in their native language for a moment before Anna turned back to Mara. "This is Lukas. He's twelve already, but stupid. Sometimes tourists have to talk slowly for him. He fails all his classes, English included!"

Anna laughed, but Lukas looked embarrassed and argued more in their language before turning towards Mara. "I understand! Anna is just mean!" He extended his hand and smiled towards her. Mara moved her sled reins to her left hand and returned his handshake. "You should lose that and try mine. It much faster!"

Now it was Mara's turn to look puzzled. Suddenly she realized he meant her sled. "Oh! I like yours too. Do the wood ones go faster?"

Lukas enthusiastically raised his hands in the air and made motions like a zooming plane. "So fast! Like rocket!"

223

Mara laughed and nodded. "I'd love to sled with you guys if that's okay." Lukas was very into his rocket imitation still. He shouted and took off in a run towards the head of the group and further up the hill. "Yes! We should go!" Mara laughed more and jogged to keep up. This was working well so far.

The tallest boy in the group introduced himself next. "I'm Nico, Lukas' older brother. If he gets too rowdy, let me know and I'll handle him."

Lukas took offense to this and shouted back. "I'm not! I'm the nice one! You guys are mean!"

They appeared to be joking in good nature, as the brothers still smiled despite their poking at each other. Mara smiled at their squabbling but noticed the other girl in the group was rather quiet. She was a little taller than Mara but didn't look that much older.

Anna saw her looking towards the girl and grabbed her hand to wave it in the air. She mocked in a higher pitch voice. "Hi, I'm Eva. I'm smart but too shy to talk to new people."

Eva swatted at her hand to free her own arm. Anna released her but kept laughing. "You know it's true!"

Chapter 5: Day Three

Eva gave her a mean look but spoke to Mara instead of replying to Anna. "I'm just not as loud as the rest of these. But it's nice to meet you."

Mara smiled. "No worries. Sometimes I'm quiet too. Thanks for letting me hang out with you guys."

They were now at the top of the hill Mara had sledded on earlier with her dad. She expected them to stop and put their sleds down, but Lukas in front was still moving forward. Mara didn't want to embarrass herself, so she stayed quiet and followed as they went higher. Were they going near the tree line? Mara hoped they wouldn't go anywhere dangerous.

"Did you meet Alma earlier?" Nico asked. Mara was surprised to hear the name but remembered some of these kids must be her grand-kids. "Yeah, she was nice. You know Alma?"

Nico nodded. "I thought so. She's my and Lukas' grandma."

Mara hoped Alma hadn't said anything too embarrassing to them. A scene played in her mind of Alma describing her to the boys. "Oh she is such a lonely kid! Drawing in the foyer by herself for hours yesterday! You two need to play with her!" Mara grimaced at her own imagined conversation. Whatever Alma said, at least they were welcoming her to join them.

225

"Alma's cool," Anna spoke up. "She likes to get us all snacks or drinks sometimes. Y'know, stuff the tourists don't use up when they leave. By the way..." The purple-haired girl slid closer to Mara. "How rich is your family that they booked up the resort for the whole week? You said it was your young cousin's wedding?"

Mara wasn't sure how to answer that. Tourist, rich, she wasn't used to those words herself. "I don't know... My parents just booked our plane tickets. They fought over it, so I guess they were expensive."

Anna eyed her. "I guess that means *you* aren't rich. But your cousin's family must be." Mara shrugged, uncomfortable with the topic.

One of the other boys with blond highlights jumped in. "Anna is obsessed with getting out of our village. If you were rich, she'd probably ask to go home with you." Anna tried to elbow him, but he quickly dodged, laughing.

Anna switched to their language to argue with him. After a moment the yelling switched back to English. "And why wouldn't I! Los Angeles will be better than this! I'll start a clothing company too and make my own money!"

Chapter 5: Day Three

"Do you sew?" Mara asked. Anna gave a blank stare and a sigh. "No, not sewing. Fashion! I don't need to sew it myself. Someone else will do that."

"Oh." Mara replied, unsure what else to say. She didn't much like fashion, or at least her grandmother and mother's take on it that usually involved fitting Mara in uncomfortable dresses.

Anna didn't mind her lack of reply and continued anyway. "People will wear them on walkways and red carpets. You're just jealous, Dominik."

While they were walking, Mara took the opportunity to peek beside Anna and look at the remaining two boys of the group. One was only a little older than Mara. He was tall and thin and hadn't spoken yet. The other looked a lot like Dominik.

"Rocket on!" Lukas suddenly shouted. He slammed his sled down and jumped on the front of it. Mara supposed that meant they climbed high enough on the hill to start sledding. Before he went down, he patted the back of his wood sled. "You going? Will be fast!"

Mara nervously shook her head. "Uh, I don't want to lose my sled if I let it go here. You go down first!" The boy didn't seem to mind her rejection, as he quickly lifted his feet and took off without her.

This started a chain reaction as the other two boys, Dominik and who Mara supposed was his brother, also slammed their sleds down and took off, whooping and hollering the whole way down.

"Don't let the boys win!" Anna shouted. Mara laughed and readied her sled too. These were a fun bunch, she thought. The girls took off at roughly the same time, and the other boys followed with Nico last.

The trail down was steep! Mara was shocked at how fast she accelerated! She was too busy talking to the group on the walk up to notice how high they had actually gone!

There weren't any trees in the way, luckily, but Mara held her sled reins hard and gritted her teeth as they raced. The wind whipped past at record speed and stung her face, but she found herself unable to pay attention to it. Laughter from Anna and Eva to her left echoed across the landscape to her. Mara's fear began leaving, and she found herself laughing the rest of the way down too.

"Wooooooo!" Lukas screamed out as he neared the bottom and tumbled off his sled. He didn't seem hurt, as he quickly stood up and raised his arms triumphantly at crossing the imaginary finish line first. "Rockeeeeeeeet!"

The two boys slowed to a stop near him, followed by Anna, Eva, and then Mara herself. She put out her foot to stop her sled but stayed sitting on it for a few moments to catch her breath. How long had it been since she ran out of breath simply laughing? Mara couldn't remember.

She started asking Lukas about his sled when suddenly his face changed to shock. He shouted in their language towards her, but she didn't understand.

SMACK! Mara went spinning, rolling further down the hill. The landscape was a dizzying sight of snow, sky, snow, sky. When the rolling stopped, she put out her hands to steady herself.

"Sorry, sorry!" one of the boys yelled. Mara hardly registered it as she waited for her head to stop spinning.

"Oskar!" Nico yelled, followed by more yelling in their language. After a moment Mara felt a hand on her shoulder. "You okay?" Lukas grabbed her arm and helped her stand up.

Mara then realized the quiet boy, Oskar, must have struck her sled with his own. She had rolled a good twenty feet and looked to see her blue sled slowly going further down. "Oh no! I have to get it!" Lukas followed her line of sight and took off first. "I get it! No worries!"

Mara checked her hands and knees, but luckily she didn't see any blood. They ached a little, but she was okay.

Oskar walked up and apologized more. "I couldn't stop, sorry! You okay?"

Mara nodded. "I'm fine. It's okay. I probably should have been looking around when I stopped anyway."

Nico firmly put his hand on Oskar's shoulder. "That was entirely Oskar's fault. But I'm glad you're okay."

Lukas returned with Mara's sled and handed the reins back. "Don't tell Alma!"

"Oh, she should tell Alma" Anna giggled. "She would give you boys a talking to!"

"Why all of us?" Dominik asked. "Oskar is the one that hit her!"

"Because," Anna sneered, "You boys get in trouble together. You're a package."

Mara put up her hands and tried to stop the argument. "I'm okay! So there's nothing to tell anyway. But..." She took a breath and looked over to Lukas. "Can I ride your sled next?" A grin came over her, and Lukas returned it. "Of course!"

The group made quick work of hiking back up the hill. This time Mara left her sled hooked on a stick and rode on the back of Lukas' sled. It was faster! They rocketed down, and she held onto his waist tight to avoid bumping off the back.

"Wooooooo!" he yelled with the same enthusiasm as the first trip. Mara laughed and joined. "Rockeeet! Woooo!" It was hard being quiet with such a loud group.

When they reached the bottom, Mara asked about the last boy's name. "He looks a lot like Dominik, are they brothers? What's his name?"

Lukas laughed at her. "They are twins! They should look similar!" Mara's face reddened. She should have figured, but she didn't want to assume. Lukas continued. "His name is Levi. They had older brother too, Nico's age. But he got punished."

"Punished?" Mara paled. "Is he not here anymore?"

"He means grounded," Eva said. "He couldn't hang out today because he set a fire."

This brought up more questions for Mara. "A fire?!"

"Only a little one!" Lukas assured. "We have bad buildings near our houses, and he set wood inside."

"Oh." Mara calmed down. "It was an accident then." Eva nodded. "But he still got in trouble. It was dangerous."

Wind picked up and swirled around Mara's face, stinging her eyes. She rubbed at them. Wait, she thought, they were talking about abandoned structures in their village. That might be the building Mara needs to find the box in!

"Do you hang out in the buildings for fun often?" Mara prodded, hoping to get to the next phase of her plan.

"Only the non-lame kids do." Anna piped up. "The lame ones like Oskar don't."

"Not Oskar's fault!" Lukas shouted. "His parents get mad, so he can't go there!" They started arguing in their language again, but Mara wanted to keep the conversation going.

"That sounds fun! I love exploring places like that. I was exploring parts of the resort earlier in the week too. Can I go if you guys are going next?"

Chapter 5: Day Three

Eva spoke while Anna and Lukas were still arguing. "It's far. Our houses are a long walk away."

Mara couldn't lose this opportunity. "That's fine! I love hikes. I don't look athletic, but I walk a lot!"

"Alma might get mad." Lukas turned back to her. "We're better meeting you and playing around the resort." He looked concerned, and Mara didn't know how to argue that without seeming suspicious, so she stayed quiet for the time being.

They walked back up for another round of sledding, but as they walked Mara got an idea in her head. It felt alien to her, but it whispered in her mind all the same. She tried to push it aside and think of something else, some other way of talking the group into letting her go with them to their village.

They reached the top, and Lukas held out his hand to steady Mara as she climbed on the back of his sled again. Despite her uneasiness, Mara listened to the whispers and squeezed his hand tighter than normal. Before they started sliding down, she leaned in his ear. "Lukas, I *really* want to go with you to your hang out spot near your houses. Please talk them into letting me go..."

His ear turned beet red and he stuttered. "U-uh, okay, I can!" Mara wasn't used to talking to boys this close. She felt her own face redden, but she fought against the embarrassed feeling and leaned into him anyway as they went down.

Once at the bottom, she grabbed his hand as they stood up. He was staring at the ground but spoke in a low voice before the other kids caught up. "Y-you have pretty hair."

"Thanks," Mara said, still not used to this tactic but wanting to see it to the end. "I like yours too."

Lukas stood next to her, blushing for a moment before he removed his hand as the other kids started reaching the bottom. To cover up his embarrassment, he raised his hands and shouted, "Letttttt's gooo! Rockettttt!" before racing back up. Mara followed.

They ran four more trips. The twins, Dominik and Levi, got into an argument about which of them was faster today. The girls stayed at the top one time to officiate the race, and the other boys joined in. Nico beat them all and scolded them for fighting.

On the last trip down, Mara noticed the time on her watch. "Oh no, I have to get back to my parents soon! They didn't want me sledding past five!"

Lukas nodded. "Then, uh, I see you soon? Will you be at resort tomorrow?"

Chapter 5: Day Three

"I'll be here tomorrow. Could... we hang out at your spot then?" He looked uneasy at the idea still, but she squeezed his hand, and he melted like fake butter. "Y-yeah! I will meet you! Outside the back, and we can walk together!"

Wow, Mara thought, this worked *really* well. Part of her felt ashamed for using such a gross tactic, but the idea did work. Lukas must have really thought her hair was pretty...

Despite Lukas agreeing to walk her to the hangout spot tomorrow, he didn't share the plan with the rest of the group. Mara was wondering if he would hide it from them, but it didn't matter to her. Once she was there, she could get the box and walk back. Hopefully Lukas wouldn't be mad... he seemed like a nice kid. She did like hanging out with him; that part wasn't a lie.

"Don't trust them!" echoed in her head, but she was conflicted. The group waved fond goodbyes as she took her sled and walked back to the booths area. Lukas waved a little more shyly.

Back near the resort, the crowds were thinning. Most of the little kids had handed in their sleds and were walking with their parents back into the resort.

Mara walked hers to where she originally got it. The same employee was there, and he greeted her a little more rudely with no other adults around. "Have fun with that one?" His tone was flat, and he didn't try to hide his frown.

"I did..." Mara mumbled, handing the reins over. Should she feel guilty for today? She looked back towards the group of kids still sledding on the high hills, spotting Lukas out in front on his rocket sled. Maybe she should.

"There you are!" David spoke, startling her. "C'mon, we're going to be late." He waved her towards him, and Mara saw her mother standing further off waving goodbye to Samantha and Ryan.

Chapter 5: Day Three

Mara followed behind, and they walked into the resort and towards their rooms. Shannon was quiet, but an angry quiet. Mara didn't care. Now that phase one was complete, her mother could do whatever punishment she wanted. Mara was still winning.

Back in their room, Shannon began shuffling hangers and shoved a shirt and tie towards David. "These are for tonight," she said and then turned her attention to Mara, "And you, you don't need your outfit for tonight!" Shannon put her hand on Mara's shoulder and steered her into Mara's room, closing the dividing door behind her.

"I saw you hanging out with those kids after I told you to stay put. You have dozens of relatives to play with here, but you run off to hang out with outsider kids? I guess your family doesn't mean anything to you, huh?" She stared at Mara with a frown, but Mara didn't reply. "You know, if you hate your family so much, I don't think you need to join us for dinner!"

She jerked her hand off Mara and began stalking around the room, looking for something.

"You also don't need your Switch." She put the game console under her arm. "Or your drawing pad, or your other toys." Shannon picked up her backpack last, and Mara became alarmed. The tape recorder!

Shannon noticed the weight of the bag and opened it, beginning to pull items out. "You stole your dad's camping multi tool? What the hell is in here?!" She took out her notebook, extra pencils, compass, and finally the tape recorder. Mara felt the hair on the back of her neck stand up.

"Where did you even get this??" Mara opened her mouth, willing an excuse to come, something to save her. But she had nothing. What would her mother believe?

Shannon immediately started pressing buttons and turning it over in her hands. "This is old. Did Grandma give this to you?! Why are you hiding it?" The device clicked as she pressed the play button, and the usual static sounded out.

Mara wanted to cry. In a moment Rudy would begin talking about the next clue, and her mother would blow a gasket and ruin everything! She had been so close!

"......" static continued, but no voice came out. Mara looked up as her mother shook the tape recorder a few times for good measure. Still nothing. She turned it off and angrily stuffed it back in Mara's bag. "Whatever you were playing with this for, it's confiscated tonight! You're going to stay in your room while your father and I have dinner with family!"

Shannon gathered up her backpack, Switch, and other items and went back into the other room. Before she closed the door she pointed a finger at Mara. "And I want you to think about why you should pick your family while you're in here alone!" The door lock clicked after her, leaving Mara alone and locked away from her gadgets.

The tape... didn't play? Mara let out a relieved breath she had been holding. She was so sure she was done for! She couldn't believe what happened. How did the tape not play? Did her mother fumble wrong buttons in her haste to mess with it? Mara hoped she hadn't accidentally recorded over that section of tape. She needed to hear the next clue after she got the box for Rudy tomorrow.

Mara unzipped her coat and sunk into her bed. If her mother thought banning her from family dinner was a horrible punishment, she might have to act out more. She stifled a laugh into her hands. Today almost couldn't get any better. Mara got to sled, play with a new cat, make... friends? And she completed phase one of her plan to get the box! Not dealing with her parents at dinner was a bonus.

The thought of the kids stuck in her mind though. Mara had a gnawing feeling of guilt when she thought of Lukas. How she had held his hand and leaned in close to him also made her stomach feel weird. It wasn't like Mara hated boys, but that wasn't something she would have normally done. She never held a boy's hand like that even.

Sure, she was old enough. A lot of her classmates had boyfriends or kissed a boy already, but Mara always shied away from that type of thing. She was happy just hanging out as friends with the rare boy that talked to her and Beth. What came over her?

It was like the idea slithered into her mind and wouldn't leave earlier. She wasn't forced to act on it, but it almost felt like it wasn't her that thought of it.

How would Lukas react tomorrow when she got her game clue and then stopped giving him that kind of attention? He would probably be mad. Maybe he would tell his older brother, Nico, about what she did. Or even Alma, Mara grimaced. Or if he wasn't mad, then he would at least feel sad and confused at her sudden change.

She was feeling like the villain in Lukas' story, and she didn't like it. Sure they had only hung out for a few short hours, but what

Chapter 5: Day Three

she did wasn't nice. It wasn't going to make Lukas' day better. It was going to make a bad day for him, and it was going to be her fault.

Mara turned on her side and stared out the window at the mountain. What happened to her being an explorer this trip? Or a cool hero detective? Part of her felt cool when she made progress and got clues like the key yesterday, but part of her felt... darker. She kept lying, sneaking, stealing, and now manipulating someone that wanted to be her friend.

She felt justified doing these things against her parents. She knew they already lied and hurt her. But was Lukas really that bad? And Alma? And Nico and the rest? They hadn't done anything to her that she knew of. But Rudy was so stuck on any of the "villagers" being bad people that she shouldn't trust! What if... Rudy was wrong?

Mara didn't like that thought. If Rudy was wrong, then maybe the game was wrong. But then what was right? Nothing had been right in Mara's life so far! She wanted Rudy to be right. She wanted it to be true that she was special, smart, and capable of great things. She wanted her parents and other mean people in her life to be the stupid villagers from the story that get fixed in the end.

241

The Red god

Mara stood up and walked to the dividing door. She put her ear against it and listened for several moments.

Nothing. Her parents must have gotten changed and left for dinner already. Good. That left Mara to do whatever she wanted.

Which... wasn't a whole lot in this room. She was left with her luggage full of clothes, the bed, bathroom, small desk, and the window. What she really wanted was to check the tape recorder to see if her mother recorded over part of the next clue. But how could she get into their locked room to retrieve it?

The connecting doorway had two doors that overlapped. They had both been unlocked and opened previously, but now the other room's door was shut and locked. It didn't even have a doorknob or keyhole from her side, so she had no chance at suddenly gaining lock-picking skills.

Mara was stubborn. She didn't want her mother to have even a tiny victory tonight. She knelt down and inspected the door frame, hinge, and threshold. It was all very snug. There was no room for sticking something between the door. Even if there was, Mara wasn't sure what good that would do. She had metal coat hangers with her clothes, but could she really daisy-chain them together and

Chapter 5: Day Three

unlock the doorknob? That sounded like something that would only work in a book or cartoon.

Oh. Mara did have the keycard for her own room's exterior door. That probably wouldn't work on her parents' door, but it was worth a try.

Mara made sure it was in her pocket and then exited the room. She looked both ways down the hall before walking to the other door. She inserted the keycard and tried turning the handle, but the indicator light only showed red. For good measure, and because she was frustrated, she removed the card and reinserted it quickly several times while re-trying the door. Red, red, red. No luck.

This was stupid! Only a few inches separated her from her things, but she couldn't do anything about it!

She sulked and stared at the door for a few moments, arms crossed. If stares could open doors, this wouldn't be a problem.

Suddenly Mara heard footsteps and talking from one of the hallway's adjoining staircases. She didn't want to stick around and find out if it was a relative or not, so she briskly walked back to her room and entered.

Upon entering, the window caught her eye. Maybe they opened and had a fire escape? She walked over and shoved the curtains further out to inspect the sides. Strike three! The window was sealed and didn't have any latch or way it opened.

Mara slumped to the floor and held her knees to her chest, thinking. She was smart, right? Rudy thought so! She should be able to do this.

Maybe more supplies would help? Mara wasn't sure, but she wanted to feel like she was making progress, so she moved to her luggage and rifled through it.

She saw her dresses, jackets, dress shoes, socks, a few hangers, nothing she didn't already know about. Well, while she was looking for magic door-unlocking supplies, she might as well check the rest of the room.

The desk had a pad of paper with the resort's letterhead, a pen, a phone, a resort brochure, and a few water bottles. The bathroom had towels, paper cups, her wet swimsuit hung up, her toothbrush, a bar of soap, and mini shampoo/conditioner bottles. Besides that, there were only the bed covers on the mattress.

Mara paced the small room, thinking about the items and the doors. Nothing was looking like it would help so far. But it would be easier to think if she wasn't so hungry. While she was relieved to skip the family part of dinner earlier, she forgot that also meant

Chapter 5: Day Three

skipping the dinner part of dinner. She glanced back at the desk and saw food on the front of the resort brochure. How much trouble would she get into if she tried to get food...?

An evil smirk formed on her lips. If she couldn't unlock the door, she could make herself even with her mother another way. This was something Mara had never done. Usually she was very quiet and avoided her when she was angry, but look where that got her. It was an exciting idea, but could she actually be brave enough to do it? If she ordered room service, would they tell her parents right away or only at the end of the resort stay?

Sometimes she did think of doing bad things when she was really angry with her parents, but she didn't do them. Like the time when her mother grounded her when she wanted to go to Beth's house, so she spent the whole day in her room imagining if she took scissors and cut up all her mother's favorite magazines. She didn't do it, but thinking about it made her feel better.

This was different though. She needed food, right? Ordering it like this would punish her mother's wallet, but it wasn't the same as something destructive just for the sake of destroying something. This felt... justified. The more she thought about it, the more she talked herself into doing it for real.

245

Mara picked up the brochure and thumbed through it as she sat on the bed. They had a mouth-watering variety of food, from steaks to roasted chicken and seafood. Then there were the side dishes and appetizers, every form of bread, potatoes, vegetables, and soups and pastas.

Even if Mara decided against trying to order food, it didn't hurt to pretend and pick something out, right?

With her conscience eased, she examined the menu pages several times and settled on a roast dinner with french fries and simmered carrots. That's what she'd get... if she was doing it.

How could she find out how the resort charges for this? She read the fine print of the brochure but couldn't find details on if the charges would be immediately noticeable or only at the end of the stay.

She could pick up the desk phone and ask them, but what if she got Alma from the front desk? Would she be suspicious Mara was doing something bad and tell her parents? Or would any employee do that? Was there a minimum age to order?

These were stupid, small problems like the stupid locked door. Small problems could cause big trouble, though.

Chapter 5: Day Three

Mara stared at the desk phone for several minutes, then the brochure, then the phone... She stood up and walked over to the desk. She could do this, as long as she worded things right.

She practiced to herself for a moment. "Hi, can I order room service? Can I get the roast dinner with fries and carrots?"

If she could keep her voice confident, the employees probably would have less chance of questioning it. And if they did question it, she could say she didn't know kids couldn't order and to just cancel it and hang up. There was no reason they should immediately tell her parents.

Mara nodded to herself and picked up the phone. She was nervous for such a small, stupid task. It didn't help that she didn't talk on phones often. They made her nervous in general.

She put the receiver up to her ear and left her other hand hovering above the buttons. It looked like she should dial 0 to get a resort employee. That was easy enough. Her finger reached for the button but didn't connect yet.

"Mara? It's okay, listen to me."

She froze. She hadn't dialed anything yet. Who was this? How did they know her name?! Her hand began trembling, still held above the button.

The voice prickled her neck and made the side of her face cold.

"Mara, don't focus on the tape anymore."

She opened her mouth to say something, but only a shuddering breath came out.

"I'll be here and find you when you get the box. Don't stop. Don't get distracted. Don't listen to the villagers. GET THE BOX!"

The scream stung her ears. "R-Rudy?" Came Mara's quiet, stuttered reply at last.

"Yes, Mara. I'll see you soon."

Mara jolted and dropped the phone receiver, letting it slam onto the desk and bounce onto the floor. A loud dial tone rung out from it. Mara's ears rung, and she lifted her shaking hands to cover them.

She sunk to the floor and stayed that way for a moment.

How had Rudy called her? She knew he must have been watching around the resort. He helped her with the chandelier after all. But how could he watch inside the room? There were no security cameras here like there were throughout the main resort areas.

Chapter 5: Day Three

But... somehow, he did call her. And he knew she was worried about the tape not playing his voice when her mother had messed with it. He knew... everything?

Mara wasn't hungry anymore. Her stomach felt as shaky as her hands. But she was confused too. Shouldn't she be happy she finally spoke to Rudy? And that he was going to meet her? But every fiber of her body tensed. She was... scared, terrified. Why?

"Mara..." came the voice again. It was barely heard over the tone coming out of the phone.

"You aren't a coward. Cowards don't get this far, solve this much, win this many times. Stop acting like a coward and get up. You're special, Mara. Keep following me."

She removed her hands from her ears slowly. Her hands still trembled, but she picked the receiver back up and held it to her ear.

"I'm not a coward." Mara began sobbing. "I'm not. I'm NOT! I'm not like my parents. I'm not like my dad! I can be brave and not be like him..."

Her breathing hitched and made her voice go silent for a moment before she could continue. "I'll get the box for you tomorrow. I made one of the kids promise to take me there! I did a good job! I'm a good girl! And brave!" She hiccuped and waited for a response. But all she heard was the phone's dial tone in her ear.

After another moment, she stood back up and placed the phone back on the base. She was stupid to be scared like this. She had to do better, or Rudy might stop liking her. She had to listen to him and stop being a coward.

She sniffled a few times and wiped her tears and snot away with her sleeve.

Was Rudy watching her right now? There weren't any cameras in here that she could see, but maybe he had his own hidden ones. Mara didn't know, but she didn't want to make him mad by continuing to cry like a baby.

She tried to stop her crying. She knew how to do this. She knew how to stop her emotions. She did it often when her mother was especially angry with her and yelling. Mara was a little gray rock. Just a rock. A calm, cold, unmoving rock. Rocks don't cry. Rocks aren't scared. She just needed to breathe.

She sat on her bed and pulled her knees to her chest. She focused on her breathing and the beating of her heart, willing it to slow down. She counted the beats and concentrated on her watch's time.

Chapter 5: Day Three

She saw 6:30 p.m. go to 7:30 p.m., and her heart beat went from rapid thuds to slow and calm. She felt exhausted. The physical exercise of sledding and running all day and the lack of dinner caught up with her. She still didn't have her appetite back, but it was just as well. Her parents would be getting back soon, and she ran out of time to call room service.

She struggled to keep her eyes open. She wasn't sure if her mother would be mad at her for napping when they got back, so she settled for laying on the bed but not under the covers. She could sit upright quickly if she heard their door open and pretend she wasn't asleep.

"Why with the lights on though?"

"She was waiting for us the whole time, what do you expect?"

Mara groggily opened her eyes. She was startled at first, but quickly realized it was just her parents standing in the now-open doorway between their rooms.

"Hey, kiddo. We brought you some dinner. Sorry for waking you." Her dad stepped in and sat a Styrofoam container on the desk.

"Did you do much thinking?" Shannon asked in a bored tone, standing with her arms crossed.

Mara thought for a moment and touched her chin. "I did. A lot. Can I have my stuff back now?" Her tone wasn't angry, but it also wasn't her usual subdued manner of speaking. Surprisingly, her mother didn't call her on this and simply left to grab her items from their bedroom.

She dropped them by the base of Mara's bed and turned to leave along with David. "Good. We'll see you in the morning then."

"Okay, goodnight," Mara called back as they shut the door.

The food wasn't roast dinner and fries, but Mara needed it to keep her energy up. Lukas did say the walk to their village would be a long one tomorrow...

Chapter 6: Day Four

Mara dreamt the whole night. Each scene was a flurry of stinging ice and whispering wind, interspersed with her dad, mother, Alma, Aunt Barbara, Lukas, and others that were more a blur than a face.

She tossed and turned but was never quite sure if she was awake or not as the dreams blended with the darkness of her room.

But a moment stood out in the whirlwind of a night. Mara was standing outside with Lukas in the snow, but it was dark. He was trying to tell her something, but the whipping wind made too much noise to be able to hear him. She was desperate to communicate to him though. She had grabbed his arm and tried yelling over the wind. Yelling that she was sorry, that she did like him, and that she didn't mean what she did.

When morning came, all that remained was that vague dream and a deep, dark pit in Mara's stomach.

She knew what she had to do today. The plan was straightforward. She had to pretend everything was normal with her parents but sneak away as soon as possible to meet up with Lukas behind the resort.

Mara felt mechanical as she got out of bed, showered, dressed, and began packing her backpack. Maybe it was the bad night of sleep that made her so tired. And the coldness of the room didn't help. She noticed after she first removed her covers that the temperature wasn't normal.

She rubbed her arms to ease the goosebumps and tried to focus on her packing. What did she really need today? Her mother had dumped everything out the night before, so it was a good chance to start fresh.

A compass would be good since she'd be walking far away from the resort. In case she got separated from Lukas, it would ensure she couldn't get too lost. The multi-tool might come in handy if she had to pry anything up to get to the box...

Mara went through each item, carefully considering its use and either packing it snugly at the bottom of her bag or setting it aside next to her luggage. The last item was the tape recorder. Mara found herself hesitant to even touch it. Rudy said to forget it; that she didn't need it anymore. She had to trust that he was right.

Instead of putting it in the other pile of items that didn't make the cut, she opted to push it with her shoe underneath the bed frame. It being out of sight made her feel a bit better, but she didn't

Chapter 6: Day Four

quite understand why. She had to shake this uneasiness and move on! Rudy needed her to act like a brave explorer today, not a scared kid.

She stood up and straightened her back with the bag in hand. It was light today. It would be good for the long walk.

After a short wait, there was a knock on the dividing door.

"I'm ready," Mara replied. The door opened and her dad stuck his head in. "You've been ready early lately! Well, good. Your mom is almost ready, and we'll head down soon."

Mara nodded and stood up off her bed. "What's the plan for today again? I think there was a movie day?" While speaking, she peeked further in their room, looking around for her mother. The bathroom door was shut, so Mara assumed she was still doing her makeup in there.

David stepped forward to lean in the doorway and continue their conversation, another sign to Mara that her mother was busy. Her dad almost never chatted with her unless her mother wasn't there. It was easier to talk more freely without her.

255

"Movie and wine day!" David replied, seeming to be in high spirits. "It should be pretty fun for you kids and us adults. Your mom and I will be hanging out on the left wing I think. They had a separate room for the kids' movies and snacks."

This should make sneaking away pretty easy, so Mara didn't complain about being segregated with the kids. "That sounds cool. When breakfast is done, can I go find Danny and Aunt Barbara or Gina?"

"Sure! If you want to walk to the kids area with them, that's good with me." David paused to shake his head and let out a low, pained chuckle. Mara was puzzled, but he motioned her to come closer and lowered his voice. "I think it's best if you go with them right after breakfast, really. Your mom is planning on marching to the front desk and giving them what-for after last night."

"Last night?" Mara asked. "What was wrong?"

David looked back to the closed bathroom door before continuing. "Our room was freezing. One of the resort heaters must have broken, but I'm sure they'll fix it. It's not that big of a deal but... You know her moods. It's an excuse to yell at one of the employees." He shook his head more and let out a sigh.

Chapter 6: Day Four

Mara didn't reply, but her mind wandered. Everything seemed cold to her lately, even her dreams.

David looked like he had more to say, but the bathroom doorknob sounded as it began opening. David jumped back a foot and spoke again to Mara in a louder voice, pretending as though he wasn't complaining about Shannon a moment before. "So that would be good. You can meet up with Danny and we'll either meet at the kids' room or our room after the movies are over."

He turned to address Shannon stepping back into the room. "Honey, will it be the usual time for dinner after the events of the day, 6 p.m. or so?"

Shannon looked dressed for the day, but her face had a distinct lack of coffee. She crinkled her nose at the question. "Why are you asking me? The events leaflet is right there. Look for yourself."

David ignored her tone and picked it up. "Yep, six should be fine. Alright, you two lovely ladies ready to head out?"

Mara thought he was laying his perky mood on thick to try and improve her mother's, but their moods weren't going to be her problem soon. She nodded and looked to her mother.

Shannon was grabbing her jacket and pointedly ignoring his compliment. "Let's go. I don't want to wait until there's a line for coffee."

In the dining room, Mara was counting down the seconds until she could leave her parents' presence. She had a plate of cherry turnovers and grapes to keep her busy, but the atmosphere was still oppressive.

Her mother had taken to complaining about the broken heater. She was winding herself up for the fated confrontation with the front desk employee after breakfast. Mara felt sorry for whoever was there today. Maybe it wouldn't be Alma.

She and her dad stayed silent besides the occasional nod or mumbled agreement to stay out of trouble.

Halfway through her second turnover, Mara spotted Danny, Gina, and Gina's husband at another table across the room. This perked her up, so she quickly stuffed the rest of her breakfast down. A clean plate would give her mother less excuse for not letting her leave the table.

Chapter 6: Day Four

"Mom, can I go over to Danny and his parents now? They look like they're getting ready to leave for the kids' room."

Shannon broke from her irate monologue to look around the room.

"They look like they just sat down, Mara. You don't need to be in such a rush!" Shannon replied.

Mara's excitement deflated, but she didn't want to argue.

Instead she spent another twenty minutes pushing around a grape stem on her empty plate, thinking. After she got the box today, what was next? Rudy said he'd find her, but was that going to be at the resort? Where? When?

What was even in the box? Mara guessed that the key she had taken was going to be needed to open it, but that didn't give her much clue about the contents. If it needed a key to open, it was probably important or expensive. Could it even be the game prize itself?!

As the morning went on and her thoughts wandered to crystal cat statues snug in mystery boxes, the pit in her stomach eased off.

When she saw Gina stand up at their table, she turned her attention back to her mother. "What about now? Can I go??"

Shannon huffed and turned to look towards their table again. "You can go with Gina, but you *will* stay at the kids' room until we pick you up before dinner."

She leaned closer to Mara and lowered her voice to a harsh whisper before saying what she really wanted. "I'm not going to have you embarrass me anymore! If I don't find you there before dinner, say goodbye to your books when we get back!"

Mara didn't care for her threat, but she didn't have any intention of failing her mission and not making it back in time. She nodded before grabbing her backpack and zooming off towards Gina's table.

She arrived at their table as Gina's husband was helping Danny off his chair. Mara couldn't recall his name, but she knew his face from past family events. He was a good half-foot taller than Gina with short dark blond hair and black rimmed glasses.

He was the first to notice Mara walking up. "Oh hi. How've you been, Mara?"

Chapter 6: Day Four

"Hi, I've been good! Hi Gina! I wanted to ask if I could walk with you all to the kids' room? My parents are still finishing their breakfast." She put on a smile and waved at Danny as well.

"Of course!" Gina replied, "We were just heading there now."

As they began walking, Mara turned her attention to Danny. She figured she may as well be nice to him while she used him as cover for the first part of the day's plan. "Are you excited for movies today, Danny?"

He shook his head and buried his face in Gina's side in response, causing Gina to laugh. "Oh, don't mind him. I think he's nervous about one of the movie posters he saw. Have you seen the Puppy Trails one?"

Mara shook her head. "No, but what about it?"

"Well," Gina started between giggles, "One of the puppies in the movie is a silly little chihuahua and..."

Gina's husband cut in, sparing Mara from having to wait for Gina's giggle fit to end to hear the rest of the sentence. "And the puppy has a weird face, and Danny is terrified of it. Gina, really, it's not funny when he's scared! It doesn't matter that *you* aren't scared of the puppy."

Mara listened to the two of them playfully bicker for a few moments before Gina turned back to Mara. "Anyway, scary and non-scary puppies aside..." She paused to grin. "I'm sure you'll be a pillar of bravery today, right? Mara the Brave!" Gina looked to Danny next. "So you don't have to be scared with your brave big cousin with you!"

Mara smiled. She liked the sound of that title. "Yeah, Danny! It'll be fine! You just have to be brave like me."

Danny peeled his face away from Gina for a moment to look at Mara. She smiled to encourage him, but his eyes widened and he quickly dug his face back in.

Mara frowned. He almost looked like he was staring at something beside her. She turned, but it was just the four of them walking, plus a few random relatives in other groups in the hall. What was he so scared of?

Soon they arrived outside one of the conference rooms on the right wing of the resort. A few employees filtered in and out, and they could see chairs and beanbags set up around the middle of the floor, half filled with kids already.

On the far wall there was a projector screen set up, although nothing was playing on it yet. Mara took in the details of the room and doors, mentally planning her later escape. She didn't know the exact time Lukas would be arriving, but she didn't want to leave him waiting.

They walked in the room and headed towards the seats in the middle.

"Wow," Gina's husband exclaimed, "You kids got the big screen! And the comfortable seats!" He prodded Danny to look. "Blankets too. If you get scared during the movie, you can pull one up. You'll be safe, Danny."

He brightened up at this and walked ahead to grab one off an unoccupied beanbag chair.

Gina ruffled his hair and gave him a kiss on the top of his head. "We'll only be in the other part of the resort. Have fun, Sweetie!" She turned to Mara. "And you too! Don't get scared of the chihuahua, Mara. You're our last hope..."

Mara touched her hand to her forehead and almost groaned at the bad joke as Gina's giggle fit started back up.

"Annnnd with that, we'll leave you kids to your movies," her husband said, gently grabbing Gina by the shoulders and steering her out. "You're going to give Danny a complex... C'mon, Honey..."

The pair continued walking out as Mara watched. Gina playfully swatted at her husband's hand, and he laughed, but she could no longer hear their conversation as they got further away.

They were... a strange couple, Mara thought. They almost seemed like they were arguing, but they kept smiling. It wasn't like her parents at all, but Mara didn't really know how to categorize it. It made her feel awkward, like she didn't know how to act. But she didn't have a bad time with them.

Mara turned back and saw Danny struggling to climb into one of the chairs. She reached over and steadied it so he could pull himself up. "Here, let me hold it."

He made it up but quickly turned away from her and pulled his blanket up. He didn't seem to want to look her in the face, which made her feel odd. She took a chair next to him and settled in. Was she especially scary today? Did she have something on her face? Mara wanted to find a mirror and check, but the whole thing was silly.

She had more important things to focus on, like timing her escape. If this was a movie event, then she assumed the employees would lower the lights when they started. That would give her the best opportunity to sneak away from the group of kids.

Chapter 6: Day Four

There were large double doors leading back into the hallway, a few fire escape doors on the opposite wall, an employee-only door off to the side of where the projector screen was set up, and not a lot else.

Normally this room probably had more tables and rows of adult chairs, but it appeared emptied out in anticipation of the event for the kids. Mara turned around and looked on the opposite wall. There were some tables set against that, but they didn't look interesting. They had cups and several large pitchers of drinks.

Mara's best hope was probably waiting until the lights dimmed and then slowly breaking away to leave through the double doors into the hall. She checked her watch. It read 9:21 a.m. The movies would probably start at 9:30 or 10:00, but either way Mara had a little time to kill.

She decided to watch the employees to make it go by faster. From what Alma told her, it sounded like a lot of the workers lived in the nearby village behind the mountains. Could more of them be Lukas' relatives?

There were two women setting up more items near the drink tables. One was a little younger looking than the other, but either could be mom-age. Mara squinted and imagined one could be

Lukas' mom or aunt. They had similar features and hair tones, but then again most of the employees did.

They were wearing the standard uniforms of slacks, red shirts with gold cuffs and collars, and name-tags. Mara couldn't read the names from here, but it didn't matter. As it was, she was just being nosy anyway. What would it matter if one of them was related to Lukas?

Instead of looking at them directly, she switched her attention to what they were doing. The boxes they moved into the room and were unpacking on the table seemed to be different types of snacks. There were bags of what Mara assumed were chips or crackers and larger trays with tiny sausages.

Mara wasn't hungry after breakfast, but she made a mental note for later. She knew who would appreciate those.

A shrieking scream startled Mara out of her people watching. She jolted to look for the source but was annoyed to realize it was only one of the kids in the group next to her.

She was a small brunette girl, maybe four years old or so. A slightly older boy stood next to her, currently pulling the last corner of a blanket out of her hands. Mara stood up before she really thought about it.

Chapter 6: Day Four

"Hey, that's not very nice! Just because she's littler doesn't mean you can take that from her." Mara exclaimed, walking over. The girl continued crying as the boy took his prize and sat back down with the stolen blanket. Mara stopped in front of the pair but looked back at the employees.

They weren't paying any attention, or rather they weren't looking to get involved in the squabble, so Mara felt justified.

She grabbed hold of the blanket on the boy's lap. "You're going to be nice and give this back, right?" Her tone was firm but not angry. She put her free hand on her hip, hoping to give herself an air of authority.

The boy was sneering at the little girl, but his expression changed when he turned to look up at Mara. First was confusion, then fear. Mara easily took the rest of the blanket from him as he released his grip. "Good!" Mara felt vindicated at her easy success. She supposed it *should* have been easy. She was twice this kid's age.

She turned to give the blanket to the little girl, but her success wasn't long celebrated. The girl had a similar uneasy look directed towards Mara. She was expecting her to be happy.

"Here." Mara held out the blanket to her. "You can have it back. It's yours."

The girl hesitated but finally took it and continued crying quietly, this time into the blanket itself.

Mara wasn't a fan of little kids, but was she really this terrible with them? She awkwardly stood there, unsure what to do. She wanted to comfort her, but she didn't seem to be doing a good job.

After a moment she decided it best to leave them to it. She walked back to her chair next to the Danny-shaped blanket that Mara assumed her cousin was still in and sat down.

Mara went to check her watch again, but the lights were suddenly lowered. One of the female employees stood near the projector now and spoke to the group. "Welcome, children! We're about to get started! Please try to be quiet for the sake of everyone watching, but let me or another worker know if you need anything! We have drinks, snacks, and extra blankets for everyone."

This calmed the kids down, and Mara noticed the two she had accidentally scared were now sharing the blanket and paying careful attention to the screen as the video came on.

The title sequence for Puppy Trails played, and Mara grimaced. She hoped Danny didn't actually need her here to make it through the terrifying film. The first puppies on scene were a black lab and Pomeranian, and Mara saw Danny slowly uncover the

Chapter 6: Day Four

blankets from the top of his face to watch. She smiled. He should be fine.

Mara pretended to watch while keeping the employees in the corner of her vision. They stood near the double doors, chatting and occasionally glancing at the group of kids to keep an eye on everything.

This was bad for Mara. She'd have to wait longer for them to move somewhere else. She hoped Lukas was enamored enough to wait for her...

Somewhere between the puppies finding the Power Stone and them reaching Dogtopia, a few kids fussing caused the employees to walk over.

They split up and each helped a kid, taking them to the bathroom or to get a drink.

Mara took one last look at Danny, happily watching the screen, before bailing out of her chair and creeping towards the double doors.

She was almost there, but she remembered something important! She crept over to the snack table and filled her jacket pocket with sausage before heading back into the hall.

Mara winced at the bright lighting once out of the room. But she didn't have time to stand around and adjust in the hallway. She had to get outside ASAP!

Luckily no employees were around. She cinched her backpack straps tighter and took off down the hall.

Mara knew there was a door nearby, as they had used it the previous day when going out to sled. She passed a few internal doors but kept running until she heard voices.

She slowed to a walk and tried to hide her heavy breathing as a few relatives walked the opposite way and waved at her. She waved back and kept walking, hoping to not draw suspicion. As soon as they were ten feet behind, she took off sprinting again until she reached the door.

It was heavy and took her a moment of struggle to push open, but once outside she breathed a sigh of relief. The annoying part of the day was over! She was far away from her parents now and was about to get even further away once she met up with Lukas.

Chapter 6: Day Four

Mara took her other jacket out of her backpack as she walked and put it on. He was supposed to be near the back of the resort, but the door she exited was more on the side.

Walking around the corner, she saw him sitting on one of the landscaping rocks. He was playing a hand-held game Mara didn't recognize. "Hey! Sorry I'm late!" she called out.

"Oh!" Lukas exclaimed, putting the game back in his pocket. "You not late! I haven't waited much."

She ran up to close the distance and noticed him putting his arms out. Mara awkwardly stared for a moment before he put them back down, realizing a split second afterward that he intended to hug her.

Not wanting to cause hurt feelings, she quickly grabbed his hand and shook it. "It's good to see you again! Thanks for hanging out!" On second thought, the handshake was probably more awkward than the hug attempt, but Lukas didn't seem to mind.

"You too! But I do warn, it's a long walk! We should start going!" He smiled and kept her hand in his as he turned to walk in the direction away from the resort's back.

The Red god

Mara smiled back and walked with him. "So, what game were you playing? Was that a new console? I have a Switch, but yours looked smaller!"

Lukas laughed and pulled out a small, rectangular device. It was plastic, purple, and had a small screen on the top half with only a few buttons and directional pad. Mara wasn't familiar with it, but it looked cool.

"It's a Gameboy. I got it from Nico! Extreme retro!"

Mara lit up in recognition. "Oh! My dad talked about those! He had one as a kid. That must be so old!"

He nodded and knocked his fist against the screen a few times. "Old but sturdy! It pretty good!"

The two were now approaching the gravel road behind the resort, and Mara supposed they would be following it for a while. She gave one last glance at the resort and swallowed. It was okay. It was going to be okay. She would get the box and come back, and Lukas didn't have to get hurt. She could still be a nice friend to him.

"What games does it have? My dad mostly talked about the graphics, and how it didn't have a backlight."

Lukas furrowed his brow for a moment. "Backlight?" He turned the console over and looked over the back, not

272

Chapter 6: Day Four

understanding. Mara laughed and turned it back in his hand. "Uhm, what's a better word for this...? The light that comes through the screen?"

Lukas appeared to understand and enthusiastically spit out what sounded like an eight-syllable word. Mara didn't catch it at all but nodded back. "Yeah! That!"

"For that," Lukas started, "I have special weapon!" He riffled through his coat pockets until he produced another strange plastic item. He snapped it onto the Gameboy frame and handed the whole thing to Mara. It was almost like a bendy straw with a circle at the end.

"Like a booklight!" she realized. "That's really cool!"

He beamed at her, very proud of his compliment.

"And for game, it has Tetris and Mario, and more, but I don't bring them all."

Mara looked at the cartridge in the back. "How does it have Mario games? I have those on the Switch. I can't believe my dad had Mario games in his childhood. That sounds too old."

She handed it back to Lukas as he shrugged. "Not same Mario, but it is old." He put it back in his pocket and shyly reached for Mara's hand again as they walked.

273

Mara felt awkward holding a boy's hand, so she tried to keep the conversation going. "How far of a walk is it anyway? I know you said long but how long?"

The road continued into the distance and around some hills, so Mara couldn't see the end of it. There wasn't anything interesting along the way either, just snow, trees, and more snowy hills up the mountains.

Lukas looked thoughtful for a moment. "Five kilometers?"

Now it was Mara's turn to not understand and be embarrassed. She knew that was under five miles, but she couldn't remember the conversion they taught her in school.

Lukas caught her confusion. "You are American! Ah, yes! So..." He began counting on his fingers. "Three bald eagles away!"

Mara wasn't sure if she was supposed to be insulted or not by the joke, but his earnest grin made her burst out laughing. "Okay, I deserve that! But that doesn't sound too bad. I'm not on my school's track team, but I like long walks!"

"What is your school like?" he asked, starting to swing their intertwined hands as they went.

Chapter 6: Day Four

Mara barely noticed the touch and movement now that they were busy talking. "Hm, it's pretty typical American school I guess? I don't know. I never really thought about it."

"What is typical?" Lukas prodded.

"Well, for me that's getting up and ready for the bus by 7. I use a different backpack for my school books." She gestured to her current backpack. "It's big and heavy... Then the school building is pretty boring. Lots of concrete and white walls with some posters and signs for school info."

Lukas nodded and waited for her to continue, very interested in her answers. "There's about three hundred kids that attend, but there are different grades too so not all of them are my age or in my classes. The classes themselves are kinda boring, except math and English. I like those..."

Lukas stopped her at this point. "Wait! You already speak English, but they make you take class?"

Mara nodded. "Well, it's not to teach us to speak English really. It's a lot of reading famous books or improving writing skills."

"Oh, so harder stuff. But English is hard." Lukas frowned.

The Red god

"You speak better English than I speak..." Mara trailed off, trying to remember what they spoke in Austria.

"German? I also speak Slovenian!" Lukas offered. Mara suddenly felt stupid next to him. She could act snotty like Anna and make fun of his small English mishaps, but he knew three languages! Mara only knew the one!

"That's really cool. I only know English, so I can't imagine how hard it is to learn."

Lukas grinned. "Not that hard, but so much time! I can't sit in class that long all days. But I'm happy to practice more for you!"

Mara stared at her feet for a moment, embarrassed she was getting so much attention from him. "Thanks, but I don't think you need more practice. We can talk fine already!"

The two walked in silence for several minutes, but Lukas was happily swinging their arms as they went.

Mara was trying to think of a new topic to bring up, but she got distracted by movement up ahead.

A bush was wildly shaking about twenty feet off the road, partially up the hill. It wasn't windy at the moment, so the movement puzzled Mara. Lukas noticed the same thing, so he gave Mara a look and they both stopped.

Chapter 6: Day Four

"What do you think it is?" Mara asked first.

"Probably aliens. There are a lot here." Lukas calmly replied.

Mara looked at him like he'd grown a second head. He said it so matter of factly it worried her. He turned to look at her too but couldn't keep up the straight face and doubled over laughing.

"Sorry! You have a good scared face! I had to!" He gasped out between laughs. Mara rolled her eyes but chuckled too. "Okay, you got me. But really, what is it?"

"I don't know," Lukas replied, "But probably nothing that bad. We have goat here, groundhog, goose, and lots of other small rodent and bird. Nothing scary like bear." He began walking closer to prove his point and picked up a stick to poke the bush.

Mara was nervous but didn't want to show it, so she walked a few feet behind him.

"Out, out, aliens! You not allowed here!" Lukas yelled as he poked at the shrub. The shaking stopped, and it got eerily still.

"Mrrroooooooo!" came a loud cry, causing Lukas to drop the stick and run back.

"Gravy!" came an equally loud cry from Mara, recognizing her strange friend's caterwauling. "I was hoping I'd see you! I brought lunch again!"

Lukas hid behind her now, trying to understand why his new girlfriend was yelling condiments at the screeching bush. "Mara, no! Wait! It sound strange! It not a goat!"

She laughed and shrugged his hand off her shoulder, walking closer anyway.

"It's Gravy! It's okay, I know him." She got a foot away from the bush and stopped to look through her pockets. Finding the sausages, she leaned down and held one out. "Gravy, it's me. Want some?"

The cat stopped its loud cries suddenly and poked its nose out of the bush. In almost cartoon fashion he smelled the sausage and was led further out, wiggling his nose in the air.

Lukas breathed a sigh of relief seeing it was just a cat. "Oh, you. We call him... uhm, what's the English? Trash dump?"

Mara let Gravy take a piece of sausage from her hand and turned to give Lukas a look. "You call this sweet boy Trash Dump?"

"Well, he eat like trash dump..." He nervously rubbed the back of his neck, hoping he hadn't offended her. Mara shook her head and offered another piece to Gravy. "It's okay. Whatever your name is, you are *very* cute."

Chapter 6: Day Four

Lukas walked up and squatted beside her as she fed the cat. "You like cats?"

Mara nodded. "Very much! I have one at home called Hershey. She's a black and brown cat, and much smaller than Gravy."

Lukas held out his hand and took a sausage from Mara to help break it up for the cat. "Like the bad chocolate?"

Mara laughed. "Like the chocolate, yes, but I do like Hershey's."

Gravy was more hesitant to take food from Lukas, but with some baby talk from Mara he began getting closer. "Who's a pretty cat? You are so pretty!"

While Lukas fed him, Mara gently stroked his gray fur along his back.

"You know..." Lukas started, "I didn't want to ask, but now it makes much sense."

"What makes sense?" Mara asked.

"Why you smell like meat!" Lukas beamed.

"...Lukas?" Mara turned.

"Yeah?"

"You knew I smelled like meat this whole walk, and you weren't going to ask?"

279

Lukas paused and held his hand to his chin, looking up. "You never ask a lady why she smells like meat."

Mara put her face in her hands and started making a noise that startled Lukas. "Ah! Are you..." Before he could finish his question, it became apparent she was laughing, not crying, and even snorted.

He joined her until they both collapsed in the snow.

"Why..." Mara started but got interrupted by another round of laughing. "Why is that something you don't ask?! I would ask you if you smelled like meat!"

Lukas took a moment to catch his breath before he could reply. "I don't know. To be honest, I like saying wild things to catch people. I never said that before. It not a common saying here!"

"Oh man." Mara groaned and sat back up. "My ribs hurt now, thanks."

"You very welcome!" Lukas quickly replied.

Mara noticed Gravy had gotten scared by their sudden outburst of laughter and had retreated closer back to the bush. "Aw, I'm sorry, Gravy." Mara crooned. "Here, we didn't mean to interrupt your lunch. You can have the rest of these."

She dumped the rest of the sausage out of her pocket on the ground before turning to Lukas with a grin.

Chapter 6: Day Four

"And now I no longer will smell like meat. So our debate on the policies of asking or not asking why someone smells like meat is now moot."

Lukas leaned in and pretended to smell the air next to her with a very serious face. "Yes, no more meat. I have no questions."

Gravy scarfed down the last of the food and turned to trot down the road towards the resort. They both waved goodbye and started their walk again.

"I'm sorry we stopped so long for the cat," Mara said, "I hope it doesn't make us late for meeting up with the rest of the kids."

"It no problem," Lukas replied, "We will make it there."

After walking another few minutes, Mara estimated they were probably a third of the way. The walk was going by fast, and she was having a lot of fun with Lukas.

Suddenly her dream came to mind from last night. Lukas and her, standing outside in the dark. She was unable to hear him, but she kept trying to apologize.

Her mind also wandered back to the entire goal of today, to get that box from his village. She really hoped the ending to this game would be kind to Lukas too. If he was one of the villagers from the story that had a problem, wouldn't his problem be fixed in the end?

Mara had to believe that she was doing something smart, something good.

As the two walked, they continued to talk. The topics bounced from Lukas' school, his brother Nico and mother Katharina, Mara's friend Beth, what their houses were like, the climate in Colorado, and what they wanted to do when they grew up.

"...and maybe a scientist, too." Lukas finished.

Mara laughed and shook her head. "I thought my ideas were crazy. But if you become a cowboy-astronaut-scientist, you should come to the US and visit me. I'm sure there are jobs for that there."

"You mean it?" Lukas asked.

"Mean what?" Mara replied, distracted by the latest structure coming into view. It looked like metal appearing over the top of the hill around the next corner.

"I could visit you in the US someday?"

Chapter 6: Day Four

Mara looked back at him. "Well, I don't know about plane tickets and all that, but if you could that would be fun. I'd love for you to meet Hershey and hang out with me and Beth. She'd like you! You're very funny."

Lukas didn't reply, but he had an embarrassed smile and squeezed her hand as they continued.

"What is that?" Mara finally asked. Craning her neck and squinting hadn't given her any clues about the structure yet, and her curiosity was killing her.

"That's the bridge. We almost there now. It's right outside the village boundary."

Mara was getting excited and nervous now.

They turned the corner and it came fully into view. It was a large metal bridge that looked like it could easily fit a big truck. It was over a frozen creek that split the road.

"Now," Lukas said, looking both ways, "We must look for car before crossing. There is room to walk on bridge, but not both."

Mara nodded and looked around too. Beyond the bridge she could see some buildings. They looked to be made from stone, but the size, roof material, and outer details varied a lot from building to building.

There was no car in sight, so the two of them began walking across.

"Where's that abandoned building you guys were going to hang out at?" Mara asked.

Lukas pointed to the left. "It beyond most of the houses that way. Not very far compared to the walk already!"

Mara hoped the other kids wouldn't be there yet. She needed to retrieve the box alone. Rudy was very insistent about that.

As they walked through the village, Mara took in the change of scenery. The streets were made of stone here, but not the kind of perfectly shaped fake ones she saw around her home's neighborhood. They looked like real creek rocks placed long ago.

Large piles of dirty snow were shoved off the street sides, making it walkable but not as aesthetic as the manicured paths of the resort. The buildings themselves had differing sizes. Some were clearly residential with colorful painted wood doors, cars or trucks parked by the side or under metal roofed carports, and various decorations or toys scattered in the yards.

One in particular had two kids' bikes laid by the driveway and red ribbons and birdfeeders tied to a large evergreen tree in front. The door was painted with bright stripes of blue and green. The

Chapter 6: Day Four

windows glowed with yellow-orange light. Mara thought it was very cute, and it brought back her earlier daydreams of a pink cottage in the woods as the game prize.

On the other side of the street were the more business-looking buildings. Some were two stories and had signs hung off metal hangers. Mara couldn't read the words, but she could guess the purpose for some by the accompanying window displays or pictures. There was a supply store with food and homegoods, a mechanic, and a clothing store.

The clothing store caught Mara's eyes, but after looking in the window it didn't look anything like the stores she was used to her mother dragging her to. The racks were mostly comprised of dark colored coats, overalls, pants, leather boots, and other winter gear. Nothing looked too frilly.

Lukas turned back to see her gawking in windows and rapidly turning her head to either side of the street to take it all in. He laughed. "Do you like it? My hometown is small, but it okay. We have lot of kids to play with here."

"It's very cool," Mara replied. "I like how the houses look! Will you let me know if we walk past yours?"

Lukas nodded. "We walk past it soon. It is on the way to the meet spot."

As they walked, Mara noticed Lukas had dropped her hand, probably as they were walking across the bridge. Was he worried family, friends, or schoolmates would see him holding hands with a 'tourist' girl and make fun of him?

Mara wasn't sure how to feel about that. It wasn't like they were really together. This was all for her to get to the box. But she hoped she wouldn't get Lukas in trouble or made fun of.

Some locals waved as they walked past, and Lukas waved back. Mara was curious how Lukas knew them, if they were family members or parents of his friends. But it was such a small town she supposed everyone knew everyone somehow.

The thought of Mara not knowing anyone here made Mara a bit shy. The last several days at the resort were the opposite for her. It was filled with relatives that knew her, at least enough to wave hi.

After a few minutes, Lukas broke out into a run up ahead and pointed excitedly. "That's mine and Nico's house! Red door!"

Mara looked and saw a house much like the other ones. The front door was painted bright red with a rack of deer antlers in place of a wreath. In the yard were the familiar sleds the boys had brought to the resort the other day. There was also a sort of wind chime on a metal pole off to the side of the driveway. It looked handmade, perhaps out of metal pipes.

Mara jogged to catch up. "Looks cool. Did your dad hunt the deer?" She pointed to the antlers.

Lukas nodded but his smile dropped. "Yeah, Mother said long ago. He died when I very young, so I don't remember."

"Oh," Mara replied, unsure what to say.

Lukas quickly changed the subject. "And! Over there is the bad building!"

Mara's eyes followed his pointing, and she saw a circular stone building several hundred feet off. It was near a tree line, and there were no other buildings close to it. The roof appeared to be partially collapsed in, and the outer stone walls were mottled with moss.

As they walked closer, Mara noticed a vibrating sensation growing in her ears. Lukas was saying something, but the ringing made it hard to pay attention. She patted at her ears beneath her hat, hoping to ease the sound. Maybe they climbed in elevation more than Mara realized on the walk.

The Red god

"...Mara!" he shouted and grabbed her arm, startling her. She almost stumbled backward, but his grip held her in place.

She looked down to see a large chunk missing out of the stone street in front of the building. She realized Lukas must have been warning her about the spot before he grabbed her.

"Sorry!" she exclaimed, "I wasn't paying attention!"

"It okay!" Lukas replied, releasing her arm. "But be careful here! It is dangerous place if you not know it."

"Here." Lukas stepped forward and held open a crooked wooden door leading inside. "I will show the danger places inside, so you can avoid."

She stepped in after him and looked around. It was darker inside, but the hole in the roof let some sunlight in. The floor was very uneven planks of wood with a few obvious rotten holes closer to where the sun shown in the brightest.

Mara was sure there were more holes in the floor unseen on the darker edges, so she followed carefully behind Lukas where he stepped.

As her eyes began adjusting, Mara noticed the stove in the middle of the large room. It was made of stone, same as the walls. It had a metal door on front and a chimney above going into the roof. The box was somewhere there... Mara knew it.

But Mara couldn't go straight to it with Lukas here, so she tried not to stare so obviously. "So what was this place?" She asked.

"Someone old house I guess." Lukas shrugged. "It's been here long time. Even the older kids not know much. But! It has bad writing! Very cool!"

He half ran, half hopped towards the far wall, excitedly pointing and dodging the holes in the floor.

"There! See?" He stopped in front of the back wall, still pointing. Mara slowly walked over, much more conscious of the holes in the floor. When she reached him, she had to squint at the wall. It was darker here, and the writing definitely wasn't in English.

"What does it say?" She asked.

"Lots of things. Different writers too." Lukas pointed to a different section. "This one like prayer. Roughly says evil never happen again here. It should be sealed."

He turned and walked further along the wall. "And this. Lots of curse words and some name! Not say much else besides the bad words."

The Red god

"A name?" Mara cocked her head. "Is it the name of the house's owner?"

"I doubt." Lukas looked thoughtful. "The name is not real, real. Very story-like name."

"The Red god..."

Lukas and Mara froze, looking at each other but not understanding. Neither of them had said that.

A prickling sensation spread from Mara's ears to her fingertips. She wanted to move her feet and run, but her legs didn't listen except to tremble.

Lukas reacted first, jumping backwards as a hand came from the shadows further in the back. He grabbed for Mara but tripped into her. Mara's back made painful contact with the floor, and the ringing in her ears returned.

All she could see now was part of Lukas shoulder on top of her and the sun streaming in through the roof's hole.

The figure grabbed at Lukas' boot and drug him roughly off of Mara. Her body thankfully let her move now, and she scuttled backwards on her elbows.

Chapter 6: Day Four

This wasn't the plan! This wasn't something Rudy warned her about! She didn't know what this was, so she did the only thing an eleven-year-old girl could do in this situation. She screamed.

Lukas was pulled into the darker area, and he began yelling in his language and struggling against the figure.

The whole attack lasted only a handful of seconds before Mara was grabbed and hoisted up from behind. She spun around to punch the second assailant but was met with a scowling familiar face.

Mara stopped her screaming and gasped out his name. "Nico?"

After Nico had set Mara steady on her feet and marched over to do the same to Lukas, he led them and the now-not-so-mysterious Levi towards the center of the room and sat them on the floor in front of the stove.

He spoke in his language, but even without understanding it Mara knew a scolding when she heard one. He pointed from Lukas to Levi, shouting at both as they sat and winced.

The Red god

At one point Lukas spoke up to defend himself. "Why mad at me?! Levi scared Mara! He did way worse!"

Levi chuckled. "You babies shouldn't be in here reading scary stories off the wall anyway! The prank wasn't that scary unless you're a baby!"

Another look from Nico shut them both up. "Both of you shouldn't be doing this!" He switched back to his language to add more, but Mara had enough.

"What did Lukas do?! He was only playing with me today!" She stood up and tried puffing out her chest and standing as straight and tall as she could. She wasn't very intimidating in the face of a much taller sixteen-year-old boy, but she had to try.

"You!" Nico pointed his attention toward Mara. "You!... Gah! You're just a tourist! You wouldn't understand the trouble your rich relatives can get us in!" He put his hand down and took a moment to breathe and calm himself.

"You're right. Levi was the worst of you three in this." Nico continued. "But Lukas shouldn't have brought you here, Mara. We could get in real big trouble. And not just us kids, but our relatives working at the resort like Alma."

Chapter 6: Day Four

Mara put her head down and sniffled. The adrenaline of the episode was wearing off, and she started feeling less indignant and more shamed.

Nico noticed her crying and softened his stance. "I don't think it's your fault, Mara. I'm sorry I yelled. But we don't know your parents or grandparents. They could sue or something if you got hurt here. It's not the same as one of us getting a scrape."

Lukas put a hand on her shoulder and cut in the conversation. "It my fault. I knew Nico wouldn't want me bringing you here. But I wanted have fun with you and show you a cool place..."

Nico crossed his arms and looked expectantly at Levi. It took a few moments of a stare-down, but eventually Levi spoke next. "I know, I know! I shouldn't have scared a girl... Next time I'll only scare Lukas. Sorry."

Nico shook his head, and Lukas turned to glare, but before another squabble could break out Mara spoke.

"I didn't mean to get anyone in trouble... But I'm already here. Can I stay and hang out a while? Lukas can walk me back before my parents notice! I'm keeping track of time, and it'll be hours before they expect me at dinner! No one will get in trouble!"

293

The Red god

Lukas joined in the begging, and Nico felt outnumbered. He sighed and rubbed his temple. "Okay, okay! But only while I'm supervising. Then you walk Mara home. And, Mara, you don't tell anyone you were here!"

The two youngest celebrated their win. Nico turned and noticed the building's door creaking open.

Anna poked her head in first. "Mara is here? Why?"

Eva then followed. "Lukas, Levi, what are you doing? I heard screaming almost all the way at my house!"

Nico explained the trios' shenanigans while Mara turned back to Lukas. "When we got interrupted by Levi being a jerk, you were reading me the writings on the wall. What did the last ones say?"

Lukas walked her back to the far wall and pointed where he left off. "The name here is Red god among the curse words. So not a real name as I said. Then the others mostly worn off except more curse words or parts of prayers. Creepy, huh?"

Mara nodded. "Very creepy..."

Why would Rudy pick such a place for the next clue? Mara supposed it would be easy to hide something here since no one lived in the building, but what was with the villagers and the superstitious graffiti?

Chapter 6: Day Four

Mara's curiosity got away from her, so she asked more questions. "You said even the older kids don't know the history of this building, but what about the adults? Like your mom or Alma?"

Lukas shrugged. "One time Nico asked Alma about it while we ate, but she got really angry and hit fist on the table! Our mom didn't know the answer, and Alma got mad at her about it too. She tell us to not ask."

"Alma, angry?" Mara questioned. "I can't picture that. She seemed really nice when I talked to her."

Lukas stood up straighter and immediately responded. "Alma is nice! All the time! She very good to us. Buys us toys, gets us snacks at resort. But... it was strange. We don't ask after that."

Anna walked up behind them. "My dad told me some stories about here."

"Not real!" Lukas groaned and rolled his eyes. "Very fake stories. We're not scared of those."

"You don't know if they're real or not!" Anna shot back.

Mara stepped between them with raised hands to stop the fight before it started. "I'd like to hear them, even if they might not be real!"

The Red god

Anna smiled and stuck out her tongue towards Lukas before linking arms with Mara and guiding her back to the stove in the middle. "I'll tell it then! Everyone should sit and listen!" A few of the boys groaned, but Mara sat on the floor as instructed.

"A long time ago, my grandpa lived two houses away from this one." Anna dramatically spun on her heel and pointed towards the direction of the closest village buildings.

"And when he was a kid, he knew the man who lived here and waved to him when going or coming back from school. The man was quiet and weird! He never waved back."

"One day while he was at school, the teacher suddenly ran back into the classroom and started barricading the door from the inside! He didn't know what to think, and his teacher yelled at them all to stay back!"

Mara gulped, recalling her school's active shooter drills earlier in the year. Did they have those back in her grandparents' days?

"The students hid under their desks, and terrible screaming came up from the town! It wasn't just outside the door. The screaming was in the village center and every direction!"

Chapter 6: Day Four

Anna twirled back to face Mara and extended her hands in front of her face like claws. She lowered her voice to accent the story too. "And the screaming didn't stop for hours..."

"They dared not look out the windows, but my grandpa knew in his heart what was out there!"

"What?" Mara leaned forward, drawn into Anna's passionate storytelling. "What was out there?"

"A giant, BIG, MEAN, SHARP WOOLLY MAMMOTH! And the strange neighbor had been the one to call it in to tear up the villagers with its tusks!" Anna punctuated the sentence with stomping her feet and making more clawing motions with her hands.

"There was blood everywhere when the screaming stopped and the teacher let them all out of the classroom!"

Mara's imagination began running wild. It was very cold and mountainous up here. Could woolly mammoths actually still be around somewhere? Would their tusks be that sharp?!

"Stupid, Anna!" Lukas shouted. "If it woolly mammoth, everyone would heard stomping all around! It make no sense!"

297

The Red god

"But my dad told me!" Anna retorted. "He heard from his dad, and there were 27 deaths in the records book for that year! It matched up!"

Nico joined in the conversation, albeit much more calmly than the two yelling kids. "That part is true. I saw the records book when our grandpa died, and a lot of pages back it had a huge number of deaths all in 1967. But I doubt it was a woolly mammoth. They probably had a flu outbreak, and some scary story spread to explain it."

Mara slouched back, mollified by his explanation.

Lukas calmed down too. "But why would Alma be so mad then?"

Nico thought for a moment before crossing his arms and shrugging. "Sometimes adults are weird. It might have been a really bad memory for her, and she didn't want to talk about it, especially when kids made up stories and asked about stupid things like woolly mammoths..."

Anna huffed but said no more. Nico, however, finished his thoughts on the story. "And the guy who lived in this building was probably just one of the first flu deaths. The people might have

Chapter 6: Day Four

written on his old home's walls afterward to try and ward off more sickness."

"Well, whatever killed him," Levi said, "he left us a cool clubhouse. Let's play cards!"

The kids sat near the middle of the floor and played cards for over an hour. Mara didn't know the game at first, but Levi was nice enough to teach her after Nico smacked his arm.

It reminded Mara of Rummy but with some different rules and scoring methods. She picked it up quickly after the first round and even managed to win once. Lukas cheered the loudest for her when she did.

At about three o'clock, Levi had to leave, shortly followed by Anna and Eva who said they had other family plans to get to.

When it was only Lukas and Nico, Mara began getting nervous. She still hadn't been alone for an opportunity to grab the box. With Nico's promise to supervise her, it was looking unlikely he'd leave anytime soon.

When Lukas got bored with cards, he pulled out his Gameboy and began coaching Mara on some of the Mario levels. Nico sat further away near the door and played something on his phone.

"You have to jump-jump here! Or the brick don't fall!" Lukas prodded her arm. Mara tried her best to pay attention and play, but her mind kept wandering. If it got much later, she'd need to start walking back to the resort. How could she get them both to leave her here?

She schemed up several plans, but they had low chances of success. For now she waited a little longer, hoping for a better opportunity or idea.

At 4:30, Nico bolted up and hid behind the door, peering out at something. "What is it?" Lukas asked.

"Alma is home early." Nico cringed. "She'll be mad if she finds us hanging out here again."

Mara walked over and peeked out the door beside him, spotting a red compact car near Lukas and Nico's house pulling up. Inspiration struck her. "Won't she be extra mad if she finds me here too?"

Nico sighed. "Definitely. We have to be careful..."

Chapter 6: Day Four

"Why don't you go keep her busy after she walks in your house and give a signal to me and Lukas when she's definitely not looking?"

Nico thought for a moment. "Yeah, I guess I should. I can try to get her to do something in the kitchen and then open and close the front curtains as the signal."

Lukas put his Gameboy away and handed Mara her backpack. "We'll be ready to run! I protect Mara with my life!"

Mara smiled but felt guilty. She wanted Nico gone because Lukas alone would be easier to manipulate. She wasn't about to do a nice thing...

After a few moments, the car door shut loudly and they watched Alma enter the house. Nico ran ahead and hoped Alma didn't walk in front of the window in time to see him exit the dilapidated building. If not, he could pretend he ran in from another friend's house.

Lukas and Mara stayed behind to watch. Nico made it to the door and entered too.

Now was Mara's chance.

"Oh no! Lukas I forgot we should have got water before the long walk back! I've been really thirsty, but I didn't want to stop playing with you early. Can you go in after Nico and fill my water bottle back up?"

She unzipped her backpack and handed it to him, hoping she wasn't laying the acting on too thick. Lukas looked between her and the house. "But we'll miss Nico's signal!"

"I won't!" Mara promised. "I'll dart out and meet you next to the clothing shop! We can walk back from there."

Lukas hesitated for a moment more before grabbing the water bottle and taking off towards the door. "Okay! It most important Alma doesn't see you! Wait for the signal!"

As soon as he exited the building, Mara raced back to the stove. There was a loose stone here somewhere. Rudy said so! She only had a moment to find it!

She wildly grasped at the stones starting closest to the floor and moving up. Each one was wiggled and tugged before she went to the next.

Her heartbeat sounded in her ears, and her hands scuffed against some of the more jagged edges.

"*Up,*" she heard in her mind. "*Higher!*"

She moved up, skipping several rows of stones and began trying again. On the third stone, she felt it giving way. She braced

Chapter 6: Day Four

her foot against the base of the stove and pulled hard. She was about to change tactics and grab the multi-tool from her bag when suddenly the stone fell out with a loud thud.

Wasting no time, she reached up and felt around. Her hand touched more cold stone and then wood. The box...

She pulled it towards herself and only gave a brief glance before stuffing it in her backpack. She didn't have time to gawk!

She pulled her straps up and ran back over to the door. Mara saw the curtains of their house repeatedly opening and closing, and she worried they had been trying to get her attention for too long.

She used her shoulder to shove the crooked door open enough and began sprinting back the way Lukas had brought her. She ran past the rows of houses, past the more boring businesses, and finally made it to the clothing shop.

Mara stopped to lean on her knees and pant. The cold air stung her lungs as she rapidly breathed, but she felt exhilarated. She did it. She got the next clue! Rudy would be so proud of her!

The Red god

She hoped she didn't look funny to any of the villagers walking by, but she swung her backpack around her front and sat clutching it, leaning against the building's display window. She only had to keep this safe until she got back to the resort and Rudy found her.

After several minutes, Mara saw Lukas jogging up. "I was worried!" he exclaimed, "You didn't leave soon!"

Mara still felt bad for tricking him, but she needed him to not be suspicious. She swallowed another lump of guilt and lied. "I'm sorry! The door was really stuck, and I couldn't get it open for a moment. I had to hit it really hard with my shoulder finally!"

Lukas reached her and handed her the water bottle. "It okay. Alma didn't see anyway, so no trouble." Mara gladly took a drink. Maybe the lump of guilt was less a metaphor and more an actual dry throat. She could hope...

Lukas sat next to her and waited for her to finish. Mara drank about half before giving up on her metaphor idea.

304

Chapter 6: Day Four

"Alright, I'm ready to walk," she said. Mara stood up and waited a moment, but Lukas was still sat and looking towards his lap. "Are you okay?" She asked, concerned.

She watched as he fidgeted with his coat hem before standing up. "Yeah! No worry! Let's go!"

The two began walking out of the village, but Mara felt he was still anxious about something. He was unusually quiet. Mara tried to fill the silence anyway with more stories about Hershey and other tales of back home.

They made quick work on their route across the bridge and back through the winding gravel mountain road. They walked at a much quicker pace since Lukas expressed worry at Mara being late for dinner with her parents. Mara didn't disagree, but she wondered if that was really bothering him.

When they finally made it around the last corner and saw the resort coming into view, Lukas stopped suddenly. Mara noticed and stood too. "Oh, I guess you don't need to walk me all the way in. But thanks for walking me so far! I had a really fun time hanging out with you, Lukas!"

He stood fidgeting with his coat again and took a moment to reply. "Can I give you something? Temporarily!" He clarified.

305

Mara gave him a puzzled look but nodded. "Yeah, what is it?"

He pulled his Gameboy out and searched his other pocket for the light extension. "Here." He handed both to Mara. "I want you keep it for now and play it... You can finish that level we started! And..." He looked down and seemed to be gathering his words.

"And we meet again before you leave the resort, so you can give me it back. I want to see you again before you leave."

Mara hesitated but reached out to take the gaming system from him. "I'd like that. We're leaving Monday morning, but that's still two days left. Maybe I can see you Sunday?"

Lukas looked less nervous now that she accepted his gift. "Is Sunday your cousin's wedding? Alma usually tell us to stay away from the resort during big events, and she already told us not to come Sunday."

"Oh. It is," Mara replied. "But maybe tomorrow or very early Monday morning? I'll look for you outside when I can!"

Lukas grabbed her hand and shook it. "Yes, it a deal! I sneak away when possible!"

Mara smiled, hopeful that they could be friends a little longer. She really did enjoy his company. He almost made her forget her parents, the fighting, the mind games of her mother.

Chapter 6: Day Four

"Well, I better get going before they find me missing." Mara turned to start walking again, but Lukas held her hand tight and walked beside her. "I walk you to door. We already came this far. It fine!"

The two walked in silence the last length of the road and arrived at the side door Mara originally exited. Before she could say goodbye, Lukas kissed her cheek and full on sprinted away. "Bye! See you soon, Mara!"

She stood, stunned as she watched him race off. Were first kisses supposed to feel so conflicting?

The shock wore off about the same time Lukas turned the corner out of view away from the resort. Mara rubbed at her cheek, sure it felt different after that goodbye.

Eventually she turned and re-entered the resort, walking the hall towards the kids' movie room, but not really thinking of what was next here.

She thought of writing down her address and putting it in the battery compartment of Lukas' Gameboy before they met next. It was okay if they were pen-pals at least, right? She could mail him pictures of Hershey and her classroom to go along with all the stories they shared. She hoped he'd write back too.

The Red god

Before she knew it, Mara was sat back in her chair next to Danny, watching the last movie ending. The kids were mostly asleep, and Mara was relieved no one seemed to miss her.

Mara's relief was short-lived. After the movie ended, she gathered her backpack and stood outside the double doors waiting for her parents.

Her mother turned the corner, and she could instantly feel the rage emanating from her eyes as they locked.

Her dad trailed behind Shannon, making no attempt to delay her stomping towards Mara. She flinched even before her mother met her and grabbed her roughly by the upper arm.

"How nice! You've been waiting right here for us, right?" Shannon sarcastically questioned. She gave Mara no time to answer, however. "Aunt Barbara told me what she saw you doing outside! With some boy!"

Mara was shocked and could only stammer and look around, hoping her mother would ease up given the crowd of relatives forming to pick up their respective kids.

Chapter 6: Day Four

Shannon did seem to read the room, but instead of dropping the issue she drug Mara by the arm further away down the hall.

Her arm began hurting, and she dared to try to twist free, but her mother clutched all the harder.

"Mara," her dad cut in, "Let's just go back to the room for now, okay?"

She resigned herself and the three walked on.

The gritted-teeth yelling her mother did once they were back in their room was a hundred times angrier than Nico's lecture.

Mara kept her head down as she sat on the end of her bed and said nothing.

"This week is supposed to be about family! And you're off like a stray cat with that foreign boy!"

There was one main difference between Nico's lecture and her mother's though. She liked Lukas and his brother Nico, so getting in trouble with them made her sad, shameful, and feel like crying.

The Red god

She didn't like or respect her mother one iota anymore, so nothing she said mattered. The worst part was just the loudness in her ears and the lack of freedom at the moment.

She hated having to wait out her mother's tantrum. Mara had important things to do! The box was still snugly in her backpack, and Rudy might be somewhere in the resort looking for her.

"Are you a FUCKING ROBOT!? Answer me! What did you think you were doing?!"

Maybe Rudy could come get her right now. Mara vaguely wished the room had a chandelier over where her mother stood, yelling.

"You know he doesn't even like you! He's a boy! He wants something from you and you're so naive!"

There was no such luck, of course. So Mara instead imagined she'd spot him at dinner. She only knew him from his voice, but he sounded like he'd be a tall man with ginger hair, maybe with a trench coat and detective hat. He had to have been like a real explorer.

"You're not going to have a chance to sneak off with him again! I'll watch you the whole rest of the week if I have to!"

Chapter 6: Day Four

Mara imagined he'd stride over to their table and tell her parents off. He'd tell them how special Mara was, how smart, how brave, and that he was taking her away from such stupid, evil people.

"There's something wrong with you in the head, Mara! You don't listen, you shut off, you can't even function like a normal kid! *You're not normal!*"

A pink cottage in the woods probably wasn't the most realistic prize, but it didn't even have to be pink.

"Maybe you'd like it if I shipped you off to an all-girl boarding school! You could sit and never speak to anyone with that damn blank stare of yours! Your brain could fall out of your head and you'd just keep staring at them!"

Hershey worried Mara though. She couldn't stand the thought of leaving her behind. If Rudy adopted her, then maybe he'd buy Mara a plane ticket to go get Hershey and bring her back too.

"Answer me! FUCKING ANSWER ME!"

Mara was halfway through another daydream when she realized her mother went silent.

From her angle looking down towards her lap she could only see her mother's legs and down in her periphery. She was still there standing, but no more yelling.

Did she finally break? She wondered if such a thing was possible. Mara wouldn't feel bad if she did break her mother. She deserved it. She deserved everything bad.

But broken or not, Mara continued to stay still and said nothing.

After what seemed like ages passed, Mara heard her dad enter the room from their bedroom and address Shannon. "Uhm, Dear, it's 6:45. We're late for dinner if you still want to go...?"

His voice was low and hesitant. Mara was sure he only dared interrupt her punishment because he couldn't decide if not telling Shannon they were late would get him on the other end of her wrath.

She didn't respond for a good 30 seconds.

"We're going to dinner. The whole family is there, and we're going. Especially you, Mara. You stay where I can see you." Shannon's voice was back to a calm but firm tone. "I can't have anyone asking why you skipped dinner twice in a row."

Chapter 6: Day Four

With that, Shannon turned and went back into her bedroom, slamming the door. Mara was alone for only a brief moment, but she savored it and let her tense body finally relax.

Her muscles ached from holding in one place for so long. She stood up off the bed and stretched.

First order of business, she wanted to steal a peek at the box, even if just for a moment.

Unzipping her backpack, she reached in and turned the wooden box over in her hand. She looked at it still in the bag, not daring to take it out while her mother was close by.

It was very dark wood with almost black-looking splotches and drips on one side. It was about the size of one of her jewelry boxes at home that had a wind-up ballerina and music when you opened it.

It had scratches and dents all around, but no other markings or decorations. On the front was a metal plate and keyhole. This was definitely what the key was for!

Mara spun around and retrieved the key from under her mattress. It would be good if both items were together now. Rudy might want her to open it as soon as he meets her.

She stuffed it in her backpack too and zipped it back up.

313

Second and much more boring order of business, she had to change into her dress for tonight and not make her parents any later...

At dinner, her parents acted as they always did. Her mother was fake nice and greeted several relatives, and her dad ignored her mood swings and asked Mara what she wanted to eat.

Mara idly ate her food once her dad returned with their plates, but her mind was elsewhere. She scanned the room for anyone she didn't recognize as family, anyone that could be Rudy.

There were some employees near the food and drink tables assisting and refilling things, but they didn't match Mara's idea of Rudy at all.

There were also a few scattered older men at tables that she didn't know, but if they were dining they must have been Ryan's family.

Waiting was hard. Mara wanted to bounce out of her seat and go shouting for Rudy in the halls. But she knew that was a stupid idea.

Chapter 6: Day Four

Near the end of the meal, Aunt Barbara and Uncle Larry walked over to their table.

"We're on our way out," Barbara started, "But I wanted to drop by and thank you for staying with Danny for the first movie earlier, Mara! I heard from Gina that he was really scared of one of the puppies!" She laughed but stopped short when Shannon didn't appear amused. Barbara gave Mara a worried look before turning to leave but said nothing else.

Mara didn't respond either. She assumed Aunt Barbara saw Lukas kiss her out the side door earlier and told Shannon immediately afterward, thinking it was a cute story. But she must have sensed her mother's anger and regretted it to be stopping by just to check on Mara.

Whatever her motivation, Mara didn't care. No one protected her except Rudy. A passing pity glance from Barbara or her dad helped nothing.

The Red god

The trio finished dinner in silence and headed back to their rooms.

Mara hoped to get some privacy tonight and look at the box more, but to her displeasure her mother insisted she stay in her parents' bedroom tonight while her dad stayed in her room.

Shannon wasn't kidding about keeping an eye on her the whole rest of the week. Under her annoyed glare, Mara couldn't do anything except put her pajamas on and climb into bed, pulling the covers over her head.

She tried her hardest to ignore her mother and hoped she could sleep despite being forced to share her bed. She was almost twelve! It was embarrassing!

Her only saving grace was that her mother didn't try to talk to her. She was on her phone or reading, ignoring Mara as well.

After a long time of daydreams far away from this room, Mara drifted off.

Chapter 7: Day Five

Mara dreamt of being watched. But even when waking the feeling didn't dissipate. If anything it got worse.

Her mother was up first, getting ready for the day. Mara heard her moving clothes on hangers and walking about the room, but she didn't see her yet with the thick covers over her face.

She supposed her mother was glaring at her the entire time. There had to be a reason for this heavy pressure she physically felt across her chest and shoulders. It was anxiety inducing, even given Mara's high tolerance for stressful situations compared to kids her age.

She hesitantly removed the covers from her head and looked around for her mother. Shannon was near the bathroom arranging hangers and grabbing makeup bags. She appeared to still be pointedly ignoring Mara, not ever glancing her way.

Mara thought she should feel relieved, but the strange pressure persisted.

It made it hard to think. What should Mara be doing today? Normally she had a plan ahead of time, where the next clue was, who she needed to talk to. Today's plan was... wait for Rudy?

She glanced at her backpack, still exactly where she left it on the floor. Luckily her mother hadn't ransacked it a second time. The box and key should be safely tucked away.

Mara was okay waiting for a while. She could be patient if she had to be. But at a certain point should she go ahead and open the box even if Rudy isn't there? What if she misunderstood his instructions and she needed to open it before he'd come find her?

Her mind raced with different thoughts, unsure what she should do. Lukas was among them too. She wondered if he would be somewhere outside the resort waiting for her today. They didn't have set plans to meet, but she didn't have a way of contacting him either.

"Get up and get showered. Don't make us late for breakfast." Her mother interrupted her planning.

She got out of bed and did as told, but she had a new thought. How could she do anything with her mother playing prison guard?

Chapter 7: Day Five

Maybe the best Mara could do was wait for Rudy to find her.

Breakfast went much the same as dinner the night before, with Mara anxiously looking around for an unfamiliar male face. But one difference was Samantha, Ryan, and one of Ryan's cousins joined them at their table.

Ryan's cousin was a lanky man. He was a little older than Ryan but had much the same facial features and beard. He introduced himself with a warm smile and handshakes around the table, but Mara's mind was far away and kept no memory of his name.

He wasn't important. Ryan and Samantha making small talk with her parents wasn't important. Her plate full of uneaten food wasn't important.

Rudy was important.

Mara's sense of uneasiness only grew as the morning ticked on. It was like knowing you forgot something but being unable to remember what you forgot. She was supposed to leave. She shouldn't be with her parents being watched right now. But she

319

didn't know where she was supposed to be or why, just anywhere but here.

She felt like a cornered rabbit. Anxiously shifting in her chair, she finally decided to try a Hail Mary to get out of there.

"Mom, can I be excused? I need to use the restroom..." Shannon didn't buy it for a moment, or rather she didn't care even if it was the truth.

"No," her mother flatly replied, "You finish your plate first. You're wasting food."

Mara normally would have scarfed the pancakes down to satisfy her mother's requirement, but she wasn't sure she could handle it today. Food didn't sound pleasant. She couldn't think of it with this pit in her stomach and pressure on her chest.

"I feel sick." She tried pushing the issue, unsure herself if this really was a lie.

Samantha took notice and paused her conversation on the other side of the table. "Aw, I hope it wasn't the food, Mara. You do look pale today!"

Not wanting to be embarrassed by further attention towards Mara, Shannon stood up. "Alright, let me walk you to the restroom."

Chapter 7: Day Five

Mara knew this wasn't a kind gesture to make sure she made it there okay. She knew her mother was still watching her, even supervising her bathroom trips apparently. But it was as good an opening as any for the moment.

The two walked across the hall to the closest ladies' room. Mara hoped her mother wouldn't actually follow her inside, but she had bad luck lately.

Mara began walking towards a stall in the far back, but her mother stopped her.

"I'll take that." She sternly commanded. Mara turned to see her pointing towards her backpack. She was hesitant to part with it, but it didn't appear she had much choice in the matter.

Mara slid it off her shoulder and held it out by the strap towards Shannon. Once she grabbed it away, Mara marched off and closed the door latch with a rougher movement than required.

Having a door blocking her mother helped a little but not enough. Mara sat on the closed toilet lid and simply breathed for a minute.

What could she do? What should she do? She was suffocating but didn't quite know why. What did Rudy want of her now?

She missed the tape recorder. The game was simple then. She had instructions, as funny as they were, to follow and keep her on track. Now she had... waiting? Nothing?

Had her mother left her with the backpack, she might have opened the box in the stall. She was dying to know what was inside, and Rudy might be waiting on her to open it first for all she knew.

But she couldn't even be left alone with that! Mara sat and stewed on her thoughts. Her mother wasn't going to win this. She was going to finish the game and make Rudy proud. She needed to.

A loud knock on the stall door startled her. "Don't waste my day, Mara." Her mother called out. "And make sure your dress is straightened out. I don't need you looking pitiful on purpose to embarrass me."

Mara gulped down a rising feeling of anger towards her and exited as commanded.

Back at the table, Shannon chatted with the group as before with fake smiles and laughter.

Chapter 7: Day Five

Samantha gave Mara a concerned look though. "Are you feeling better now? It's no trouble if you can't finish breakfast and need to rest, you know. Don't feel like you need to entertain me and Ryan."

Ryan jumped in too. "Oh yes, don't worry about it! Sam can entertain enough for all of us."

Samantha giggled and faked jabbing him with her elbow. "Okay, okay. I know my puns last night were bad, but you don't have to go asking for more!"

Before Mara could answer, Shannon replied for her. "She's better now. It's fine."

Samantha didn't look entirely convinced, but she didn't push the topic. Conversations continued, except Samantha gave Mara looks every now and then.

After another twenty minutes Ryan's cousin stood up first. "I can't wait to see the event booths today. It's about time for them to be opening. Want to head over and check them out?"

Samantha stood to follow. "Yeah! I think they'll have a lot of jewelry among the shopping booths! We definitely need to check that out!"

The Red god

The group walked out of the dining area and began down the hall, but Shannon paused for a moment. "I'll meet back up with you. I have to drop Mara off at the children's room."

David looked towards the vise grip Shannon had on Mara's hand and thought better of asking if she'd rather he take her instead. He merely nodded. "We'll be near the back conference room I think. That's where they had banners for the Culture & Shopping event."

The group split, and Mara felt hopeful for the first time today. If she was getting dropped off, she had a chance to sneak away! As long as her mother didn't take her backpack again, she could get away and open the box. It was pressing on her mind more and more.

They turned the corner and Mara saw the room up ahead. There was already a group of young kids sitting in a circle inside, but she didn't see Danny this time.

Shannon kept her grip on Mara up until they were fully inside the room. Then she turned to talk to one of the workers, a young woman with her hair pulled back and a red and gold apron tied in front of the usual employee uniform.

324

Chapter 7: Day Five

Mara vaguely heard her mother instructing the employee about watching her specifically, but her attention was on checking the room out.

It wasn't big like the dining room or conference rooms. The side walls were lined with bookcases and cubbies for the children's personal effects. The back wall had a chalkboard and a little raised stage area. Mara wondered if this room doubled as a classroom sometimes.

There were also colorful cartoon characters, suns, animals, and flowers made of paper hanging around the ceiling as decorations. It was very juvenile, but Mara supposed it was cute for the little kids. She was just too old to be here.

"Mara," her mother turned her attention back to her, "I *will* be back here to pick you up. The worker will watch you. You won't be pulling anything." The last words were spoken in a low tone, and Mara understood the vague threat. She nodded to get her mother off her back, and Shannon then finally left.

Mara clutched the strap of her backpack. She still had it, and she still had hope.

The employee instructed her to sit anywhere comfortable in the middle among the other kids. They had some small wooden chairs, beanbags, and other mats to sit on. Mara opted for sitting cross-legged on a mat near the back of the group. She had to start strategizing for how she could leave.

The employee settled the rest of the children and took her seat in the back, facing the children. "Now, we should start with a story! But which one? Did you have a favorite from the ones we told on the first day?"

One of the little girls in front raised her hand the highest, and the employee pointed to her. "Yes! Which one did you like?"

"The one! Uhm..." She seemed to struggle to remember before enthusiastically belting out details she remembered. "The one with the wind!"

Mara looked up from fiddling with her backpack strap. Another story about the wind? She wondered if that was a common theme for the locals. Rudy really emphasized that in his story too.

"Okay, I'll tell it then!" The employee walked to the left wall and picked up a big book from near the middle of the bookcase. She walked back to her stool in front of the children and held it open to show the pictures as she retold the story.

"There once was a little boy who lived in a cozy village."

Chapter 7: Day Five

"He stayed inside away from the other kids quite often because he got ill easily. But he loved to watch out the window as they played and wished he could join."

"As time went on, the boy's parents had to work more and more. They were almost never home, and he became very lonely."

"He only had his books for company and his favorite window. He read and re-read the books, but one day it wasn't enough, and he opened the window to at least hear more of the children playing."

The page was turned, and the image was of the boy peering out the open window with a dark swirl just outside.

"Now, the boy had heard from his mother and father to not talk to anyone they didn't trust. But the boy was so lonely, he forgot this."

"A faceless voice spoke from outside the window, and the boy listened."

Mara felt ice grab her neck. "LEAVE!" An urging came into her mind. But she couldn't move without the employee immediately stopping her.

"The boy talked to the voice all day long, but that night he lied to his parents that he hadn't done anything new."

327

The page turned. The dark whirl was now inside the house, whispering into the boy's ear as he slept.

"The faceless voice misled the boy and spoke evil to him all night long. He let it speak and listened."

The pressure on Mara's neck and shoulders was near unbearable now. She hardly breathed.

The page turned. The house was now empty in the picture, except for the boy standing alone among a giant black whirl, enveloping him.

"The evil was so strong his parents had to flee to save themselves. The boy was swallowed by it, and he regretted not listening to his parents. He regretted believing the lies."

"LEAVE! LEAVE AND DON'T LISTEN TO THEM!" The urging screamed louder, and Mara recognized this as not her own thoughts now. Terror gripped her, and she lowered her head and covered her ears with her hands to stem the panic. The employee didn't seem to notice since she was towards the back.

These... these were the stories that the front desk employee and porter pushed her so hard to listen to that first day at the resort. They tried to make it mandatory for all the children, and Mara had run away that day and not stayed for them.

Chapter 7: Day Five

"Now!" The employee closed that book and stood back up. "Which of you can tell me the moral of the tale?"

A few hands shot up. The little girl from before spoke first. "Don't talk to strangers!"

"That's good, yes. But there is more. The boy was foolish for believing the voice, but he was a sad character as well. The root started with his parents. They knew he was vulnerable, lonely, and unable to play with the other kids."

"They could have stayed with him more or found a childminder for times when they had to work so long. But they didn't. He was left alone all day, every day, for a long time..."

The employee gave a sad look. "So the root was with them too. They should have taken care of him, and the boy should have told someone and tried to get help if he could. So if any of you feel too sad, scared, or lonely and can't get your parents to help, please try talking to another relative, teacher, friend, or even one of us. We all need to help each other."

Tears stung Mara's eyes. It wasn't fair. None of it was fair. Ask for help? FROM WHO? Her dad knew and didn't care! Her grandparents knew and didn't care! Aunt Barbara saw it herself and didn't care! No one stopped what her mother did!

329

"I will help, Mara." The voice came again, whispering in her mind. "Leave! Leave here and open the box!"

She clutched her ears tighter and stayed paralyzed. Everyone would hate her. No one would help. What could she do?!

"Excuse me." The employee had walked over and bent down near Mara without her noticing. "Are you okay?"

Mara looked up but only saw a dizzying black and red. Her vision swam.

"LEAVE! THEY WILL KILL YOU! THEY ALREADY HATE YOU!" Mara listened this time and bolted up and out of the room. Her vision cleared and her heart raced. She heard the employee yelling behind her and a few startled gasps from relatives as she sprinted past them down the hall, but she didn't stop. She couldn't.

She reached the door to the outside and shoved it open and ran.

Her breathing was quick and painful. Her legs ached. Her ears hurt from her fingernails digging into them. But she ran.

"LEFT!" The voice screamed. Mara went left and ran up a small hill off the side of the gravel road behind the resort. She tried to think. She didn't know what to do. She briefly thought of

Chapter 7: Day Five

Hershey and wished nothing more than to cry into her soft fur again.

There were no people in this area of the mountain. Only trees, rocks, and snow. The voice urged her on.

She climbed higher on an outcropping of exposed rocks and slid back down, scraping her knee. The child inside her wanted to sit and cry, but she couldn't be a kid anymore. She wasn't normal. Her mother was right.

She climbed again and continued running. The voice directed and hours passed before she came upon a half-rotten wood structure among some trees.

"Go inside!" The voice barked.

It looked like a small lean-to built for hunting a long time back. It was barely big enough for one person, but she crawled in and shut the door.

It was dark. And quiet. All she could hear was her own sobbing for a moment. Was Rudy even real, Mara wondered. Or was he someone in on this?

The voice answered, seemingly reading her mind. "Rudy? You still want to meet him, don't you?"

The Red god

For the longest time, Mara didn't answer. She stayed still and breathed. Eventually she spoke, barely above a whisper. "Rudy liked me..."

"I like you, Mara. I'm the only one that does." Understanding then dawned. "Are... you Rudy?"

An echoing laughter broke out, seeming to come from all around her. Mara instinctively covered her ears again and shut her eyes tight, shaking.

"I am many names. Rusalka, Rubrum, Fonos, Krvavitev Ena, Red God, and now... I suppose you call me Rudy."

The voice continued, not caring that Mara was unable to respond due to her fear.

"I will be everything to you, Mara. I will be your Rudy. Your mother. Your father. Your god. Take the box and open it."

When it didn't get a response, it changed back to a soft whisper brushing past her ears.

"I will kill your mother for you. Her harsh words will die in her throat as she falls in front of you."

Mara opened her eyes. "I... I don't want that. I hate her. She is terrible, evil, mean to me, but I don't want to kill anybody!"

Chapter 7: Day Five

"Then she will be made to bow before you instead. You will have your own followers, too. You will wield power with me, Mara."

Power... The word made Mara think of the desires and problems she had written down for her family, particularly her grandmother who had it written as her ultimate desire in life. Did this voice have her investigate those to better manipulate them?

It manipulated her... all along. Everything it had her do. Everything it had her believe.

She was a fool. She was stupid! She was never smart or special! Just like her dad telling her she was mature for her age whenever she had to deal with her mother's episodes, it was a lie. She was just a young kid, and she couldn't handle this!

For the longest time she stayed curled up, sobbing and shivering. The voice was relentless.

"You don't have a choice but to throw your lot in with me now, girl. You let me do what I want, and you have many things. You disobey, and everyone you call family still hates you. You are shameful! You are ruined!"

"They will not even blame me! They will blame you for what you have done! You cannot go back. You cannot try and tell them

333

now! They will toss you outside like dirt and throw rocks until you are dead!"

"You asked for this, too. It was you that sought it out! You wanted to grow up. You wanted praise. You wanted away from your family. I merely gave you a chance..."

"I wanted..." Came Mara's small, racked voice. "I wanted someone to think I was special, and love me, and not be like my parents. It was supposed to be better..."

She thought of seeing Gina holding Danny's hand, and her and her husband playfully bantering and laughing. She was so filled with envy that she hated to see it at the time, but she lay broken now. Admitting to herself and this... being... that that's what she always wanted.

"It is better." The voice persuaded. "You will never get that with them. No one will love you but me. You are a disgusting, shameful creature now without me. Now, open... THE... BOX!"

The shouting made her tremble again, but she stayed where she lay and made no move to obey it. It was a sad irony that her mother's screaming episodes made her able to withstand this better. She was used to being screamed at. What difference did it make if it was this thing or her mother?

Chapter 7: Day Five

She withstood it the whole day. It screamed, it commanded, it threatened, it lied, and finally it went back to whispering.

The little crack of daylight Mara could see through the wood door faded into gold and then black. The coldness crept in all the more with the sun gone.

Mara wondered if this was it, if she should die here from the frost and not bother anyone anymore. Maybe her family would be happier like that.

"You can live forever if you open the box for me, you know. It is an amazing gift."

Living forever sounded like torture to Mara now. Who would want to live like this?

But her thoughts drifted to Hershey and Beth back home. She wanted to see them again. She didn't want to make them sad.

Would any of her relatives be sad if her frozen body was found here tomorrow? Her despair told her no. No one was looking for her. Some of her relatives and the employee definitely knew she ran away, but many hours had passed with no rescue party. She never thought to expect one, but still her heart ached with a longing to be wrong.

The Red god

"I can make them regret abandoning you." It taunted, but Mara still shut her ears to the whispers.

When the moon crossed the night sky further, a tiny ray of light re-entered the shack and shone near her backpack.

Mara stared and moved for the first time in hours to reach for it.

"Yes, yes. Open it now and be warm with me! Let us start!"

Mara pulled the backpack closer and fumbled with the zipper for a moment. Her hands were stiff from cold and couldn't move right.

"Hurry and do it!"

Eventually she got it open and plunged her hands inside to retrieve the item.

"And the key! Take the key!"

A loud shrieking erupted as Mara pulled Lukas' Gameboy out instead of the box.

"STUPID! STUPID GIRL! THEY WILL KILL YOU BY MORNING IF YOU DON'T DIE OF ICE! OPEN THE BOX!"

Mara winced from the loudness but otherwise focused on ignoring the voice.

Chapter 7: Day Five

She wished her hands weren't so ruined by the cold. She ran her fingertips along the plastic of the console and over the buttons, but she couldn't really feel it.

Lukas would hate her. Not only had she lied and tricked him, she also in essence stole his cherished game by taking it with her. She wished she could have at least kept her promise to return it. He deserved so much better.

"HE WOULD JOIN THEM IN STONING YOU! THE WHOLE VILLAGE WOULD!"

Mara managed to turn the game on with her numb fingers, and the light lit up the shack. She ran her fingers over Lukas' light attachment. He even included that when he loaned it to her.

In the corner of her eye, she saw something dark illuminated by her tiny source of light. Curious, she turned around and grabbed at it, tugging.

A stiff fabric came up, and Mara saw more underneath. She pointed the Gameboy and looked further.

It was a large pile of thick burlap cloth.

"That won't save you! It is but rags!"

Mara was beginning to think she should do the exact opposite of whatever the voice was telling her. She pulled the cloths loose and began piling them on top of herself, covering even her head and pulling her hands inside.

It was still frigid, but ever so slowly she could feel her hands again. She kept the Gameboy in front of her in her makeshift cocoon and stared longingly at it. She couldn't really save herself. She knew that. Even some temporary warmth tonight wouldn't save her from the deadly punishment that likely awaited tomorrow. But... maybe she could keep her one promise to Lukas.

If she lived through the cold, she could set out at first light and make it to the village and leave the Gameboy there. If Lukas himself joined in and killed her, she could at least know she tried to fix what little she could.

The warmer she got and the longer the night drug on, the softer the whispers became. Mara didn't know when she fell asleep.

Chapter 8: DAY SIX

Mara didn't dream, but she awoke with a startled gasp. Her cocoon had gone dark, likely from the Gameboy losing power. She didn't know how long she had slept.

She pulled the cloth from her head and was surprised to see sunlight once again. This was it, her last day. She had only one task, and this time it was her own and not Rudy's.

She sat up and carefully placed the Gameboy back in her backpack before zipping it up.

"You will open the box before they kill you. You *will* do it."

Mara ignored the voice and the growing fear in her stomach. Death was a lot easier to face when it was a day away instead of today.

She slung her backpack on and opened the shack door to leave. Before walking out, she took careful account of the surrounding area. The snow still had her tracks from the day before, but there were no new ones. There was no sign that anyone had came near looking for her.

Mara hoped she could find her way back to the road from here. She could follow her footsteps, but that would take her back towards the resort. She needed to take the closest route to the village.

The Red god

She looked around and tried to estimate how far she had gone. If her sense of direction was right, then she might have ran closer to the village than away from it.

She set her face to the right of the shack and started walking.

"Death is very painful, you know. It will not be quick and easy. I have seen many. You will not be able to stand it."

Mara tried to ignore it, but the idea made her heart race more. For all her imagining herself as a hero, she was a coward. She didn't need the voice to make her fear what was coming. She already did.

Slowly she climbed hills, slid down rocky faces, and navigated through patches of trees. If what was coming would be violent and painful, she would savor the little bit of peace she had now.

Birds flitted overhead and chirped happily. The sun shone. The breeze was soft and gentle.

Mara had only ever been to one funeral in her life, her grandfather's on her dad's side. But she liked to imagine she at least knew a little of what funerals were. Goodbyes, crying, and happy memories all swirled into a few hours.

If everyone hated her, she would consider this her funeral, the slow walk among nature before her journey ended.

Chapter 8: DAY SIX

She had some good memories to think on. Every moment laughing with Beth. Playing with Jace when he was still with them. Cuddling Hershey all night. Rare moments of her dad joking with her.

There were a few even rarer ones with her mother. Mara didn't think of them often. When she was very little, maybe Danny's age, she had memories of her mother playing with her and laughing, genuine laughing. Her brain couldn't make those memories coexist with the rest of her mother, so she mostly kept them locked away.

Today was the last day though. So Mara thought she should let anything locked away come out. Why not let her memories walk her funeral with her.

There was another of her mother buying her candy at a store after a long day shopping. She hadn't gotten mad at her that day. She asked what Mara wanted near the checkout and didn't scold her or refuse when she pointed to a box of candy canes. It must have been near the Christmas season for there to be candy canes there, but Mara was so young she didn't remember anything but a blurry recollection and smiles exchanged.

Anger towards her mother had been building so high during this trip, but Mara was too tired to keep it stoked now.

341

She thought of trips to the zoo, school plays, and the state fair at the end of each summer. Memories from later years were more mixed. Maybe there was an hour of smiles followed by the usual arguments and fights for control.

The mixed memories made Mara wonder if her mother had her own voices she was listening to. Maybe there was an explanation for her behavior. But in the end, Mara couldn't do anything to help. The voice talking to her now couldn't either. There was no magic to fix what her reality was.

Despite trying to focus on happy memories, Mara found herself sobbing as she marched on. She wiped her tears with her sleeve and kept walking.

Her thoughts drifted to the future she wouldn't have. She had started conversations with Aunt Barbara and Uncle Larry days ago about life desires and dreams. She thought of her own now.

Despite her bitterness towards the idea of romance and marriage, she wanted her childhood fairytales of love to be true. She wouldn't have admitted that before. But if she had any dream, it would be that it could exist.

Chapter 8: DAY SIX

Maybe if she hadn't messed everything up she could have been happy with someone like Samantha was with Ryan. Or maybe it would have ended like her parents' marriage.

Whatever the future would have been, it wouldn't be anything now. She added her daydreams of the future to her funeral procession walking beside her.

Despite being alone, she felt less lonely to imagine walking with these memories.

She climbed another hill and saw the gravel road below. It was too soon. She wasn't ready... but there was no ready about today.

She clutched her backpack straps and slid down to meet the road. Looking ahead, she saw the metal structure of the village bridge around the corner.

She made it. Despite the voice whisper-screaming to the contrary, she did one small thing that she could do.

Mara carefully looked around and crept closer to the bridge. She probably didn't stand much chance walking all the way to Lukas' house, but there was only one way in and out of his village. He was sure to find it.

She left the Gameboy carefully perched atop the bridge railing and gave one last look before turning away.

The Red god

"There is still time! They have not caught you! Hurry with the box!"

Mara began walking the road back towards the resort. If there was punishment waiting, it should be there rather than the village. Being hurt by her parents was a less sad prospect than being hurt by Lukas.

She marched on.

Her memories of her life caught up to the present at the same time as the resort coming back into view. It was a few hills away still, but she saw a corner of the back above the hill.

She wasn't ready. She wouldn't be. But she walked slowly still.

The voice now laughed, slow and low, and then louder.

Mara wasn't sure why. It begged her to not go this way before, but maybe it enjoyed her pain all the same.

Mara stumbled on part of a rock and caught herself suddenly. She looked towards her foot and saw blood.

But... it wasn't hers.

She covered her mouth and held back a choking gasp. Several feet ahead the blood trail continued until it reached a small mass.

"No..." Mara begged. "No... not him. Not him!"

Chapter 8: DAY SIX

She ran ahead and stopped on her knees in front of it, a mass of tangled red stained fur.

"Gravy." She sobbed. The voice's laughter echoed off the surrounding hills.

"What did you do!?" She screamed. Frantically she patted at the fur, rolling part of it over to reveal Gravy's face. He was not in one piece and long gone.

"WHY? WHAT DID YOU DO?" Mara stood up and screamed. She spun around in a circle, looking for the voice, trying to catch some visible form it had to funnel her fury.

But her screams died down. There was nothing there. Nothing she could fight. Nothing she could do.

She fell once more to her knees, sobbing in front of Gravy's body. The voice's laughter stopped, and it became quiet except for her own crying.

Mara was convinced the voice entirely left her as she stayed there, staring at the remnants of her friend.

But the smallest whisper returned.

"I can fix it."

This time, the broken girl made her worst mistake. She lifted her head and listened.

345

The Red god

"Open the box, and I will fix it. All your mistakes will be wiped out with my power. Even your friend's death."

"What... what can you really do?" She whispered back.

"Your friend died trying to cross the road to find you. You were responsible for this too. But I can erase things. I can make them happen or not happen. I have all control."

Wind swirled around Mara, gently at first and then gaining speed. She was lifted to her feet and then turned back to look at the cat on the ground.

Things couldn't end like this. At least not for Gravy, not him. It wasn't fair. Mara would have understood if she needed to be punished like this, but not him.

She slid her backpack off and unzipped it.

"I will be gentle. It won't have to hurt much." The voice almost caressed her ear.

Mara took out the box and the key. As she already knew, the key fit the slot perfectly and turned with a small clink.

Shaking, Mara lifted the box's lid. The inside was padded with some cloth carefully inserted. It was stained in parts, but it still held its treasure.

Chapter 8: DAY SIX

Mara slowly breathed out and lifted the item from the box. It was a small knife, made of dark metal and a leather-wrapped handle. It had no gold or jewels. It was not valuable looking, nor was it pretty to look at. But this had been the end of the game.

"Take the knife and slice your hand, Mara. Do it soon. People from nearby have already heard your screams and are coming this way."

Mara looked between the knife and Gravy for a moment that felt like an eternity. Her breathing slowed. The wind stopped.

And she sliced her hand.

Time seemed to stop, but the wind moved.

It swirled faster and faster, enveloping Mara. She looked to see blood floating from her hand into the air, joining the swirling wind.

She screamed and fell backwards, looking up in horror as the voice now formed a presence.

Her blood continued to pour out, building droplets in the air. The droplets crystallized in some areas and formed a circle near the ground and got narrower as it went up.

The Red god

As Mara's eyes followed, she saw it became pale white legs, a dress, pale arms, and finally the head.

The voice now had a face.

"Oh, my. It's been a *long* time." The Red god spoke. The voice was familiar but now obviously feminine, or as feminine as this revulsion could be.

The figure stretched and formed her hands as the last of the blood whirlwind found it's place in her body. It was unnaturally slender and tall. Pale, almost white, skin covered it but was marred by bright red and black veins spider-webbed throughout.

It had the face of a woman with dark black eyes and crimson lips, but the proportions were slightly off. Everything about the being screamed terror, but Mara couldn't look away.

Black hair flowed down from its head, and at last it seemed satisfied with its stretching and preening.

"I've missed this form so. You know, men used to fall dead at my feet every day. I didn't have to work for it so much then."

It twirled, experimenting with the movement and looking in glee as its dress floated with it. It was a gradient of bright and dark red, formed of crystallized blood. It was larger at the very bottom and became skin-tight at the calves and up. A large 'V' shape was

348

cut out from the chest of the dress, and the shoulders were gravity-defying spikes jutting out and then flowing down behind like pieces of a cape.

Pressure seemed to emanate off the being. Even being several feet away, Mara could feel the power and danger.

"N-now..." Mara stuttered, still fallen before the being. "Y-you fix Gravy?"

The Red god turned and faced Mara. A smirk formed on its lips, and it reached a sharp-nailed hand to place on its hip.

"Now, why would I do that? I kill things. I don't fix them."

This time Mara couldn't even scream. She stared with her mouth open as it turned and walked towards the resort. Her vision faded, and her head crashed back onto the gravel road.

Mara came back to consciousness to the sound of screams. Her head pounded, and her hand pulsed with pain where it still bled.

Her vision was blurry, but her adrenaline rush snapped her back. The realization of what she had done flooded her body. This wasn't a movie or a book. This was real life, and a monster worse than she ever knew existed. And SHE was the one that set it loose!

She rolled over and lifted herself off the ground. Each scream pierced the snow covered landscape and brought to Mara's mind a different relative. Was that scream Gina? Her mother? Aunt Barbara?

Before she realized her legs had moved, she was racing towards the resort. Her mind was empty of plans, but her body screamed at her to move and do something.

Upon turning the corner the back of the resort came into full view, and Mara came to an abrupt halt. She could only stare at the scene unfolding.

Samantha's perfect wedding had proceeded. The bride and groom stood at the alter beneath a white arch flowing with purple flowers. The red carpet stretched from them to the resort's back door, and on either side were rows of chairs that contained half the guests...

The other half were running already.

The tall, red being was behind them in the middle. Mara watched it bend back and then snap forward with an unnatural ease, striking a running man and spreading blood onto the white snow.

Vomit splattered the ground in front of Mara. She fell to her knees as the screams faded to the background. She could hardly hear them over the ringing in her ears.

She was dizzy. She couldn't breathe. Once the vomiting stopped, the screaming got louder again. It took Mara a moment to realize the louder screaming was her own.

"How fucking DARE YOU?" The Red god's voice now boomed out. Mara lifted her head in time to see one of her mother's cousins, a petite woman in a dark gray dress, being drug backwards by her ankles.

The being yanked her violently as she tried to claw herself free, digging fruitlessly at the snow. The name Judy came into Mara's mind, but just as soon as she had remembered the woman's name she was snuffed out. The Red god dropped her legs and stabbed her with a spear of crystallized blood. The weapon had formed in her hand as she moved to strike.

Judy's screams peaked and ended as fresh blood poured from her back. The Red god slowly straightened back up and began turning.

The Red god

Like a hunted animal, fear overrode all of Mara's senses. Her shaking legs pounded the ground as she ran to hide. Off to the side of the wedding was a large decorative boulder.

Before reaching it she stumbled and rolled partway down the hill. Her left arm wrenched behind her as she fell, but the pain didn't register in her brain. It had no room with the overwhelming terror before it.

She shoved herself back up and dove behind the boulder. Her breathing was shuddered gasps, and now hidden she desperately tried to stifle them to be silent.

"I will have WHAT I WANT! AND YOU WILL STOP FLEEING LIKE *ROACHES*!" The voice commanded.

Mara found herself praying it wasn't talking to her directly. She was fast. She was good at hiding. It shouldn't have seen her. She begged for it to not have seen her!

Screams from her relatives climaxed and were quieted. With the new silence, she could hear some sobbing. But no sounds got closer to her.

Mara's breathing still came in rapid bursts, but a thought came in her mind to look around the boulder's edge. Were her parents there? Were Samantha and Ryan okay by the altar?

Chapter 8: DAY SIX

"Listen to me and less of you may die! If you have half a thought in your meat bags you'll kneel and wait before me!"

Rudy, The Red god, whoever or whatever this thing was, it definitely didn't see her yet. It was addressing the crowds.

"My kind and your kind have lived side by side for eons past! You are my lesser! Lowly, beastly creatures! But..."

The voice trailed off, and Mara tried forcing herself to turn and look at what was happening. Her attempts faltered each time for fear. She was a coward! Why did she think she could do anything?!

The being made no sound when it moved. Whether it walked silently or hovered above the ground, Mara did not know. But the voice was twenty feet to the right when it spoke next.

"...I have some use for you." The tone was strangely soft now. Mara couldn't imagine what it was doing.

"If you will submit to me, I can raise you higher. You would be far above a normal human if you were beside a god like me. I would graciously grant you your desires."

The next voice that spoke was not the being, but it made Mara's heart drop more than she thought possible. How could someone with no hope lose more?

The Red god

"H-How can one submit to you? W-What can I do?"

She found it within herself to look now, or rather she couldn't stop herself even if she wanted. A man was knelt in front of The Red god, gazing up, seemingly awestruck by the female form.

Mara wanted to tell herself that she couldn't see well enough from here, and that the voice was misheard. But she knew it would be a lie.

The man fallen before it was her dad.

"It is quite simple." The Red god purred, touching David's chin with a spindly finger to lift his head up further. "Give yourself to me, starting with your mind now and your body later. I will fetch my knife for the bodily binding when I am ready."

David spoke again, but Mara couldn't comprehend how he had breath left in his body while staring into the eyes of that... thing. "A-and I can have my desires? I-is that money? Or more?"

The Red god threw her head back and bellowed a shrieking laugh. Mara flinched, covering her ears momentarily.

"Oh, you are a fast one! I rather like you!" It now cupped his cheek with its palm and grinned widely as it looked into his eyes. "Yes, money and more. I have no use of it myself, but power comes

354

in many forms, and I will have it all through those bound. But first..."

The Red god's head swiveled to scan the rest of the group. "I will check more of you before deciding on who to bind. I need not settle for the ugly or scrawny among you."

Mara squeezed her eyes tightly shut as new tears filled her vision. She was so dehydrated she didn't know how crying was still possible.

Memories of her dad flickered before her mind. She let them race past her, taking in the themes but not grasping a particular one. Her brain was trying to find a pattern, a hidden remembrance, something that would explain his behavior.

He had tossed her and her mother aside for this creature so gladly! He had kneeled and gazed longingly! Shannon crouched not even two feet away, hiding in terror behind part of her chair. And he did not so much as turn his head to glance at his wife!

Mara knew her parents hated each other deep down, but she didn't expect him to turn on her even then. He had always deferred to her and tried to keep her happy. Even at Mara's expense he adhered himself to Shannon, through each and every tantrum and screaming match Shannon started.

The Red god

Mara opened her eyes and once more looked at her dad, still kneeling and facing away. This was who David was. Someone who kneeled to whoever screamed the loudest or gave him the best false promise of consort. Whatever Mara believed of him as her dad didn't matter. This was him.

Mara turned her attention back to watching The Red god as she strode away from David. She appeared to be sizing up other relatives. They remained scattered beyond the overturned chairs, to the left of the wedding setup, kneeling wherever they fell after their attempted escape.

Fear once again seized her as she watched the being pass by Aunt Barbara and Danny. She hadn't noticed them before, but Barbara was huddled on elbows and knees with Danny shielded beneath her. Even at a distance, Mara could see her limbs shaking, but Barbara was quiet.

The Red god stopped just after them. It stared at a clustering of people, but Mara couldn't tell who the couple in front were. Perhaps a husband and wife from Ryan's side.

Mara knew who stood up behind them though.

"I don't need power from you," her grandmother stated. Mildred was eerily calm, both in her movement as she stood up

356

straight and her voice as she addressed the being. "I get power for myself. It's the only proper kind for a *Hausfeld*."

Mildred dared to tip her nose up as she finished, locking eyes with The Red god in defiance.

In response The Red god let out a haughty laugh. "And *I* don't need someone so old they're practically a walking corpse! In fact, let me help you with that..."

Mara tightly covered her mouth with her hands to suppress her cry as The Red god jerked forward and put its hand straight through her grandmother's chest.

Mildred wheezed and coughed, sputtering blood onto the couple below. A fresh chorus of screams rang out, but Mara still heard The Red god's voice rise above them. "Now you're just a corpse! No more walking!"

It lifted Mildred's body with ease and flung it off to the side. The corpse hit a young woman, knocking her back and covering the front of her dress in red.

The woman cried aloud and shouted a name, causing a nearby man to rush to her. Mara blinked and missed The Red god's next movement, but the blood-formed spear was still through his chest suspending him above the ground until his body slowly slid down it.

At once there was fresh panic and running. Mara caught herself wanting to call out towards them, to come hide with her, but she couldn't move.

The being was in a frenzy now, whipping left and right to strike down those that ran. It no longer used its hands or a spear but instead shot spikes through the air. Each made an unworldly whistle of undulating high pitch tones as they quickly met their victims and pierced through them.

Mara now saw Uncle Larry further in the back running towards his wife. The screams, whistles, shrieking, and sounds of falling bodies was too loud for Mara to hear anything, but she saw him shouting as he reached Barbara and Danny and hoisted them up to run.

The trio began running towards the resort. Blood was everywhere now, so that Mara couldn't distinguish between snow and the red carpet that once made up the aisle runner, but she mentally urged them to reach it and escape.

Barbara stumbled on a body, and Mara lost them from her vision as they reached nearer to the resort doors. She quickly turned to look around the other side of the boulder, but the scene had already changed in that one short second.

Uncle Larry was now face down in the mire of blood, but his hand remained raised towards Barbara for a moment more before falling. Everyone... everyone was going to die.

"BLOOD-FILLED SACKS! THAT'S ALL YOU ARE!" The Red god shrieked as she spun around.

She was now facing the alter. Mara saw Ryan tightly clutching Samantha. Her wedding dress was unstained by the blood where they stood. Amid Mara's panic, her mind floated a most useless thought to her. Her cousin really made a beautiful bride.

The Red god reared back to fire another set of spikes.

Had they actually gotten married? Time seemed to slow as Mara watched them. The priest stood further back hiding behind part of the arch. Maybe he had listened to their vows minutes before and declared them husband and wife.

If Samantha died as Mrs Jansen, would she at least take a little bit of happiness with her?

An older man barreled from the left and knocked into the couple, shoving them off to the side of the alter as he shouted.

The Red god

Mara only recognized him as Ryan's dad after he was halfway slumped to the ground, filled with gaping holes from the being's attack.

Ryan rolled to cover Samantha and held her near the ground. The priest sprung from his hiding spot and ran at that moment.

The Red god took special notice of him and charged forward, not bothering to send spikes for a quick death. With four large strides it had him held up high by the throat.

"Oh I *really* hate you spiritual types. You are always so annoying even after bindings are secured. I still don't understand why you think throwing water on me would ever help you..."

It smiled as it slowly crushed the man's windpipe. His hands frantically tried to pry the being's off of him, but the movement could hardly even be considered a struggle against the power the being displayed. It was like a mouse fighting an anaconda.

A crunch echoed out, and his head lolled to one side.

What could stop this? What could Mara do? She watched half the wedding party be turned to a slurry of red. Everyone was powerless.

A sudden force yanked Mara off her feet, and she screamed and covered her face in instinct.

Chapter 8: DAY SIX

"You! You need to leave with me NOW!"

Mara removed her arms from her eyes and tried to blink to be sure of what she was seeing. Alma stood in front of her, hair disheveled, eyes wide with wild fear. She kept a firm hold on Mara's sleeve and drug her towards the side of the resort, away from the wedding turned war zone.

Mara didn't have a choice in leaving with Alma. The older woman was strong despite her stature, and it was just as well considering Mara couldn't seem to move her legs on her own.

She was drug into the resort side door, into an employee-only hallway, and finally into an inner storeroom. The screams of her surviving relatives got quieter the more doors they put between themselves and the outside, and in the storeroom it was silent.

Alma roughly threw Mara into the room and hurriedly turned to lock the door behind them. Mara stumbled and caught herself on a pile of cardboard boxes. She watched as Alma talked to herself quietly in her native language and frantically looked around the room.

She began shoving heavier boxes and furniture against the door to barricade it. Only when it was completely blocked did Alma take a few breaths and turn to look at Mara.

"You were *bound* by it. I knew it had to be you." Alma's voice faltered towards the end. She looked at Mara with a strange mix of fear and pity. Mara wasn't sure if her face was wet with tears or sweat.

Alma kept talking, but it seemed as though she was talking to herself more than expecting Mara to respond.

"Your mother didn't even let us look for you yesterday. She said you were being punished in the room and not really run away... We could have stopped it. We could have held you away from it...!"

So... her mother lied to the employees after she ran away into the snow. Mara easily pictured her mother trying to save face by doing such a thing. Shannon probably fumed all day imagining Mara was with Lukas yesterday and didn't want such a scandal being heard by the family, so she lied and said she was grounded in her resort room.

That explained why there was no search party and why Samantha held her wedding as normal. No one thought she was gone or missed her.

Chapter 8: DAY SIX

The information would have sent Mara into a spiral under normal circumstances, but the shock of the day and blood loss from her hand didn't allow her to do much except slump to sit on the floor and stare at her shoes.

She idly wondered if there was more blood from Gravy on them or one of her fallen relatives.

Alma slowly walked closer, seemingly afraid to approach Mara despite her earlier rough handling. She knelt a foot away and looked her over. Mara had no proper winter coat after her frantic exit yesterday. She had dirt smeared across her dress and face. Her hair was wet with sweat and grease and stuck to her forehead and side of her face.

Alma looked to her shoes and noted the caked snow and blood.

Finally her eyes looked to her hands too. She shakily reached out and grasped both of Mara's wrists, turning her palms up to see.

Mara expected Alma to begin yelling, to hit her, to threaten to kill her. Surprisingly, Mara didn't flinch from her touch. She felt herself emptying now. Even adrenaline couldn't keep her going forever. If Alma wanted to kill her, maybe that was how this story ended.

363

But Alma didn't. Instead she carefully looked at the knife cut, still steadily bleeding droplets of blood that ascended into the air and dissipated. Mara assumed it was continuously being drawn to The Red god, fueling its physical form and strength even while she was some distance away.

Alma gently put that hand down and moved to inspect her left hand. Mara numbly noted it too was covered in blood. She didn't know from what, but it didn't matter.

"Your finger is badly broken." Alma shifted to reach into her pocket and pulled out a handkerchief. She slowly wrapped Mara's middle 3 fingers with it, attempting to stabilize the break.

Oh. She did fall on it earlier when running to hide. Chaotic, broken memory fragments flashed to remembrance. She supposed she broke it then.

Alma held this hand after the wrapping was done, and she lifted Mara's chin to look in her eyes.

"I'm sorry it has come to this, child. You have limited options now. But you are so young, younger than my grandsons even, I-..." Alma's voice cracked and she took a moment to compose herself. Fresh tears escaped her eyes before she continued.

Chapter 8: DAY SIX

"I want to tell you everything. We don't have much time, but it is the very least I can do for you now."

Mara finally spoke, numb but wanting to know where this would go. "Are you going to stone me?"

Alma seemed unable to speak for a second but shook her head and wiped away the newest tears. "That is very painful. We do not have to do it that way... But let me speak what I know."

Mara nodded and listened.

"That being is known to my people, to my grandparents and their grandparents for as long as my village has kept records. It has had many names given to it, Rusalka or The Red god being some."

"What... what is it?" Mara asked.

"A spirit that sometimes can take a body. I do not know much more of its origins, except it probably predates even our village of hundreds of years. Perhaps it walked with the first men, or even before them."

"What I do know is it preys on the ignorant, the outcast, or the abused. It needs human blood, a binding, to keep its physical form and have power. Right now it is... using yours."

Mara looked to her right hand and hid it behind part of her dress in shame.

365

"Tell me, child, how did it speak to you? More knowledge may help us prevent the next occurrence."

Mara curled her hand into a fist and tried not to cry again. She was so, so tired.

"I found a tape recorder in one of the store rooms like this one. It had a man named Rudy playing a game. It made me find clues around the resort and... give it information about my family."

Alma nodded and broke her eye contact with Mara to give her a little room to tell her story.

"And it told me other things..." Mara's voice cracked, and she couldn't finish her sentence. Hot tears stung her eyes and rolled down her cheeks, adding to her feeling of shame. "...It told me not to trust my family, or you, or the other people here. And I believed it..."

"It told you to steal something from my office that day we talked, didn't it?" Alma questioned in a low but soft voice.

Mara moved her knees to her chest to hide her face now. "Y-yeah. I stole a key from a drawer. And then it had me take a box from an old ruined house."

Alma was surprised at this. "Old house? Were you at the village?" Mara replied with a nod, face still hidden by her knees.

Chapter 8: DAY SIX

"I see. And the box had the knife within it?" Mara moved her head again but didn't speak.

"Then that was our fault we missed it. We try to cover up its attempts as much as possible, but we did not think the binding knife was still in the village. It has a habit of hiding things like that for the younger to find."

"Like the paper or stones with writing on them?"

"Things like that, yes. Did it take you to the original boundary wall to the west of the resort?"

"I... think. There was a rock wall with chiseled stones and one with smooth writing."

Alma sighed. "Yes, that was it. It writes on the stones every several years, and me and the other elders chip the writing off whenever we see it return. But... we hadn't checked it again this year."

Mara felt a little relieved to hear Alma and the elders, whoever they were, had been fighting this thing already. Maybe there was hope for her yet.

"Are the elders other adults from the village?" She asked.

Alma affirmed. "They are. There are only three of us per generation that are entrusted with the knowledge and records about

367

the being. The rest of the village and our families are not told about it."

Mara thought that would explain why Lukas, Nico, and the other kids played in the ruined house and only had rumors and stories about The Red god. They were kept in the dark.

"Why not tell everyone? Why not warn them?" Mara felt angry now. Why did she have to fall for this trick? Why did it have to be her set up to fail time and time again?

"It is not so easy." Alma shook her head. "Six generations back, they tried that. One of the elders made the knowledge of the being widely known. It was explained to the children as well as the adults, and..." She trailed off and looked at Mara again.

"And one of the adults, a greedy man, was excited to hear of it. He sought it out on purpose and made an agreement with it. He wanted power and affluence, and he gladly bound himself to try and get it."

"This tale has repeated many times. You are not the first host and will not be the last. When he was bound, the records say over half the village was slaughtered. He was a strong man already, and he grew in strength using the being's agreement."

Chapter 8: DAY SIX

Mara thought of Gravy and The Red god's false promise to her to fix him. "I thought it didn't help anyone. How did the man get stronger through it?"

"It... keeps some promises... for some hosts. But please, dear child, it is never worth it! For that man, he used the power to conquer two other nearby villages and rule over them. He gathered large stores of food, clothing, housing, women, and slaves. He ruled over other humans cruelly for a generation and a half, but he was not really a human himself by the end of it."

Mara wondered what promises it did have the power to keep. She feared and hated it, but the stories captivated her. "He became immortal through it?"

Alma looked concerned at her curiosity but answered anyway. "He was not immortal. He lived over a hundred years and aged very slowly, but he died a painful death. Several of his enslaved people banded together and killed him before the being could strike them all down. Which brings me to the last time this occurred..."

"I was thirteen years old. I did not know the stories and records at the time, and I also did not know that my grandfather was one such elder who did know. I was just a child in school,

369

worried about my hair, my clothing, my scores, and the boys in my class."

Mara had a hard time picturing the older woman at that age. It almost seemed a mystery that adults used to be kids. What was her mother like when she was her age? Was she awkward? Happy? Angry? Was she like she is now, even back then?

"I was in class when it happened. Even after all these years it seems fresh in my memories. The boy I liked sat three desks ahead and one to the right. Our languages teacher was droning on and writing on the board. I paid him no attention as I fiddled with my hair and thought about talking to that boy later..."

Mara tried to read Alma's expression as she talked. She held a small smile, but her eyes showed pain.

"...and then the screaming started. I was one of the first to the window to look out. I did not see the being itself, but I saw crowds of adults forming towards one end of the village and more running away from there. Another teacher ran into the room and made us all hide beneath our desks and shuttered the windows."

Alma's smile was now gone.

"And the screaming continued and got much louder. It seemed all around the school building. We shook in fear, and I held my best girl friend. We stayed quiet for what felt like most of the day, but it may have only been two or three hours."

"At the time, none of us knew what it was, and most of them never really knew even afterward. When the screaming stopped and the teachers let us out, we were led straight to our homes in pairs. They instructed us to stare at our shoes the whole way, but even then I saw the blood in the snow. All in all 27 people were dead."

Mara looked away from Alma and towards her shoes again. How many of her relatives were dead now? And now? Were they dying even as she selfishly waited and spoke to Alma?

"We burn our dead here. That may be an odd custom to you, but it is our way because of the deep frozen ground. The fire that burned the dead was larger than I had ever seen before or since. The other children and adults were split into groups by the elders in the days ahead. One elder spoke to each group in turn."

"But when my group was about to hear our elder, my grandfather came and took me from the group back to our house. When it was just us, he told me everything. He told me about the being itself, the purpose of the elders to keep this knowledge of the being, and their ways of protecting us as best they could."

The Red god

"He told me they picked new elders ahead of time, and it was time for him to pick his successor too. I don't know why my grandfather chose me. But I took the responsibility seriously and listened carefully."

"The truth of what had happened that day was that a man by the name of Jakob lived in a house on the outskirts of the village. He had grown up there mostly alone. Both of his parents had died by the time he was sixteen, but he continued to live in the house alone since he was almost an adult."

"By most reports, he had a strange personality even in his younger years. He avoided everyone and did not speak unless necessary. I was aware of him a little myself, as most of my classmates avoided walking past his house towards the later hours and told exaggerated stories of him, saying he was harsh to the children or secretly a monster."

"In truth, he probably needed help after what happened to his parents, and the village as a whole failed him. Whatever the case though, he must have started talking to the being, either understanding what it was or being tricked as you were."

"And that day... he did the binding. The Red god came to physical form and began killing. My grandfather banded some of the strong men together and convinced them to fight it. Gathering them and meeting the being took some hours, but they came together..."

Alma sniffed and wiped her face. She sat up straighter and put on a very serious look.

"Mara... child, I need you to listen to this with care. I know you are frightened. But you must pull all your strength with me." She reached out and pulled Mara's hands to her own, holding them tightly.

"When the men came together, they went not to kill the being, but to kill Jakob. It is all we can do. The being itself cannot be killed, only the host..."

Mara couldn't respond. She met Alma's kind eyes but stayed quiet. Her heart should have known there was nothing for her after what happened...

"So that is what they did. Jakob was killed, and The Red god lashed out with the remnants of its power and killed the men too. Only my grandfather ran enough to be out of its range by the time it winded down and went back to nothing but a whisper in the wind."

Alma squeezed her hands.

The Red god

"I wish it were different... My God you are too young for this fate..." The older woman paused to wipe further tears away, and Mara reached her hand out.

Alma was startled when the girl's hand touched her cheek, but she calmed and put her hand over Mara's smaller one cupping it.

"I-I can't lie and say I'm not scared." Mara stuttered. "But I don't want anyone else to be hurt because of me! If you have to do it, I... I want you to do it. This is my fault. All of it..."

Before she could finish, Alma lurched forward and enveloped her in a tight hug.

"I don't want it to end like this. I was appointed an elder for a reason, and I must hold my duty as best I can. Part of that may be gathering more information and trying new things..."

Mara could no longer hold back her sobs, but Alma continued.

"At the time of the last incident, my grandfather worked to kill the host and lead the other elders to tell the groups cover stories. They were told that a large wild animal ravaged the village and killed many, even the strong men. They told them many other lies in response to disbelief and questions, and they charged everyone not to speak of it more."

Chapter 8: DAY SIX

"Curious adults and children alike were punished by the elders if they questioned it. They had to keep a lie believed to avoid another tragedy like the strong, greedy man who sought the being out on purpose. I continued the lies when I grew up and took the mantle of an elder myself."

"We only speak the truth in part and in stories. You skipped the children's room stories until yesterday, didn't you? We tell the partial truths there, that our children would be warned against the voice and get help from those who should look out for them and love them."

"Some days I wonder how long we have been telling these stories unknowingly even. A common saying in school when I grew up was to ignore bullies, and they would not hurt you then. But as any child knows, that does not work on bullies. They come at you still and harm you with words or actions..."

"I think... these are even older stories passed down. 'Ignore the voices, and they will not hurt you.' It was never meant for human bullies but for this being. How long have we fought to keep our children from it?"

Alma pulled back and looked Mara in the eyes. The older woman's eyes held determination, fear, and love. Mara was sure she'd never seen that look directed at her before, certainly not in her parents or relatives.

"I want to help you fight, Mara. But I also must fight for my children and grandchildren too, you understand?"

Mara wasn't sure she really did understand, but she nodded. She wanted to trust Alma now and do whatever she thought best. She didn't know what else to do...

"Good, then we need a strategy to fight with and... contingencies in case we lose the fight."

"What should I do?" Mara asked. She leaned closer to Alma and gripped her arms, recoiling when she realized she was getting blood stained on Alma's sleeves from her wound. But Alma still held her eyes and didn't move away from her.

"The most important thing is the knife. It has used the same knife in the last bindings we have recorded. Only we thought it had been lost during the last incident. We did not find it in Jakob's house... Do you know where the knife is, Mara?"

Mara sorted through the last hour's painful memories.

"I sliced my hand with it near the road to the back of the resort, but then I passed out. I'm not sure if it's still there."

Chapter 8: DAY SIX

Alma thought for a moment. "That's okay. We can't be sure about everything, but we have to try. You will run there, avoiding the being, and try and get the knife. We have to prevent it from binding any others. Then you run, Mara. You run as fast and far as you can away from here!"

"This is something we never tried before... so it might not work, but I want to try for you! You run all day and all night! If by the next morning the blood from your hand stops absorbing into the air, then I think distance is a factor for the being. That would mean it cannot draw power from you if you are far enough away."

"And then, what do I do?" Mara questioned.

"There are more villages to the west of here. If it indeed cannot draw power from you anymore, you can assume it will wind down here and the rest of us alive will be okay. You keep running until you reach the other village. You tell them you need help and that you are an American lost. If they can contact another family member in the US, they should get you home. The most important thing is that you never come back to the resort in case it can resume drawing your blood."

"And what about the knife?"

Alma shifted and pulled her phone out of her pocket and started looking through it. "I have some contacts for the other villages. If I can talk to someone we can trust, I can tell them to take it from you and destroy it in a forge."

Mara nervously tugged at the handkerchief Alma wrapped her left hand with. She was beginning to feel the injury in full force now that they had been talking for a while.

"And what if... the blood doesn't stop flowing into the air?"

Alma sat the phone down and tried to meet her eyes again, but Mara kept her head held low.

"Then... we can assume the being is still drawing power from you despite the distance. It... It will be important information for future elders to have. And it will be good that we tried it, to keep future generations safer with more knowledge."

Alma reached out and squeezed Mara's shoulder to get her to look up.

"And I will be grateful to you for trying this with me. And... I ask your strength to protect us too. You would still have the knife at that time if the blood is still flowing, and... I will show you where to cut deeper to have it end with the least amount of pain for you. Can

Chapter 8: DAY SIX

you agree to this, Mara? None of this is fair to ask you, but I must also protect my people."

Mara thought of Lukas. His toothy grin was forever etched in her memory. She had so much fun with him these last days, but now it felt like a knife was already in her heart to think about him being hurt because of her.

"I... I understand. Show me where, and I know I can do it if the blood doesn't stop. I can't be a coward anymore."

Alma gave her a small, sad smile. "You are no coward, child. You are young, and you have been burdened and mistreated more than ever should have happened. Your mother and father should have protected you instead of pushing you away. I don't know the full story of what happened with you, but from your mother's lies I can tell they did not love you right. The being specifically targets victims like you, and I am sorry no one truly helped you."

Mara took a deep breath, wiped away a few lingering tears, and stood up.

"Please show me and let's hurry. I don't want any more victims if I can help stop it."

Alma stood up too and put her hands on Mara's shoulders one last time, pushing them back straighter.

379

"Stand up tall, and you can face this. Let us do the best we can, together."

Mara walked with purpose now, head held high despite her shaking legs.

Alma had removed the door's barricade and let her out. Alma wouldn't follow her through the resort and to the knife outside, but she wished her well and embraced her one last time before Mara began her task.

The hallways were completely empty, but there was evidence of the panic before the remaining employees hid: Cleaning supplies dropped by the side, scattered papers, a lone shoe, all things Mara didn't notice on her way inside with Alma.

Almost all of the hallway doors were shut. Mara wouldn't have been surprised if they were barricaded from the inside as well.

As she walked, she wondered if they heard her soft padding on the hallway floor. Did they tremble in fear of her? Did they seethe in hate, knowing what she caused?

Chapter 8: DAY SIX

She couldn't very well blame them for either, but there was no use in dwelling on such self-pitying thoughts. She knew the only thing she could do to help now.

As her legs stabilized and she felt confident she wouldn't collapse, her gait sped up. By the time she reached the main guest hall, she was running so fast she narrowly made the hallway's turn.

Her heart pounded, and her breath quickened. Fear still kept a firm hold on her heart, but she ran all the faster. In the back of her mind she recalled a line from one of her books: "Bravery is not the absence of fear, but action in spite of it."

She had to choose bravery now.

Mara reached the resort's foyer. It was lit by the same sparkling chandeliers, roaring fireplaces, and bright red carpet as when she first entered those doors with her parents. But nothing else was the same. Everything was wrong now. She could hear the screams again with less doors and walls between her and the outside.

She reached the front doors and shoved them open. This was the longer route to the back gravel road, but it was her best chance at avoiding being seen before she reached the knife.

The Red god

The sudden cold air stung her face, but she gritted her teeth and ran. She ran for Lukas, for Alma, for Barbara, for Gina, for Danny, for Samantha, and for her parents if she could save them.

The screams grew in volume. Their earlier high pitch turned more into a wail of mourning now. Mara didn't know if The Red god had continued killing or had gathered them for 'sifting' a final time, but the pain in the cries was piercing to her soul all the same.

Mara turned the resort corner and saw towards the back. The wedding was not in view yet, but part of the road was in the distance.

She didn't stop to creep around corners and try and see where the being was. She kept sprinting and did her best to pace her rapid breathing.

The gravel road grew closer and closer, as did the wailing on her right. She couldn't stop. She couldn't look. She had to leave, for them.

Mara spotted Gravy's blood trail on the road ahead and knew she was close to where she used the knife. She prayed someone could forgive her for what she let happen, what she caused, for Gravy, for Uncle Larry, for her grandmother, for everyone.

382

Chapter 8: DAY SIX

It was a selfish thought, forgiveness. She felt shame and self pity creep in again but pushed it aside. It wouldn't help them now, only running could.

She only stopped once she reached Gravy's body. The road looked as she left it, blood trailed around mixed with snow and gravel and slush. She hurriedly searched the ground a few feet ahead on hands and knees.

Her mind raced with thoughts of the next step. She had to run after she found the knife. She had to get as far away as possible to protect them. It was all she could do. She wouldn't know of her family's fate afterward unless they came to her away from the resort. The thought of not knowing was a crushing pain in her chest already.

Her searching eyes and racing thoughts abruptly stopped. She had found it. The knife was a few feet further, the blade glistening with her blood.

She stood up off her knees and stumbled the last few feet before grabbing it. She expected to feel a surge of power, of weakness, of something once her hand touched the handle. But the only thing she felt was coldness from the contact. Whatever ability the blade held, she gripped it tight and stood up to begin the next phase of her task.

"I knew you were a smart girl, Mara. I didn't lie about that."

Mara didn't need to turn around to know the voice now. She began to run away from the road, away from the resort, but a clawed hand ripped into her shoulder and threw her backwards with ease.

She hit the gravel road on her back and felt all breath leave her lungs.

"But because you're smart, you should know how this ends. How do any interactions with your kind end? Though you are young in years, you have already seen your own blood leave you to me. You are mine, Mara."

Although The Red god lied to her in the past, Mara knew not everything it said was lies. She couldn't wait for her parents to save her. They would not be doing that. She coughed and turned back onto her side and then shakily pulled herself to standing.

"I know some of them wronged me in the past... I know some of them defended my mother and enabled what she did. But I won't join you. I won't hurt people out of hate!"

Chapter 8: DAY SIX

As Mara spoke her words, she found herself staring into the face of The Red god with less fear than she thought. It didn't seem as tall now. If it killed her, it did, but she wouldn't go without a fight for those she cared about and that cared back.

The Red god's face twisted in rage at her defiance. The red and black veins pulsed in its forehead and neck. It screamed louder than Mara had heard yet.

"THERE IS NO HOPE FOR YOU! YOUR STORY HAS ALREADY BEEN SET! I WROTE YOUR LAST CHAPTER! IT IS MINE TO TAKE!"

"No..." Came Mara's small reply, "I listened to you for the last time!"

Mara ran again. She gripped the knife tight to her chest.

The Red god flashed like lightning to grab her. Mara screamed and kicked wildly, making contact with the being's arms.

It began dragging her back towards the wedding party, but Mara fought on.

"You're not going to use me to hurt more people! I'm not going to be a coward and let you!"

The wailing of the remaining guests quieted as they saw The Red god returning with its prize. It strode into the middle of them.

The Red god

Mara now noticed they had been made to kneel in groups again. Her mother, dad, Samantha, Ryan, Barbara, and other faces flashed before her as she was carried past.

In the corner of her eye, Mara also spotted Alma near the resort's back door, watching the spectacle in fear. She stopped her kicking and screaming for a moment to catch her eye. Was... this it? She could not ask Alma what to do or for help.

Alma only gave a small, sad nod as they locked eyes, confirming what Mara already knew about the older woman's backup plan.

The Red god addressed the cowering group, dropping Mara in front of her in the center.

"This is the source of your strife and misery! I bound her, and she has brought your death!"

Mara's ribs hurt where she hit the ground, but the emotional pain of looking up into her family's eyes was by far the worst. Fear, disbelief, and anger emanated from most where she looked. She felt utterly naked and alone.

Mara said nothing to defend herself. She only gripped the knife tighter and tried to clear her mind and recall Alma's last advice.

Chapter 8: DAY SIX

"But, luckily some of you will be bound to replace her and will serve me better!" The Red god's wide red lips contorted into a crooked smile, and she looked into each terrified face, searching for her next favorites.

While it looked away, Mara breathed in, breathed out, and steadied her hands. She lifted the knife high and took aim at herself. There was still a chance she could be quick and cause the being to lose power before it could bind anyone else.

Time slowed as Mara tightened her arm muscles and pulled them towards her with all her strength. She thought once more of Beth and Hershey, of Lukas and Nico, of a future she wouldn't get the chance to explore. Her heart hurt so much, and the knife hadn't even made contact yet.

A scream rang out, and Mara felt a heavy weight topple her. She felt a wetness reach her chest, but she couldn't process if she had been the cause.

"No! NO! You.. you don't have to do this! I'm not going to watch you do this!" Mara knew the voice, but she only saw a sea of white when she opened her eyes.

387

The Red god

"I-I don't know how it happened, but I'm sorry I wasn't there to stop it." Samantha sobbed, holding Mara tight. "But I'm here now, and I'm not going to stand by and watch!"

Mara pushed her away as much as she could, but Samantha held her still. Mara could see she stopped the knife with her own hands and had blood freely flowing down them onto Mara's chest.

"You don't understand..." Mara cried, "If I don't do it, everyone will die. I have to!"

The Red god watched and began a slow, low laugh. It didn't reach out to separate them nor grab the knife. It was amused at a scene it had never seen, but it didn't appear concerned.

"I don't know who told you that, Mara, but that's wrong." Samantha pulled the knife out of her grasp now and looked her firmly in the eyes. "You don't have to do that, because I'm your family, and I'm going to help."

Samantha dropped the knife to the side of her and reached back over to grip Mara's bleeding right hand. She clutched it tightly in her own to stem the tide of blood still flowing into the air.

"You are my family! And you do not belong to that *thing*! You belong with us!"

The Red god stopped its laughter and looked startled.

Chapter 8: DAY SIX

Mara looked at her hand in disbelief as the blood no longer flowed to the being. Samantha turned her body, still gripping Mara, and looked to the other family members. Some turned away and hid their faces. A few stared back with shame, and a few others with nods of agreement.

"YOU DON'T HAVE ANY RIGHT TO HER! SHE IS MINE NOW!" The being shrieked and lurched forward.

"She is my FAMILY!" Samantha shouted and turned back to completely shield Mara. Ryan jumped forward and shielded Samantha without hesitation.

The Red god first slashed at Ryan's back, but Barbara joined and took part of the attack to her arm. Gina took the right side of the group and latched onto Samantha's right arm to help protect her.

"YOU ARE NOTHING! YOU CAN'T DO ANYTHING AGAINST ME! DO YOU KNOW WHO I *AM*?"

Attacks from the being came in rapid succession as Gina was joined by Samantha's dad, Mara's grandfather, and Ryan's cousin.

Blood splattered to the ground around the family, but no one dropped. The Red god was losing power.

389

It gathered its strength for another barrage when David stood up. He did not join the group enveloping Mara from harm, but he spoke to the being directly. "I will still bind myself! I am here, waiting. I did what you said and waited!"

The distraction caused The Red god to turn its head towards him, and at the same time Shannon launched herself at the being in fury. She screamed and clawed in incoherent rage.

Mara could only see a small portion of the scene around Samantha's shoulders and the other adults huddled around her.

"...GOD DAMN YOU! MY FUCKING...!"

Mara thought she heard a few more words and her dad's name from Shannon's manic frenzy, but nothing was clear.

What she did see was The Red god's right forearm being raised up and transforming. It took the shape of a long blade and was brought down across Shannon.

Shannon's neck to her waist was split in two, and she slumped to the ground, making no more sound.

"SHUT UP, SHUT UP, SHUT UP! I WILL KILL THE LOT OF YOU!" The being screamed and whipped around to resume its attack towards Mara.

Chapter 8: DAY SIX

The group held their line and took it. Blood dripped from Ryan's back, Gina's side, Barbara's arm. But they held still.

Mara could only cry in the center, watching her hand as Samantha kept it clutched tightly.

The Red god's shoulder spikes were the first to fall. They crumbled and disappeared as its screeching lost momentum. Then the bottom of the dress began dissolving upward. The being's long black hair fell out and disintegrated before it could reach the ground.

It screamed and struggled still, but soon it was only half of the physical being it was. "You can't! You fucking can't!" The volume of it decreased rapidly.

"Hey," Samantha whispered to Mara, "Remember when we were younger and I played hide and go seek with you?"

Mara remembered that day well. It was at another relative's wedding, and the two of them were playing games while the adults dined and talked about boring adult things.

"I... think I understand why I found you hiding alone with your scraped knee instead of coming to ask for help." Samantha continued. "Your parents didn't help you with things like that...

They didn't help you with a lot of things. But that doesn't mean that no one will. Me and Ryan will. And others, okay?"

Mara looked at her cousin. She had her wedding makeup smeared, her beautiful red hair curled and pinned in place. But Mara really looked into her eyes. She had a determination and love that she didn't notice before.

Mara dropped her head in shame. "I should have asked you for help... It wouldn't have come to this."

"It's not your fault, Mara. I and others should have noticed sooner. What matters is what we do now. We can both do better and get through this. I'm here with you."

Mara hesitantly nodded and looked back to her hand.

"It doesn't hurt anymore...!" She exclaimed.

Samantha gingerly removed her hand and noted the wound was no longer bleeding even when uncovered.

They turned to see the last of The Red god dissolve into nothing more than an angry breeze, and then there was silence.

Ryan locked eyes with Samantha, and he moved to stand up.

"Are you alright?" Samantha asked, worry evident in her voice. She then spun around and looked to Mara, Gina, Barbara, and the rest. "Stupid question! Is everyone alright??"

Chapter 8: DAY SIX

"Mostly alright," Ryan answered, checking his back. "Nothing that some bandaids won't fix." He chuckled, which was an odd sound to hear after all the screaming.

Mara noticed him looking back towards the altar, where his father lay dead after saving them earlier. Ryan was clearly in tremendous pain, but he forced a brave face for Samantha and the other living relatives.

The others slowly stood up and checked each other as well. There were a multitude of injuries in the survivors, but nothing fatal.

Alma came hurriedly from behind the resort. "I-I can't believe you stopped it! You *lived*!" The older woman looked to Mara and cried anew. "I am sorry I did not help you more...!"

Samantha put a hand on Alma's shoulder, worried that she would fall from her trembling. "Let's get help for anyone bleeding. We can talk more afterward."

Alma, Ryan, and a few of the other less injured helped everyone inside the resort.

Alma called out as they went through the halls towards the foyer, asking the hiding employees for help and that it was safe now.

Slowly more and more of them came out with supplies, medical kits, blankets, and bottles of water. They spoke in hushed tones as Alma gave instructions not to go to the resort's back and that they would speak further after the immediate injuries were treated.

They were sat in groups in the foyer. Each person was assessed and helped as best they could. Low murmurs and quiet sobs echoed in the large room as everyone settled.

Mara, Samantha, and Ryan sat in one group nearest the fireplace on the right of the foyer entrance. Mara glanced over and saw her dad in another group, but he did not look her way and kept his head down.

Soon, Alma joined them and helped Samantha bandage Ryan's back wounds. When he was tended, Alma moved to re-bandage Mara's left hand and latest scrapes.

Mara was quiet as she worked, unsure what to say after everything that happened. Alma took the initiative though.

She stood back from Mara and addressed her. "I will do this properly now..." She kneeled in front of her and held Mara's hand to her forehead. "I am ashamed, and I apologize to you and your family. I almost caused your death had your family not intervened."

"Why do you say that?" Samantha asked.

Mara shook her head. "Please sit with us and talk instead. You don't need to apologize. So much of this was my fault."

Samantha looked between the two of them and then at Ryan. "Can we get an idea of what happened out there? What *was* that?"

Alma stayed kneeled but let go of Mara's hand and looked towards her lap, gathering her words carefully.

Ryan looked towards Alma as well and spoke in a low voice. "We need to know. So... so many of our loved ones just *died* out there. You know something."

"I will tell you the truth..." Alma switched her volume to almost a whisper. "But not everyone can know in full. Not everyone can be trusted to handle it."

She turned her head up and looked between Samantha and Ryan. Confusion was evident on their faces, but they nodded and waited for her to continue.

"My village has known that being for many generations. As I told Mara, it has many names, but a recent one was translated as The Red god."

Ryan quickly shifted forward. "Wait, you've known about it for that long?! How could this happen then? Why do people even come to this area? You opened a resort for tourists! Are we nothing but sacrifices to it?!"

Samantha placed a hand on Ryan's shoulder and gently pulled him back, sensing his frustration and pain might hamper getting answers. "This has something to do with Mara. The being tried to take some ownership of her, and you already spoke to her about it. What did it want with my cousin? Why her?"

Mara saw Alma shift uncomfortably on the floor, so she stood up and held a hand out to her. Alma took it and sat next to her to continue.

"The elders of my village kept records of The Red god and the hosts it chose. More often than not, the victim was young and already known to be in a vulnerable position. It has this type it prefers, and Mara fit the type unfortunately."

Samantha pulled Mara closer to her side and wrapped her arm around her. Mara was glad for the warmth. Something about it made her eyes give in to the exhaustion she had fought over the past days. She leaned into Samantha and stayed quiet as the adults talked.

Chapter 8: DAY SIX

"Then it's always dangerous here for people," Samantha stated, "Why stay here? Or why not warn everyone?"

"Everywhere has danger." Alma sighed, not out of annoyance of the question, but out of a weariness that spanned longer than any of the young adults could know. "If my people left here and went elsewhere, there is no guarantee it would not follow us. Or more like it may exist elsewhere. Evil is not local to us only. But we live, and we fight it, same as other families do."

"We warn people in our own ways, but we can't tell the truth to everyone, or we find those that will seek the being out on their own are far more dangerous." Alma paused to look over at David, and Samantha gave a sad nod of understanding.

"What... should we do about him?" Ryan asked. "Is it dangerous if he stays here? Can he bring that horrible bitch back?"

Samantha gave Ryan a sharp look for his word choice, but he shrugged in return. "I don't think she's going to need therapy for hearing a curse word.." Samantha looked like she wanted to respond, but her mouth only opened and closed.

Alma ignored the couples' squabble. "I will tell the other elders what happened, and to instruct people to keep a close eye on

397

him until you all are going from here. We will not give him a chance to get back to it."

"But... to get back to your other question, no, we do not sacrifice to the being. The resort is a strong source of income for many of my village's people, my family included, but we never intended on bringing tourists into danger. Resort Ruhe has run for almost 75 years without incident. We were as careful as we could be... but I understand your anger at our part in this. And I cannot offer any restitution that would matter to you for the loss of your family members. I am so sorry."

Alma continued to tell them the other stories she had previously told Mara in the storeroom, stories of The Red god's previous attack, the greedy man who sought it out generations back, and more. Samantha and Ryan patiently listened and gained more understanding of the scope of the thing.

At the end, the tired couple looked at each other and had only one last question. Samantha asked it. "What happens now?"

Alma looked across the room, taking in the busyness of the employees as they fetched more bandages, water, and other assorted supplies and tried keeping the guests comfortable where they sat. "Now, I will get back to leading my people through this. The other elders will know in full what happened and will help me keep the story straight with everyone else."

"If you're not telling them the truth, then what story is that?" Ryan asked.

"I will decide on a story with the other elders, but it may be that a single human was responsible for this, or a large wild animal, or something else. Those that witnessed it themselves will be harshly warned to not speak of it more or ask questions. If I have to tell your surviving relatives that it was an evil spirit and nothing more of the bindings and promises it makes, then hopefully that will be enough to scare them to never return and attempt contact with it."

"I don't think you have to put any more fear into them," Ryan responded. He looked over the room and saw his surviving cousin, his grandmother, two aunts, an uncle, and two friends from his side. Anyone not in his view was dead outside in the snow. It was a somber fact to face that he'd never see them again.

"Yes... we will be careful with our wording as we separate and speak to everyone. And I will also document what I have learned today." Alma looked to Samantha with a gaze of wonder. "Today, you did something my village had failed to do for countless generations. You *saved* a host. I will *never* let that be forgotten to time. We will write it and rewrite it for the future, to save as many as we can."

Samantha returned a small smile and looked down at Mara, who appeared to have fallen asleep against her. "I... know what it's like to be the vulnerable one of a family. A long time ago some people helped me, and I had to help her."

"Speaking of which," Ryan interjected, "How did that work? I thought... uh... you were adopted, Sam? Mara's not your blood relative, so how were you able to claim her away from that thing?"

Samantha chuckled and shook her head at his question. "My parents did adopt me, but I of all people know blood doesn't always make family. It doesn't matter. She's my cousin."

Ryan sheepishly rubbed his beard. "Yeah, stupid question, sorry. You are an amazing person, Sam. I should never be surprised at anything you do."

Samantha smiled. "You can keep being surprised if you like, but you're along for the ride with me now, Mr Jansen."

"Yes I am, Mrs Jansen." He replied, returning the smile.

Chapter 8: DAY SIX

Alma took this as her cue to leave. "I think I have explained all I can for you. I will speak with the others and get back to you. Please rest as much as you can."

Samantha said her thanks, and Alma walked away to speak to the employees.

Mara felt like she was floating in a warm sea. She dreamed of sunshine on her face, and a gentle tide holding her up.

The horrors of the day only returned to her mind as she awoke and blearily looked around. Relatives still huddled in corners, wearing blood-stained suits or dresses and quietly talking or sobbing. She was still in the foyer next to the fireplace, laying against Samantha.

She straightened up in her seat and let the past hours' memories replay in her mind. They were safe, but they were the only ones to have made it. Outside was dozens of relatives from both sides of the aisle, including her grandmother, Uncle Larry, Judy, and... her mother.

The Red god

A strange feeling washed over Mara as she thought of her mother's last moments. Her attack on The Red god was over in only a few fleeting seconds. Despite the briefness of the event, Mara knew deep in her heart that she'd pour over every detail of it for a long time to come. It was a memory she would not easily be rid of.

She did not immediately cry for her mother. She also was not glad of her end. But the room was quieter without her, and she was glad for the peace.

Samantha broke from her quiet conversation with Ryan then, noticing Mara had awakened. "Hey, how are you feeling? You should drink some more water."

Mara gladly took the bottle from her and drank. "How long was I asleep? What's going on now?"

"Maybe two hours. And nothing much." Samantha replied. "Alma told us everything and then left to speak to her people. They're going to get some stories straight and then get us out of here as soon as possible."

Mara wondered what leaving here meant. Would she go home to Colorado with her dad? She watched David from across the room. He was half slumped on the floor, back leaning against one of the couches. His face was downcast to the floor, but Mara didn't think he was asleep in that position.

On either side of him were resort employees. They didn't stare directly at him, standing guard, but Mara got the impression they wouldn't let him move if he had tried to.

Had he already cried for Shannon? Mara didn't know.

Out of the corner of her eye, Mara saw a new clustering of people enter the foyer. They all appeared to be locals judging from their complexion and hair color, but not all of them wore resort uniforms.

Samantha and Ryan noticed the same and sat up straighter to watch.

Alma and two others stepped towards the front of the group. One was a woman a little younger than Alma. She wore a thick brown coat and insulated work pants. The other was an older man. He wore a business suit with a non-matching blue coat thrown haphazardly on top. They all wore grim but determined expressions.

"If I can have your attention, everyone." Alma started. "We want to bring what calmness and understanding we can to everyone after the tragic events of today. The employees here already know me and our other two leaders, but I will introduce them for the sake of our guests."

"This is Bernhard, a police chief in our nearby village, and Hilde, our village's record keeper and financial manager of Resort Ruhe. And I am Alma, another manager at the resort and community planner for our village. We are here to help you all."

There were quiet murmurs among the guests, but the employees stood in quiet respect listening.

"To start, I, Bernhard, and Hilde will assist our resort employees in gathering you in groups to talk at lengths with each of us. We understand we have much to explain, and we will talk in small, manageable groups to ensure you can also speak up with questions. We thank you for your patience with this, and I assure you everyone will be arranged a swift, safe transport back to your respective home countries afterward."

As Alma finished her initial announcement, she waved over particular employees and spoke in hushed tones in their local language. They began moving guests into other rooms, and Alma strode over to Mara's group again.

"Since you all know everything already, we won't pull you into a separate room. However, I want to warn you of another plan we

Chapter 8: DAY SIX

have. I and the other elders decided we need a larger cover up for the wider community and countries of origin for your many family members that died. They cannot question this event and come find out the truth or we would all be in danger."

"In perhaps an hour, you will hear a tremendous rumbling and shaking. We have some trusted people from our village that are planting explosives high on the two mountains. They will trigger a controlled avalanche and bury the dead for some time. Outside police and investigators will hear of the avalanche, and we will particularly ask for their help in rescue efforts."

"How will that explain the condition of the bodies?" Samantha asked. "They... did not die normally. There are large physical wounds."

"And there are metal chairs, tent poles, and many other objects with sharp points scattered around the resort. We will place even more strategically before the explosions are begun. It will look as though they were pierced and slashed by these as the snow tumbled into everything with a high force, like a wooden pole can go through a house during a tornado."

Samantha looked to Ryan and gripped his hand. "Okay, we will expect the noise."

"I am sorry you do not get your dead back for burial sooner and that they will be subject to more brutality..."

"We understand why," Ryan replied. He kept his head down and avoided making eye contact, but he didn't fool Samantha who knew he was fighting back tears.

"And," Samantha jumped in, "We will lay them to proper rest in some time. We'll do it right, then." She squeezed his hand, thinking of his father. Samantha was lucky both her parents survived. Losing aunts, uncles, cousins, and friends was gut-wrenching, but she knew it wasn't the same as a parent. She looked to Mara as well and wished she could offer more comfort to the girl.

Alma gave a sad nod and turned to leave again. "We will hurry with everything, and you will leave soon after."

Little by little the groups in the foyer were rotated out, led back to speak in separate rooms and then led back to sit and rest.

Mara wasn't sure if they returned with calmness or understanding, but they certainly returned with less murmuring. They seemed to know keeping quiet was good for now.

Lastly, her dad was also escorted to a back room. Mara wondered what Alma or the other elders told him. Did they

Chapter 8: DAY SIX

threaten him to never return? To never seek The Red god? Did they attempt to comfort him over his loss as well?

Like many things today, Mara didn't know the answer. He returned with his escorts and sat back in a chair without argument, face still steadfastly focused on the floor.

It was then that a rumbling was felt, and Samantha and Ryan both reached for each other and Mara. They huddled tightly in their little corner of the foyer and rode out the shaking and deafening roar and cracks that sounded like thunder.

The guests screamed and clutched each other as well, not understanding the sound.

It went for 30 seconds or so and was ended with a finale of a jolt that moved them from their seats.

"I think it hit the resort too," Samantha said, a new shakiness evident in her voice.

"It definitely did." Ryan stood up and helped her and Mara back up from the floor.

"Was that an avalanche?!" Someone screamed out, and several employees rushed back in the room along with Alma.

"It is okay!" Alma addressed them. "It was, and it hit the back of the resort. But the front is fine. You all can leave out the foyer

407

doors safely still. I've spoken to our emergency numbers, and they are sending helicopters now in case the mountain road was affected."

There was a new wave of worry, crying, and talking among her relatives, but Mara's little corner stayed steady. Ryan had a protective hand on each of their shoulders, and they waited for their promised transport.

"Hey Samantha..." Mara hesitantly asked. "Can I stay with you and Ryan for a while? I know you don't want me following you both around. I-I caused trouble. And you want to do married people stuff now, but..."

"Mara, you can ask it. Go ahead." Samantha encouraged, giving her a small smile.

Mara wiped away a few tears and started her sentence over, this time with a little more confidence. "But I need help. Please, I want to ask you for help now. I can't stay with my dad. I can't...!"

Samantha shifted and hugged her. "I know it's not easy to ask for help, but I'm so proud of you for it. I will never not help you, Mara. And yes, you are coming with us. If they try and separate us on the helicopter or plane, I'm biting someone!"

Ryan chuckled. "I would absolutely not be surprised by that."

Chapter 8: DAY SIX

"Why wouldn't you be surprised by that?" Samantha laughed and turned back to him.

"Because! You literally came back from the dentist that day after your braces removal and told me you turned down their teeth smoothing procedure!"

"Oh... that."

"Yes, that! You said, and I quote, 'I didn't let them file them down because those are my *biting teeth*.' And that you needed your biting teeth!"

"Well, I do need them! Look at my scrawny arms! I couldn't fight off some robber or kidnapper with these! I would have to bite someone to have a chance! And you know, they only offer to smooth out your teeth, including your canines, to make you look cuter if you're a woman. Screw that, I'm already cute!"

Ryan laughed again. "Yes, you are. As long as you don't bite *me*."

"Oh, never." Samantha pushed on his chest playfully. "You only get kisses, no bites."

Mara watched the two of them and smiled. The tragedy of the day still weighed heavily on her, but there was hope peeking through.

As the sun began setting, a whirring was heard overhead. Employees rushed around organizing everyone and directing them where to go.

The more injured were taken first, but when the third helicopter arrived, Alma waved Mara's group over.

"This is yours. It will take you to the hospital nearest the airport, and then you will have tickets booked for you back home. I know you understand what happened here, but I will repeat this so there is no misunderstanding... You cannot come back to the resort, and you cannot tell others the truth of what happened. This is the safest way for all of us."

Mara nodded. "I know... and thank you for helping me. Can I ask one other thing?"

"What is it, child?"

Chapter 8: DAY SIX

"I left Lukas' Gameboy on the bridge railing. Can you make sure he finds it? And can you tell him I'm sorry?"

Alma looked pained but gave a patient reply. "You know I cannot tell him the truth of what happened either. He will hear of the avalanche and that the surviving guests were safely transported home."

"I understand, and I know I can't talk to him again... It wouldn't be safe for him."

Mara hated goodbyes, but she found something she hated more: A lost chance to say it. She didn't get to say goodbye to her mother nor Lukas. Their endings were not the same. Lukas would live on in his village, just not seeing Mara again, but it still made her sad.

Alma hugged her and whispered one last parting in her ear. "You did good, child. You stay with your cousin, and I will make sure Lukas finds his Gameboy and knows that you said goodbye. Have a good life, Mara."

Ryan put a hand on her shoulder, and Mara pulled away from the embrace. "We better go, kiddo. We shouldn't hold up the rescue efforts."

The Red god

The three of them walked out Resort Ruhe's foyer doors for the last time and walked towards the waiting helicopter. A man in a bright orange jumpsuit hopped out of the side and led them to their seats, securing each belt and giving the go-ahead to the pilot to take off.

As they ascended into the air, Mara saw the mountains and resort from a new perspective. The sun was just below the horizon, leaving stripes of gold and red spanning the lower sky. No blood could be seen in the back of the resort. Everything was covered in thick piles of snow, even up to the back of the resort roof.

The evil that occurred there had been covered in pure white, giving an impression that it never even happened, but Mara still knew the shame, pain, and death underneath it all. It would take the rescuers a long time to dig out the bodies, but it would take her an even longer time to dig out her trauma and guilt.

Samantha leaned over and squeezed Mara's hand as she stayed mesmerized by the departing scene. "We're starting a new chapter now. It'll be a better one, I promise."

Mara nodded. For the first time in a long time, she trusted someone. It was possible for things to be better.

Chapter 9: A Better Chapter

Mara scrunched her nose and stared at the math equation in front of her for a few moments more before leaning forward to quickly scribble more numbers.

Satisfied, she smiled and brushed her hair out of her face. It was much shorter than it was a year ago. The brunette strands barely brushed her shoulder. It was a lighter feeling than she was used to, but Samantha encouraged her to choose more of her own style. Her mother never let her cut it where she wanted, after all.

But... her mother wasn't here to decide everything for her anymore. It was a thought Mara had often with a strange swirl of sadness, relief, and guilt.

Mara traced her fingers on the surface of the large dark wood dining room table she sat at, getting distracted from her homework. Whenever her thoughts went back to what happened at the resort, her therapist recommended trying to ground herself. She should know by heart the exact steps of the technique he recommended by now, but she often forgot if it was to touch three things, look at two, smell or taste one, or if she had it backwards.

The Red god

But it didn't matter. She knew the gist of it. Her fingers now traced the edges of her math book, and she focused on the sharp contrast in feeling from the smooth table.

When they arrived at the hospital in Austria before flying home after the nightmare events, the doctors were worried Mara might lose a fingertip or two to frostbite. Everything hurt from the time she had run away from the resort and stayed in that frigid hunting shack. She hadn't noticed the damage to her fingers before they pointed it out.

But time heals *most* wounds. She regained full use of her fingers, sans her broken third finger on her left hand. It was amputated after they determined it was already infected and badly torn.

Mara supposed that explained why she was less good at math now. She could only count to nine.

She chuckled aloud at her own musings and picked her pencil back up to work on the next problem.

"Mara, girl!" A voice startled her out of her thoughts.

"I can't believe you're doing homework on your birthday! You can have fun, y'know!" Samantha smiled as she walked further in the kitchen towards her.

Chapter 9: A Better Chapter

"Well, I want to do better this year..." Mara fidgeted with her pencil. "Last year I think my teacher thought I was stupid... I want to make up for it and catch up."

Samantha pulled out a chair next to her and sat down, dumping an armful of mail onto the table as she did so. "You know you're not stupid! Last year was just... a lot of catching up on other things you needed too. We all needed it."

Mara sat back and let her eyes wander to the kitchen window above the sink. The sun was brightly streaming in, and she saw nothing but blue skies above. "I know. I liked the counselors and lady from child services. I just need more time for school now."

"You know what that is?" Samantha asked, patiently folding her hands in front of her.

Mara furrowed her brow and looked closer towards the hedges peeking beyond the bottom window edge. "No, what do you see?"

"I see progress, Mara. You're doing well."

Mara rolled her eyes, hiding her embarrassment of misunderstanding the question.

"Look at that! It is your birthday! You must be 13 to be rolling your eyes like a teenager!" Samantha laughed as she teased. "And

415

since it is your birthday... you have to open your cards, girl! You got so many!"

Mara looked towards the pile of mail, taken aback. "Is that what all this is? Are... they all for me?"

Samantha grinned and nodded, beginning to pick a few from the pile. "There's one from Beth, your grandfather, Aunt Barbara, your paternal grandma, my parents, your doctor's office... Although that one might be a little generic."

Samantha's smile faltered as she came to the last one. "...and your dad."

Mara reached out and took one off the top. This was the first time her dad sent her something. They had a few brief visitations over the past months when Samantha and Ryan were handling things with the family court in Colorado, but he never looked her in the eye or spoke directly to her. He only followed the legal requirements and made things easy for Samantha to get guardianship.

"I want to open Beth's first!" Mara exclaimed, trying to force thoughts of her dad out for now. Bad things didn't always need to overcast the good. The good could have its time to shine.

Chapter 9: A Better Chapter

The envelope was bright sky blue, and as Mara turned it over she saw sparkly kitten stickers on the front with her name and their new address.

She was still getting used to seeing South Carolina on things. Samantha and Ryan's home was in a beautiful city about a two-hour drive away from the coast. It was a lot different than Colorado, especially the weather. But Mara liked it. It was warm. She needed warmth now.

Samantha sat the other letters back down and watched Mara open them. "We'll have to plan a trip soon so you can visit together! I know it must be hard not seeing her in person."

"I miss her." Mara sighed. "But at least we can text too. We send pictures and jokes all the time."

Samantha studied Mara's face as she read Beth's card. The front was a Siamese kitten coming out of a birthday cake. It must have had better content inside though, as she started with a small smile that grew to a grin and laugh at the end.

"Beth must have worked on this for a week to get that many cat-birthday puns. She's gotten really funny. I hope she's making more friends at our old school."

"I'm sure she is," Samantha replied, "but not one that will replace you. I never get half the jokes you send back and forth. You guys have your own language!"

"The language is called memes." Mara laughed. "And I probably shouldn't show you any more if they confuse you too much."

"Noooo..." Samantha whined. "I like the dog ones! Even if I don't get the captions."

Mara sat Beth's card aside carefully and moved onto the next.

The envelope was light yellow, and it had fancy scrawled longhand writing on front. Once Mara opened it, she promptly turned it upside down and shook a few times.

A ten-dollar bill fluttered out, and Samantha exclaimed. "Hey! Don't just shake your Grandma's money out! You have to read it first!"

Mara laughed and put the money to the side before opening the card. "I read it after! It's fine!"

"Grandma says she's doing well and has always been thinking about me. She said she's sorry she couldn't send a book this year, but I can get one with the money."

Chapter 9: A Better Chapter

Mara smiled and looked at Samantha. "I don't have the heart to tell her ten dollars doesn't buy a whole book anymore. She's been giving me the same amount since I was five."

"Oh, it's the thought that counts!" Samantha chided. "And she does think of you."

"She does." Mara agreed. "And I'm not complaining. I'll have to write her back in a few months and tell her what book I buy next."

"Do you have one in mind already?" Samantha asked.

Mara blushed in response. "Uh, yeah. But I can get it myself when we're at the store. You don't have to help."

Samantha caught on quickly to the teenager's ploy. "One with romance, eh? You don't have to be that shy! You're the age girls start looking at prince charmings! I was only four years older than you when I met Ryan. Oh he was a dear even at first meeting..."

"Alright, alright." Mara pretended to shield her ears. "I've heard the story of you guys kissing before. One more time and I might bleed little hearts out of my ears!"

Samantha playfully tapped her arm. "Oh, act embarrassed now! You'll fall in love one day and tell that story to your kids a dozen times."

The thought made Mara pause, but not as much as it would have a year ago. Maybe she would get married one day. It wasn't terrible watching Samantha and Ryan interact when they were all together. They showed a love she never saw with her parents.

Mara picked up the card from her doctor's office next. It was a generic happy birthday cake with an annual appointment reminder inside as well. She felt herself lingering on it just for the sake of procrastination. There were a few cards at the end that she felt the need to gather strength before reading.

She didn't know if Samantha sensed this, but her cousin didn't push her to hurry to the next ones. Instead she filled the silence with small talk.

"By the way, my parents will be in town next month. I figured we could all drive to the beach while we visit. You won't have homework to do all weekend, right?"

"I'm sure I can finish before that weekend," Mara replied. "The beach sounds fun. You better make sure Ryan puts on sunscreen this time though."

Samantha laughed and quickly covered her mouth with her hand before she snorted. "I don't think he'll let me forget to help him with that! His back was peeling for weeks! Oh, poor guy."

Chapter 9: A Better Chapter

Mara picked up the card from Samantha's parents now. That was also a safe one to read.

She never spent much time with Aunt Kathy and Uncle Mike before, but since moving in with Samantha they had visited several times and intentionally talked with her and took an interest in her hobbies and school plans. Overall, Mara liked them a lot. They were nice like Samantha was.

The envelope was rather plain, but the card inside was very reminiscent of where Samantha got her bubbly personality from.

It was a rainbow cake, complete with sparkles and candles that moved when you opened or closed the front of the card. Normally Mara might have thought it looked a little juvenile for her, but the cheerful well wishes handwritten inside made her shyly smile without complaint.

A very familiar thought for the past year came to Mara, that she didn't deserve such bright people being kind to her. That she should have died at either their hands or the hands of *that thing* like so many of their relatives had. Or that they should have hated her ever since she survived.

It was a long battle to win against such thoughts. Her therapist used the term survivor's guilt. Mara understood the theory of it a bit, but in the beginning she still fought that the term shouldn't apply to her. She argued her personal guilt in the events as much as she could, session after session.

But Samantha never let it fly. As much as she wanted to fall into a pit of guilt and depression and never climb out, Samantha was there to keep throwing her ropes or hold out her hand.

Eventually Mara stopped fighting and started taking those ropes and hands. There were bad days, certainly, but there were more good days.

Samantha was now looking over her parents' card and commenting on how cute it was, how excited she was for their visit and the beach, and also moving on to talking about summer plans in general.

Mara was glad for her company as she faced the last three cards.

These held something deep in common. Her grandfather had lost Grandmother Mildred. Her Aunt Barbara had lost Uncle Larry. And her dad... had lost everything. Reminders of that, even in the form of letters, brought pains of anxiety at times.

Mara took a moment to plan the order and then picked her grandfather's to open next.

Chapter 9: A Better Chapter

The envelope itself was plain white and a standard card size, but the heft of it was unusual. Mara wondered if he had included a longer letter inside, and if so, what would it say.

She took her time ripping the envelope open and apprehensively slid the card out. It looked like a happy, normal card on the outside. It was decorated with bright pink and purple flowers and said Happy Birthday in a fancy scroll.

As she opened the card's face, a darting movement caused her to flinch in shock and drop it to the floor. Mara realized what it was a half second later, but that didn't help her now racing heart.

"Oh!" Samantha yelped, standing up from her chair. "I didn't expect that either! It's okay!"

Samantha put a supportive hand on Mara's shoulder before stooping down to pick up the paper butterflies that had shot out of the card and fluttered to the floor.

Despite Samantha's reassurance, Mara felt embarrassed for her overreaction. She was jumpier ever since the resort.

Mara stood up and helped Samantha pick up the last few escaped butterflies and the card itself. "I wonder if Grandpa had someone help him pick this out, like his work assistant. It's awful fancy for a card."

423

"You never know." Samantha put her handful on the table in front of Mara and returned to her seat. "Maybe he spent a lot of time looking at the store for the perfect one for you."

The thought should have made Mara smile, but she caught herself countering it in her mind: 'Why would someone that should hate me do something extra nice for me?'

She knew these ruminations weren't helpful. Her therapist called them intrusive thoughts. Knowing that gave her techniques to fight against them, but it didn't take them away entirely.

For this thought, she focused on the realities instead. Her grandfather had gotten her a very nice birthday card. He had mailed it with intention so that it arrived on her birthday and not later. She could only take that at face value as a token of care.

The inside of the card was as fancy as the front, with flowers and cursive letters spelling out happy wishes. But what caught Mara's attention was the handwritten note.

It read "Happy Birthday, Mara. I am sorry I could not visit in person. I hope Samantha and Ryan are treating you well. I will speak to them soon about arranging a visit to Florida."

Chapter 9: A Better Chapter

The signature was signed 'Love' to Mara's surprise. Her grandfather was never a very affectionate man, although Mara couldn't remember any particularly bad memories with him either.

He was always busy or quiet back when she would visit with her parents. But... things were different now. His wife, Mildred, was gone. His daughter, Mara's mother, was gone. And he seemed to be reaching out more.

Mara wasn't sure if it was out of regret for the past or current loneliness. She felt guilt either way, but she was relieved he didn't hate her. If he wanted to invite her to visit in Florida, she resolved herself that they would have another long talk, a better talk than the ones they had at the resort.

Mara turned the open card towards Samantha. "Grandpa said he'll talk to you and Ryan about scheduling a visit."

Samantha smiled and took the card to read. "That would be great! It's been a little while. But we'll have to plan it around your school. No more extra vacations!"

Mara nodded in agreement. "I don't want to take off school for it. I have to focus more this year. But it would be nice to fit it into some other days off."

The Red god

With a lighter mental load now that one difficult card was down, Mara picked up the envelope from Aunt Barbara.

"I hope nothing jumps out of this one." Samantha chuckled.

"Yeah, I'd be okay with that." Mara smiled.

She slid the card out and saw a cartoon-style puppy face. The card opened at the bottom, and when Mara moved it she noticed an equally cartoony bright red tongue moved in and out of the puppy's mouth.

"I would say Danny helped her pick this out." Mara grinned. "But I don't know if he ever got over that fear of dogs."

"Awww, it is cute though!" Samantha put her elbows on the table and leaned forward. "Y'know, just because you're growing up doesn't mean you have to stop liking cartoons and cute things."

"I know," Mara replied, "but it's also okay if I branch out to other stuff. This is cute though. I'm glad Aunt Barbara sent me a card."

She opened it fully to read the inside. There wasn't much room beside the large Happy Birthday text, so it looked like Aunt Barbara had written extra tiny to fit it all in: "I hope you've had a good year and a happy birthday! I can't believe you turned the big one three! Make time to enjoy silly things still!"

Chapter 9: A Better Chapter

Besides the "Love," sign-off Mara saw a neatly signed "Aunt Barbara", "Gina", and a large sprawled "DANNY".

Mara felt a warmness settle into her chest at the signatures. She didn't know what she expected with these last cards. Obviously no one would send her one and write something nasty if they hated her. Her intrusive thoughts were once again proven wrong.

"Hey, Samantha." Mara questioned.

"Yeah?" Samantha answered.

Mara looked up to catch her eyes. She had a bad habit of being unable to look at people in the face when asking for things, but she was getting better about consciously letting herself meet their face.

"Didn't you talk to Aunt Barbara on the phone a lot months back? I never asked what she talked about and... I don't know if it's my business, but I was curious. Did she talk about me? Has she been okay?"

"Hm..." Samantha put her hand to her chin to think. "I mean, she definitely did talk about you. But it was mostly asking me how you were. I did talk to her about some things we were doing together, like time off school earlier in the year or making time for counselors. But I didn't get into too many private details of course!

I just wanted to reassure her that you were being taken care of with me and Ryan."

Mara nodded and went back to playing with the pop-up feature of her puppy card. "That's okay. I don't mind that. I guess I was thinking... I don't know, never mind."

Samantha gave her a look. "Girl, you know you can be honest with me. If you want to ask something else, please do."

Samantha had a way of breaking down Mara's defenses in a blunt but encouraging way. Sometimes it annoyed Mara. It meant she had to talk more, grow more, try new things, trust more. But so far she never regretted when she did trust her. It was a peaceful thought.

Mara's reply was quiet but exactly what she wanted to ask. "So... did she ever talk about Uncle Larry or what happened with me back then?"

Samantha gave a sad smile. "We did talk about Larry a good bit too. She misses him terribly, of course. She told old war stories about him, when they were dating, and when they were raising Gina. But she never blamed you, Mara. The only concern she had was if you were okay after everything."

Chapter 9: A Better Chapter

Mara stayed silent. Samantha was about to reach out to her, but the young teen lifted her head finally and looked her in the eye. "Thanks, Sam."

Samantha returned an understanding smile.

"I want to open this last one in my room." Mara stood up and grabbed her dad's card.

Samantha thought it best to give her space. "Of course. I hope nothing pops out of that one either! I'll see you later."

Mara's room at Samantha and Ryan's house still felt a little foreign to her at times. The room itself was amazing, but it wasn't the room she expected to be in when she awoke each morning.

Her brain was still stuck in her old life and old home in many ways.

She had gotten the opportunity to decorate this bedroom how she liked, or rather Samantha had encouraged her to and gave her 'that look' when she said she didn't need to bother them with paint and furniture changes.

The Red god

The floor was hardwood like the rest of the house, but there was a large area rug beneath the bed. Mara chose it because of the blue and green watercolor look it had. She wanted the room to have a calm spring vibe, the furthest thing away from red and winter.

The walls were painted a light sky blue. On the furthest wall next to her bed's headboard were two matching low bookcases.

Only the right one was filled so far. It was mostly comprised of her old childhood books and a few new ones she got over the past year. But she hoped to fill the left one too. There was still nothing like a new book to Mara.

The bed was pretty average, a wooden frame and headboard. But the bedspread was also picked out by her. It was the fluffiest comforter she could find. It was a dark turquoise color with lighter blue quilted patterns throughout.

Mara sat her dad's unopened card on her bed and turned to look at the window on the right.

"You are certainly at home here, Hershey." She remarked, walking closer to stroke the cat's sun-warmed fur.

Mara requested a desk for her room as well, and Ryan had helped her pick it out from a salvage store. They actually looked at a few furniture stores before they found this one.

Chapter 9: A Better Chapter

Mara didn't tell Ryan exactly why she kept declining other fine-looking desks, but he might have figured it out once they got her chosen one home and Mara put it into place.

This older desk was a little shorter than the standard desk height, and it fit right up against the window's bottom edge. It gave Hershey the most perfect spacious sunning spot a cat could meow for.

Mara supposed picking out furniture with the cat in mind wasn't the most normal thing to do, but it made her happy. And Hershey was happy.

As Mara pet her chocolate-colored friend, her thoughts drifted as they often did to another gray cat.

She wasn't able to help Gravy in the end, but she hoped he was somewhere peaceful like this. There were a lot of jokes of dogs going to Heaven and cats ruling Hell, but Gravy would have been welcomed into Heaven, Mara was sure.

Hershey trilled and snuggled further into her own tail, not bothering to open her eyes as she basked in the pleasant strokes and warm beams.

A grateful smile spread across Mara's face as she remembered the day she was able to get Hershey back.

The Red god

It was the first visit back to Colorado where Samantha had to take care of some filings with the local court for her guardianship. She hadn't spoken to her dad on that trip, nor on the two subsequent ones, but he let them in the old family house to gather some things, and Mara ran straight to Hershey.

She had expected to beg Samantha to let her take the cat to their house. She wasn't in a position to demand more favors after everything Samantha was already doing for her, but she would beg and bargain for her furry friend if she had to, if nothing else than for the fact that she didn't trust her dad to take care of Hershey.

But she hadn't needed to beg at all in the end. Samantha saw her embracing Hershey and crying into her fur and had immediately asked Mara where the cat's carrier was. She wasn't about to ask Mara to part with something she loved so dearly.

None of the days and weeks immediately after the resort were easy, but things got warmer once Hershey was with her again.

Mara ceased her strokes of the cat's fur and waited a moment to see if she would stir and complain at the withdrawal of affection. But Hershey stayed still, happily napping.

She supposed now would be a good time to stop procrastinating and open her dad's card. In her heart she didn't hold much hope for a long letter or flowery language, but maybe this would finally be their break in the long silence.

Mara walked over and sat on the bed, sinking deep into the thick, soft comforter. She picked up the envelope as she did so.

It was plain white with the address, return address, and a standard stamp on the outside. It gave no hints as to the contents or intentions of the sender. It was very much like her dad this past year, a vague blank look and no emotion.

Since it had no stickers on the plain envelope, Mara felt no guilt in letting it tear as she opened it.

The card itself was a picture of a cake and 'Happy Birthday' in big pink letters. It gave her a similar feeling as the generic card from her doctor's office.

Still, Mara stared at it a few moments longer than necessary, steadying herself before opening the front.

Upon opening it, Mara looked it up and down, then turned it to the back and looked there as well.

There was one line of generic birthday wishes printed in the card inside, but no handwritten letter. There was but one word, "dad", signed at the very bottom right corner.

The Red god

When Mara was sure her eyes hadn't fooled her and that she hadn't missed any writing on it, she closed it and sat it on the far end of the bed away from her.

She sat, leaned back against the headboard, and stared at the ceiling for a good while in silence. Even her usual rapid or intrusive thoughts eluded her. She supposed it was hard to think negative thoughts when she was given nothing at all from her dad.

Nothingness was a void that sucked things out of you. It didn't give anything, negative or positive.

Was that what her dad had become to her? A void in space? A dad-shaped hole with no actual presence existing inside it?

Mara counted imperfections in the ceiling's popcorn texture and tried to decide how she felt or even how she *should* feel.

Was it disappointment? Not exactly. It became hard for her to be disappointed by him. Her low expectations did a good job of accurately matching her reality with him.

If she was correctly predicting him, then maybe she truly did know him, and this was all there was to know: That he drifted in life needing a strong-willed woman to give him some purpose. And that without that woman he had nothing much of substance.

Chapter 9: A Better Chapter

Had he always been like that, even from a young age? Of course Mara didn't know much about her dad's childhood other than a few stories and old yellowed photos from her paternal grandma.

Even if she knew all the stories her grandma ever told, it wouldn't have been enough to know his childhood. It would have to have been something he himself told, and he wasn't that talkative.

Maybe it had nothing at all to do with his childhood. Maybe Mara's own mother was the catalyst that caused these traits in him to be cemented. She certainly had done a number on Mara's thoughts and habits.

But it wasn't fair to blame one person for your whole being. People weren't robots programmed for one thing with no hope of changing.

They could change, although it was very hard. Mara was learning just how hard over this past year. Therapy and opening up to people felt like being rung out like a wet towel. It was exhausting and at times painful in the moment.

But after her fresh tears would dry, she often felt better. It was like something long ago injured had been re-broken and healed correctly. Little by little things were becoming correct for her.

But the same was not happening with her dad. There had been no change since the moments at the resort. The same lifeless stare he had in the resort foyer after the survivors had been gathered together was present today.

What did that mean for Mara? Could she do something for him? Should she?

She would be lying if she said there were no traces of resentment still lingering towards him. She hated that he was who he was during her childhood. Thinking back, he never filled the father role much even when they lived together.

He was a co-hostage along with Mara who braced against Shannon's moods, but he was different than Mara. He was an adult. He had more choices he could make. He just didn't make any of them.

And no one could force him to make those decisions. Not even his daughter.

Chapter 9: A Better Chapter

About the time Mara ran out of ceiling to count, she had made up her mind. In one swift movement she rolled off the bed and stood up to open a drawer in the desk.

She had a nice collection of stationary and colored papers there. She had picked them out at a craft store during the first few months after coming to Samantha and Ryan's house.

Originally she was meant to use them for journaling and therapy homework, along with writing back home to Beth, but she liked them so much she used some for schoolwork or crafts as well.

Mara flipped through a few stacks before finding the one she had in mind. It was white, lined paper that looked pretty plain except for the variety of cat silhouettes across each header.

She took out two pages and sat at the desk to begin.

If her dad wouldn't talk to her, she would at least try to talk to him herself. There was a line somewhere in the monumental stretch of distance between them that Mara would hold as a personal boundary, but she would respect that line when she came to it.

For her that meant she would not reach out an unlimited amount of times only to receive a sucking void back.

The Red god

She would send some amount of letters, carefully knitted from her feelings and things she needed to not go unsaid. But eventually she'd see the line and stop the letters.

Her time, emotions, and overall life would not go forever into a void. She would treat herself better than that and spend time with people who returned her love.

Her therapist had a saying that she took to heart: 'Boundaries are not barbed-wire fences with which we attack people. They are safe nets which protect us. They are not wrong to use.'

When she first picked up her pen, she thought this would be a great undertaking, a task to fight to finish. However, as soon as the pen began its smooth glide across the first page, she realized she was wrong.

It would have been harder to stop writing her feelings. There were so many from so long ago, locked away and stuffed down low in her soul.

She didn't want to merely vomit her emotions on paper though. She intended this to be something he read and could think about and reply back to. So she wrote first about how she was doing better, how good Samantha and Ryan were being to her, and a little about school, Hershey, and keeping in touch with Beth.

Chapter 9: A Better Chapter

The second page is where she went back to the before times. She wrote of her feelings of their old home life, his place in that, and her mother's too. She wrote an apology for her part in the resort's terrible events.

After all, she was not a robot that was programmed only to make that mistake. And she knew the mistake she made in not trusting other adults and telling them sooner, even if a lot of events collided to make that an easy mistake for a young child.

At this point she felt her hand cramping, but she had more words desperate to get out. Mara pulled a third and fourth sheet of stationary out of the drawer and continued.

She wrote about things she wished he had said or done and things that she needed from a father figure. She asked some questions about himself, how he was currently doing, if he would consider talking to someone, and what he himself wanted from their father-daughter relationship, or if he wanted one at all.

On the last page she slowed. Her emotional load was lessening, and she felt at peace with what she had penned. Her last comments were well wishes for him and an invite to send a letter back and not wait for some special occasion like her birthday.

439

When she had finished and set the pen down, she carefully folded the four sheets closed.

If she was being honest with herself, she didn't expect him to write back. She expected a short excuse and a recurrence of his same tendencies she knew and predicted well so far. But Mara wasn't a mind reader. She wasn't God. If he wanted to change, it was going to be up to him, and she would have to wait and see.

But she wasn't going to put her life and emotions on hold to wait. She would move on and work hard on her own change in the meantime.

Satisfied with her decision and letter, she left it on the desk and pet Hershey a few more times before reclining on her bed again. She would ask Samantha to take her to the post office tomorrow to mail it, but not today. Today was her birthday still, and she would spend it how she liked.

Mara found herself listening to more music lately. She had a pair of white headphones that lived on her head most days when she was studying or journaling in her room.

She pulled the headphones off the right bookshelf and plugged them into her device before also grabbing a journal.

Chapter 9: A Better Chapter

On the outside it looked rather boring. It was dark purple with a clear absence of glitter, cat stickers, or flower designs. But it became a very special item to her. It was the first journal she ever wrote in.

When she lived at her parents' home, she didn't dare write any of her feelings down on paper. They could be read easily, and she feared punishment from her mother the most. But in her new home, she was safe. She could write now, and Samantha encouraged her privacy to do so.

The journal was filled about two months after the events of the resort. She probably wrote the last half of the pages in one week alone after the stopped emotions began flowing.

She felt freer with the words on paper. But sometimes on rare occasions, she did take it out to read. It showed her progress compared with her current thoughts and going-ons.

Some pages were filled with Lukas, some with Alma, some with acute guilt, shame, and self-loathing, some with lingering fears of a red being, and a lot with her mother.

Her mother was still a weird mix of emotions to her at times.

Shannon's chapter was closed over a year ago. She was dead. There would be nothing more for her, nothing negative, nothing positive, no hope of change now that she was gone. But that didn't mean Mara didn't pour over past talks and interactions a million times over to try and understand her better.

She had somewhat settled on some thoughts of why her mother became who she was. There were obvious patterns with her own mother, Mildred, that she continued. But the ending was more up in the air.

Her last action on this earth was to lunge at The Red god in full fury. If she described that scene to ten different friends or therapists, they would probably all tell her that she meant to protect Mara and did so with her last breath.

But Mara knew so much more context herself. And the context was a painful picture.

Shannon was controlling, jealous, vindictive. She saw The Red god take control of her daughter and husband, and she was outraged. Did any of the outrage stem from a tiny sliver of real love? Or did it stem from anger that they were hers to control?

Mara stayed awake at night thinking of that more often than she wanted to admit.

Mara was only human. She had no way of one-hundred percent telling that answer. Maybe there was a sliver there. She had seen it a few rare times in her earlier childhood she thought. But was it enough to motivate her to attack the being out of an instinct to protect Mara?

On most nights, her thoughts leaned on the answer being 'no'.

One infuriating thing about life is that there will sometimes be things you will never, ever know for a fact. You can only make peace with the possibilities and move on.

What Mara did know is that Shannon had opportunities to love and protect her for her entire childhood, and she continually chose the wrong ones.

Mara resolved herself to not become her mother. If she had a husband and a family in the future, she would try her best to love and protect them. She would be everything her mother wasn't and everything she had needed during her childhood.

People do make mistakes. She wouldn't be perfect, but she could admit her mistakes and try harder. She had to. The cycle would stop with her.

Mara let herself drift with her music, sinking further into the coziness of her comforter.

When she dreamed, she dreamed of her old room again. It was a recurring theme for her. The room itself was exactly as she remembered, except for a dark gray tint to the scene. Dust was visible in the air, and everything seemed frozen in time.

The door to leave was always locked, and none of the light switches worked. There was a faint rumble of noise heard from beyond the walls, which she understood as her parents' arguments, although she never made out any particular words.

But something was different this time. Her window from her current room was inside her old room. It glowed brightly with sunlight.

As she walked closer, she could hear other voices, but they weren't muffled like the arguing. She made out the first one clearly as Samantha's, giggles included. The second was Ryan's.

They came from beyond the window, and as she peered out she saw Hershey basking in the sun right outside too. Mara jiggled the window, and to her surprise it wasn't locked like the door had been. It opened freely, and the gentle warm breeze wiped away the last traces of the muffled arguing sounds.

As she climbed out, her eyes fluttered open back in her room, and she smiled at Hershey who lay curled up on her chest.

Chapter 9: A Better Chapter

"Mara, I'm home! Are you ready to go?" Came Ryan's chipper voice through her door. Mara thought she must have heard him and Samantha talking when he arrived through her dream.

She regretfully picked Hershey up from her cozy spot and stood up to put her headphones and journal back.

"Yeah, I'm ready! Just a minute!" Mara replied, excited to remember the plans they had.

She joined them in the hallway leading to the front door and did a playful spin before stopping in front of Samantha and Ryan. "Ready and waiting!"

Samantha laughed and held out a canvas tote. "Me too! I got all the important things."

"And by important things," Ryan asked, "do you mean chips, candy, sports drinks, and sunglasses?"

"Of course!" Samantha beamed. "Only the necessities for a road trip and a day walking around the zoo."

Mara grinned and leaned forward to check the wares in the bag. "Looks very necessary to me."

"Alright, then let's hit the road!" Ryan retrieved his car keys and held the front door open for the ladies.

As they walked out and the door shut behind Mara, she had only one prominent thought: Good days were ahead.

END.

Author's Note

I hope you enjoyed the journey! And thank you for reading!

I'm the type of peculiar person who needs a very solid ending to stories, so it is my hope that my fellow peculiars got sufficient closure from the last chapter. If you had any open questions, please feel free to reach out:

Email: jennarecktenwald@gmail.com

Website: https://jennarecktenwald.com/contact

I'd also like to take this opportunity to give my perspective on the story for anyone curious for more.

The Red god started as a dream of mine. Growing up I always had a very vivid imagination and spent hours upon hours building worlds and adventures in my mind. This carries over to my dreams occasionally, so I like to use them as book inspirations.

In my original dream, someone handed me the book. It was a finished paperback with the same title. The front cover was a snowscape with red streaks of blood and claw-marks, as though someone were dragged backwards bleeding and digging at the ground to stop their being moved.

Author's Note

I read the book in my dream and saw flashes of the important scenes and the girl. The dream ended with me throwing the book down a staircase to get it away, as it was quite frightening.

The dream did not include 98% of the finer details, such as the main theme of cycles of abuse in families, character names, or the ending, but I quickly filled in the details as I thought about it more.

I wanted this book to be a story for someone like me. Although the events depicted are complete fiction and fantasy, the themes are my own childhood and common struggles of children that grow up in dysfunctional family cycles.

One reason I daydreamed so often as a kid was to escape the tense, angry, controlling environment I was trapped in. It seems fitting that I come full circle as an adult to use that imagination to write something that may help others with their own escape.

Mara's character is easy to place in the story. She is you. She is me. She is whoever struggled as a child.

The Red god can be more difficult to place. A side effect of growing up in an abusive household can often be vulnerability to future abuse, whether that be from another extended relative, family friend, pastor or priest, teacher, or romantic partner.

The Red god

The Red god was meant to be someone close that took advantage of that vulnerability for further abuse. But if this doesn't fit your story, maybe your Red god was emotional, mental, or physical side effects of the original family dysfunction.

Whatever your Red god was, you did not deserve it, and it was not your fault.

In the last chapters, I wanted to give hope of change. Although the abuse is never the victim's fault, we can have power as we grow and escape it. We can take power back away from the abusers. I wanted to show that with Mara learning boundaries, trusting other adults like Samantha, and realizing she could have talked to Samantha earlier.

I hope this is not misunderstood as Mara being to blame for her situation. I wanted her to grow and find better paths than the cycle of her family. It is something hard learned in my own life, and I hope to encourage others to seek help, have hope, and become cycle breakers.

To those whose pasts still linger, there's help. I won't pretend to know what you as an individual need, and I will state clearly that I am not a therapist myself. But as an individual who cares, please seek out someone. That could be a registered therapist, psychologist, spiritual leader, other family and friends, support groups, help books, journals, or something new that you haven't tried. Keep trying. You are stronger than you think, and there are better days ahead.

To those who see abuse, suspect abuse, or a person that could use some help, please take some action. I wish someone had taken action for me. Too many people "mind their own business" when they see child abuse instead of helping. Children can't help themselves. It is up to those around them to help. It takes a village, but sometimes one villager can get the ball rolling and speak up.

In a 'perfect' situation victims of abuse are obvious because they speak up and ask for help, but that doesn't always happen. It doesn't always look like classic abuse either, but it can be just as damaging. Be kind, and be open to others. Again, I cannot speak as an expert authority on the exact action to take, but if you seek resources and ask them for guidance you can make a mountain of difference for someone. You could be the Samantha that prevents a bad ending.

I will include some resources at the end, but please don't think this list is exhaustive. If a particular hotline is unhelpful, there are more to be found online or from support groups.

To close, I'd like to dedicate this book to my husband, Sam. I am sorry I made your inspired character a giggling red-headed woman who resembles you in no way. My writing is funny like that. But your love and patience towards me is the same as her. Thank you for encouraging me to finish this book.

For my lovely daughter, you are my biggest inspiration to break my family's cycles. May you never have to guess our deep love for you, and may you have a happy, carefree childhood free of even the thought of some of the themes of this book. Maybe I'll let you read this when you're *a lot* older. I love you.

Thank you also to the furry inspirations behind Hershey and Gravy that kept me sane in hard times. You will always be loved.

For more:

https://www.jennarecktenwald.com/personalprojects/books

Resources

These are gathered from online sources, and I cannot make guarantee as to their accuracy. I am not personally affiliated with any of them. I hope one may help you get the ball rolling on any need you or a loved one has.

National Child Abuse Hotline

1-800-4-A-CHILD

Operates 24 hours a day, seven days a week, and receives calls from throughout the United States, Canada, the U.S. Virgin Islands, Puerto Rico, and Guam.

Learn more: http://www.childhelp.org/

National Domestic Violence Hotline

800-799-7233

SMS: Text START to 88788

Hours: 24/7. Languages: English, Spanish and 200+ through interpretation service

Learn more: https://www.thehotline.org/

National Sexual Assault Hotline

1-800-656-4673

Hours: Available 24 hours

Learn more: https://www.rainn.org/

Resources for finding a therapist or psychologist:

- https://www.mhanational.org/finding-therapy
- https://locator.apa.org/
- https://www.findapsychologist.org/